NOMINATED SERIES

her strong, witty w...
...ng about Cozies

A Time to Swill

Sherry Harris

A Chloe Jackson, Sea Glass Saloon Mystery

Don't Miss the First
Chloe Jackson, Sea Glass
Saloon Mystery!

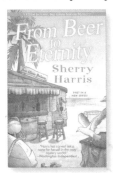

And the Sarah Winston Garage Sale Mysteries!

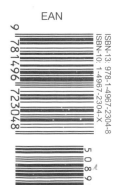   

Praise for *Sell Low, Sweet Harriet*

"An incredibly enjoyable book." —*Mystery Scene*

"Canny hints for garage-sale success blend nicely with two difficult mysteries for the intrepid heroine to unravel." —*Kirkus Reviews*

"Harris has carved out a name for herself in the cozy mystery world with her engaging, humorous Sarah Winston mysteries." —*Washington Independent Review of Books*

Praise for *Let's Fake a Deal*

"Who knew organizing garage sales could be a dangerous occupation?" —*Kirkus Reviews*

"I just love Sherry Harris's *Garage Sale* series. It's provocative, well-written, and always entertaining." —*Suspense Magazine*

Praise for *The Gun Also Rises*

"A roller-coaster of a mystery penned by a real pro. This series just gets better and better. More, please!" —*Suspense Magazine*

"Author Sherry Harris never disappoints with her strong, witty writing voice and her ability to use the surprise effect just when you think you have it all figured out!" —*Chatting About Cozies*

"This series gets better with every book, and *The Gun Also Rises* continues the trend. If you haven't started this series yet, do yourself a favor and buy the first one today." —*Carstairs Considers*

Praise for *I Know What You Bid Last Summer*

"*I Know What You Bid Last Summer* is cleverly plotted, with an engaging cast of characters and a clever premise that made me think twice about my shopping habits. Check it out." —*Suspense Magazine*

"Never one to give up, she [Sarah] continues her hunt for the killer in some unlikely and possibly dangerous places. Fans of Harris will appreciate both the clever mystery and the tips for buying and selling at garage sales."
—*Kirkus Reviews*

"Each time a new Sarah Winston Garage Sale Mystery releases, I wonder how amazing author Sherry Harris will top the previous book she wrote for the series. I'm never disappointed, and my hat's off to Ms. Harris, who consistently raises the bar for her readers' entertainment."
—*Chatting About Cozies*

Praise for *A Good Day to Buy*

"Sarah's life keeps throwing her new curves as the appearance of her estranged brother shakes up her world. This fast-moving mystery starts off with a bang and keeps the twists and turns coming. Sarah is a likable protagonist who sometimes makes bad decisions based on good intentions. This ups the action and drama as she tries to extricate herself from dangerous situations with some amusing results. Toss in a unique cast of secondary characters, an intriguing mystery, and a hot ex-husband, and you'll find there's never a dull moment in Sarah's bargain-hunting world."
—*RT Book Reviews*, 4 Stars

"Harris's fourth is a slam dunk for those who love antiques and garage sales. The knotty mystery has an interesting premise and some surprising twists and turns as well."
—*Kirkus Reviews*

"The mystery of the murder in *A Good Day to Buy*, the serious story behind Luke's reappearance, the funny scenes that lighten the drama, the wonderful cast of characters, and Sarah's always superb internal dialogue, will keep you turning the pages and have you coming back for book #5."
—*Nightstand Book Reviews*

"Sherry Harris is a gifted storyteller, with plenty of twists and adventures for her smart and stubborn protagonist."
—Beth Kanell, Kingdom Books

"Once again Sherry Harris entwines small-town life with that of the nearby Air Force base, yard sales with romance, art theft with murder. The story is a bargain, and a priceless one!" —Edith Maxwell, Agatha-nominated author of the Local Foods mystery series

Praise for *Tagged for Death*

"*Tagged for Death* is skillfully rendered, with expert characterization and depiction of military life. Best of all Sarah is the type of intelligent, resourceful, and appealing person we would all like to get to know better!" —*Mystery Scene Magazine*

"Full of garage-sale tips, this amusing cozy debut introduces an unusual protagonist who has overcome some recent tribulations and become stronger." —*Library Journal*

"A terrific find! Engaging and entertaining, this clever cozy is a treasure—charmingly crafted and full of surprises."
—Hank Phillippi Ryan, Agatha-, Anthony- and Mary Higgins Clark-award-winning author

"Like the treasures Sarah Winston finds at the garage sales she loves, this book is a gem." —Barbara Ross, Agatha-nominated author of the Maine Clambake Mysteries

"It was masterfully done. *Tagged for Death* is a winning debut that will have you turning pages until you reach the final one. I'm already looking forward to Sarah's next bargain with death." —Mark Baker, *Carstairs Considers*

Mysteries by Sherry Harris

The Chloe Jackson Sea Glass Saloon Mysteries
FROM BEER TO ETERNITY
A TIME TO SWILL

The Sarah Winston Garage Sale Mysteries
ABSENCE OF ALICE
SELL LOW, SWEET HARRIET
LET'S FAKE A DEAL
THE GUN ALSO RISES
I KNOW WHAT YOU BID LAST SUMMER
A GOOD DAY TO BUY
ALL MURDERS FINAL!
THE LONGEST YARD SALE

And

Agatha-Nominated Best First Novel
TAGGED FOR DEATH

A Time to Swill

Sherry Harris

KENSINGTON
PUBLISHING CORP.

www.kensingtonbooks.com

KENSINGTON BOOKS are published by

Kensington Publishing Corp.
119 West 40th Street
New York, NY 10018

All Kensington titles, imprints, and distributed lines are available at special quantity discounts for bulk purchases for sales promotion, premiums, fund-raising, educational, or institutional use.

Special book excerpts or customized printings can also be created to fit specific needs. For details, write or phone the office of the Kensington Sales Manager: Attn.: Sales Department. Kensington Publishing Corp., 119 West 40th Street, New York, NY 10018. Phone: 1-800-221-2647.

The K logo is a trademark of Kensington Publishing Corp.

First Printing: August 2021
ISBN-13: 978-1-4967-2304-8
ISBN-10: 1-4967-2304-X

ISBN-13: 978-1-4967-2306-2 (ebook)
ISBN-10: 1-4967-2306-6 (ebook)

10 9 8 7 6 5 4 3 2 1

Printed in the United States of America

To Bob
The perfect man, at least the perfect man for me
and to Clare
The Angel on my Shoulder, I miss you

Heritage Businesses

Sea Glass—owner, Vivi Jo Slidell

Briny Pirate—owner, Wade Thomas

Redneck Rollercoaster—owner, Ralph Harrison

Russo's Grocery Store—owner, Fred Russo

Hickle Glass Bottom Boat—owners, Edith Hickle, Leah Hickle, Oscar Hickle

Emerald Cove Fishing Charters—owner, Jed Farwell

CHAPTER 1

My shoes slapped the wet sand as I tried to make out what was up ahead of me through the swirling fog. I'd just arrived back in Emerald Cove, Florida, late last night. I'd driven through a dense fog the last thirty miles. When the advisory popped up on my phone, I'd thought, *how bad could it be?* Very bad was the answer. I'd crept along. Driving through gumbo would have been preferable. My hands still ached this morning from gripping the steering wheel of my vintage red Volkswagen Beetle.

I'd planned to sleep in. To unpack my worldly goods, which filled my car. Emptying my old life in Chicago into my new life in the Florida panhandle. But loud, angry waves pounding outside my two-bedroom beach house had other plans, so I'd gotten up, pulled on my running gear, and set out just before dawn. I squinted my eyes, but the fog danced and shifted like flowing Arabian head scarves, changing the view. There. There it was again, thirty yards ahead.

It looked like the mast of a sailboat angled oddly. Way too low for a boat to be upright. I tried to speed up, but the sand pulled at my shoes like wet hands trying to drag me under. Usually I found hard sand to run on, but this morning I hadn't found any. A groan and a creak floated across the air. The sound wasn't one I normally heard on the runs I'd taken to over the summer months. No one else seemed to be out. But the early hour and fog explained that.

The fog opened up just long enough for me to see a massive sailboat, listing to its side bobbing on the water.

"Hello?" I called as I got closer. I ran my hand through my short, brown hair. It curled wildly in this humidity. The boat was between the two sand bars that ran along this stretch of beach. The groan and creak seemed to be coming from the boat. A muffled cry sounded from inside the boat. A baby's cry. I whipped out my cell phone and dialed 911.

I thought of Julia Spencer-Fleming's opening line in *In the Bleak Midwinter*. "It was one hell of a night to throw away a baby." A terrible morning here.

"Where's your emergency?"

"Delores." Thank heavens it was someone I knew. "This is Chloe Jackson."

"What's wrong, honey? I didn't know you were back." Delores's voice was sweeter than the Mile High Pecan Pie she served at her diner when she wasn't working as a dispatcher.

"There's a sailboat that seems abandoned. It's stuck between the two sandbars. I heard a baby cry."

"Where are you?"

"The fog's so thick I'm not sure. I left my cottage about seven minutes ago and ran west toward Vivi's house. But I can't tell if I'm to her house yet or not."

"Okay, well, stay put while I get someone from the Walton County Sheriff's Department out there."

"Will do." I hung up and shouted again, "Anyone here?" I peered at the boat. The cry sounded again and tugged at my heart. I noticed a rope ladder dangling off the back end. It was like fate was telling me not to let the baby wait alone. I took off my shoes and dropped my key ring with its Chicago key chain in the toe of one of them. It looked like high tide, but I wasn't certain. I ran up the beach a few yards and left my shoes so they wouldn't get wet. There were marks in the sand like the boat had been farther up onshore.

I splashed through the water until it was waist deep and swam the last bit. I tried to keep my phone out of the water doing an awkward, one-armed stroke and kicking hard with my legs. The boat was farther out than I'd originally thought. It tilted up a bit, but I managed to catch the rope ladder and scramble up. As I boarded, a wave smacked the boat. It knocked me off my feet and I landed on my rear end, jolting every bone in my body. My phone flew out of my hand. I grabbed at it in midair but missed. A plop sounded in the water.

"No, no, no." The boat righted itself and I slid across the deck. My shoulder slammed into the side of the boat. *Ouch!* I gritted my teeth together. Another bounce, and it tipped precariously away from the sandbar. I clutched the side, managed to stay on the deck, and clung. The crying got louder, but now it didn't sound as much like a baby as it had from the shore. An animal perhaps? The boat began to move away from the shore and out to sea. What had I done?

CHAPTER 2

"Help," I yelled toward the shore. But the fog wrapped around my words and muffled them. No one yelled back. The boat moved quickly, probably caught up in a rip current. I eyed what bit of water I could see through the fog. Jumping in and trying to swim out of the current didn't seem smart, even though I was an excellent swimmer. I could become disoriented in the fog. The boat lurched in the waves. If I jumped, I couldn't be sure the boat wouldn't change direction and run me down.

The only thing worse than jumping in would be being tossed overboard. The boat tipped and tilted like the carnival rides I loved as a kid. Then there was the cry to think of. I couldn't abandon a baby if there was one. Moving would be perilous, but not moving wasn't an option.

A door that must lead to the cabin below banged open and closed with the motion of the waves. I eyed the distance. Standing would be foolish, but maybe I could slide over on my stomach. A wave pitched, I let loose. For a second I thought I was going in, but the boat rocked the other way. I took advantage and slid and scooted to the door. It banged shut behind me as I rolled down five steps, landing on the floor of the interior.

It took a minute for my eyes to adjust to the dim light that came through narrow, rectangular windows. I was in a living room, dining room, kitchen combo. The boat was a mess, with trash and clothing on the floor. The cry came from a room to my left. I stood and careened toward a door, staggering worse than any drunk I'd ever seen. I pushed on the partially opened door. A gray cat with long, white socks leaped off a bed and into my arms.

Not a baby, then. A cat. The boat pitched and we landed on the bed. I rubbed my cheek against the cat's head. "So, you're the one who caused me all this trouble." If not for the cry, I'd still be onshore. And my phone wouldn't be dead in the water. Literally. The cat purred and settled into my arms. The prudent thing seemed to try to wait out the waves down here now.

My stomach started to feel a little woozy even though I'd never been seasick before. I closed my eyes and tried to calm my breathing and heart rate. Both were banging along in double time.

"How did you end up on this boat?" Maybe the poor thing had climbed aboard when the boat was onshore. The door could have slammed shut when the boat was being flung around as it went back into the Gulf. The cat continued purring.

"Anyone else here?" No response. This room was a mess too, as if someone had tossed it or the boat had been whipped around by the Gulf for a long time. Clothes, bedding, and shoes were strewn everywhere. I hoped we'd be out of the riptide soon. Most riptides only went out about twenty feet. I prayed that's all this was.

Besides, Delores would have people looking for me. I hoped the waves wouldn't obscure where the boat had disturbed the sand. Maybe my phone would wash up on-shore and someone would spot it, or my shoes. I wouldn't think about a scenario where none of those things happened and everyone assumed I'd gone home or continued my run. In that case, it would take hours for someone to realize I was missing.

I talked to the cat until I ran out of things to say trying to keep my mind off the dire situation we were in. We continued to be bounced and pitched at the whims of the Gulf. Down here the boat creaked and groaned like banshees had taken possession. My fear level was high as I wondered if the boat would hold together. I said some prayers and stroked the cat. I'd read in books that people said time had no meaning and finally understood what they were talking about. Then, at last, the waters finally calmed. Now what?

I was chilled because of my damp clothes, even though the air and water temperatures averaged in the eighties during October in this part of Florida. I grabbed a floral shirt off the floor and put it on. It was mildewed and the smell made my nose itch. I picked up a straw hat, with a tall, stiff crown and crammed it on my head.

"Let's go see where we are," I said to the cat and it followed me up onto the deck.

I gazed about trying to figure out where I was, disheartened to see that I was way farther away from the shore than I'd hoped. In three directions I saw endless views of the Gulf of Mexico. At any other time I'd admire the sparkling water and enjoy the warmth of the sun. Ominous clouds hung in what must be the southwest. Maybe that was what had passed over and tossed the boat around. *Please, don't let them be headed this way.* The fourth direction—north, I assumed—I could see fog still obscured the shoreline. It looked like I would have to save myself.

I stayed still for a couple of moments to get used to the gentle rocking. I wasn't sure I could sail a boat this size even though I'd been on plenty of sailboats on Lake Michigan. These sails looked ragged anyway. But if the boat had a working engine or a radio of some sort, maybe I could get help. I pictured myself sailing back to shore like a modern-day, older Pippi Longstocking. Hailed as a hero.

I went to the helm and put my hands on the wheel at two and ten. *This isn't driver's ed, Chloe.* The wheel spun a full circle, so it must have been disconnected from the rudder. That was no help. Even if I found a working engine, I couldn't steer the boat back to shore.

"Is there a radio around?" I asked the cat. It didn't answer but followed me as I went back below.

I opened doors off the main cabin. One of the doors opened to a bathroom, or the head, as my uncle always called it. I tried to open a second door, but something behind it wouldn't let me open it fully. I peered through the one-inch crack. This was another cabin with a bed. It too was in terrible condition, with things all over the place.

Wood paneling that probably once gleamed was now dulled by sea air. What had happened to this boat and how had it ended up here?

The cat sat in front of a door at the far end of the main cabin. I threw it open. A skeleton sat at the head of a bed. I shrieked. It wore a hat and a dress. Its bony hand stretched out toward me. I stood as if someone had glued me to the floor. The skeleton's jaw had dropped down in what looked like a creepy grin. I slammed the door closed.

How could someone have died on this boat long enough ago for their bones to remain, yet this cat still be alive, meowing away? Never mind that now. I needed to find the radio. I scanned the room. There. There it was.

The radio was built in to a wall. If the battery that ran it had any juice, it wouldn't have much. I needed to try to figure out how to work it before I switched it on. A mic was attached by a curly cord to one side. I found the On/Off switch and a volume knob, which I turned up. It looked pretty basic. I hoped it was tuned to the right channel. But what to say? Something short and sweet. I took a deep breath, grabbed the mic, hit the On switch. Nothing happened, but I went on anyway, just in case. "Mayday. Mayday. Adrift off the shore of Emerald Cove. Mayday, Mayday—"

I hoped you were supposed to say "Mayday," and that wasn't just something you read in books or saw on films like *Jaws*. Ugh, why did I have to think about *Jaws* at a time like this? I released the button and listened. No staticky crackle. No calm voice assuring me they'd heard the message and help was on the way. Nothing but the sound of the ocean and the creaks of the boat. The cat meowed.

It was clawing on something wedged under the counter.

It glinted in the dim light. I leaned over and saw a ring. It looked expensive. I pried it out and tucked it into the little pocket in my sports bra. I looked at a stain on the floor. Maybe it was only some dinner spilled, but I scooped up the cat. Where would help come from? A helicopter? A boat that heard my message? A plane? The Coast Guard?

How could I make myself more noticeable? A mirror or something shiny to reflect off the bright, bright sun? I searched the bedroom. It had a mirror securely attached to the wall. I crossed to the bathroom. It had an old mirrored medicine cabinet. I tugged on the door, trying to pull it off, but the rusted hinges fought back.

A crowbar would work, or a screwdriver. Tools? Where would they be? My uncle's boat had a storage space below the main cabin so I went back out. I scanned the floor, kicking stuff out of the way until I found a hatch. I pulled it up and looked down into the dark space below. It was small. Probably where the engine was. I lay on my stomach and dropped my head down. It was hard to see anything in the dim light. But as my eyes adjusted, I saw the outline of a toolbox sitting on a metal table and tools latched to a pegboard.

I eased myself down, dropping the last bit. The waves felt rougher down here, and I staggered a bit as I grasped the toolbox. I carried it back to the opening, lifted it over my head, and managed to get it out onto the floor. I went back and studied the tools. I picked out a hacksaw and a crowbar. I shoved them through the opening as another wave jolted the ship. The hatch cover creaked.

"No, no, no." If it slammed closed, I'd be stuck down here in the dark and could soon become the next dead body on this boat. I leaped for the edge, pulled myself up, and rolled away as it crashed back down. I lay on the floor for a minute until the cat licked my face in a time's-a-wasting message.

I opened the toolbox and found a couple of flares and the gun that shot them. They looked old, and I knew from my uncle that old flares could be dangerous. I picked up some tools, and the cat followed me to the bathroom, where I pried the mirror from the cabinet.

I took the mirror up to the deck along with the toolbox, which I set down. I almost blinded myself when the sun hit the reflective surface. Okay, so this might work. As long as I didn't look at it. I scanned the horizon again. The fog seemed farther away. I hoped that meant it was receding and not that I was farther from shore. I spotted a tanker on the horizon, but it was so far away that I doubted it would be able to see the tiny speck I must be in the vast Gulf.

Usually when I ran on the beach I saw fishing boats dotting the horizon. None were out today. Maybe the fog had kept them in their harbors—the small one at Emerald Cove and the much larger one in Destin. Joaquín, the head bartender at the Sea Glass Saloon, where I worked, fished every morning before coming to work. Was he out here someplace? Did he know I was missing? News traveled faster than a radio message in a small town like Emerald Cove.

My shoulders slumped as I realized no one was racing to my rescue. The cat meowed something that sounded like *don't give up*. Or maybe it was just a plain meow and I was losing it.

I held up the mirror and turned in a circle, hoping as I wiggled it around it would catch someone's attention. My arms ached, but I kept at it. I saw two fighter jets scream by overhead. Probably from Eglin Air Force Base. They'd be too high to see me. But it was a good sign that the fog was dissipating. Otherwise they wouldn't be flying.

The bad news was, I couldn't see fog or shore. I'd drifted farther out to sea.

CHAPTER 3

I had to set the mirror down because my arms trembled from holding it up. I propped it up in a spot where the sun hit it. I looked out again and spotted a small, red speck heading this way. A boat! I grabbed the mirror and found a spot where the sun struck it. I lifted it up and down so the light would be like a beacon. It didn't look like the boat was getting closer.

I set the mirror down and scrambled for the flare gun and flare. I looked at the cat. "I hope this works and doesn't backfire." Literally, if it did backfire, it could injure us or start a fire. I aimed skyward and shot. The flare went up like it was supposed to. No way the red boat could miss that.

I shaded my eyes to watch the red boat. It turned away from me. Turned away. It couldn't have missed the flare.

Why was it leaving? I drooped with disappointment, swallowing some curse words no former children's librarian would ever say at the library. Why would it do that? I couldn't come up with any good reason. I could, however, come up with a lot of bad ones—pirates, smugglers, drug runners, human traffickers. Of all of them, the last one scared me the most.

My mouth was so dry it felt as if I'd been drinking salt. The cat and I headed back down below. I wiped at my face, finding tears I didn't know I was crying. "We have to be strong," I told the cat. But I knew the chances of our rescue diminished with each passing hour. We went into the kitchen and found bottles of water in a cabinet. I took a cautious sip. It tasted fine. My hand trembled as I poured some in a bowl for the cat. I finished the bottle quickly as I watched the cat's little pink tongue dart in and out of the water.

I leaned against the cabinet for a minute. The boat was swaying harder than it had a few minutes ago. Please let it be the wake of a rescue boat.

The cat and I ran up the stairs to the deck again. But no. I didn't see a rescue boat or plane or helicopter. What was in sight were black clouds gathering and swirling off to the south. At least I thought it was the south. The clouds I'd noticed earlier that I'd hoped had been moving away from me. Great. Perfect. What was next, sharks? Another wave buffeted the boat. The cat and I were thrown to one side, and the mirror was sliding toward the edge of the boat. I dove for it and managed to pull it back so it didn't tumble overboard.

I sat hugging the hot mirror for a minute. Even though it was warm out, I was shivering. *Fear*, I told myself.

Adrenaline. Think. Don't let the fear rule. It was a lesson I'd learned at ten, when I'd almost drowned in Lake Michigan. I thought about sailing on my uncle's boat, and the time the wind had quit out on the lake. I'd panicked, but my uncle had laughed and said not to worry. He had two backup systems for the sails, a motor and a generator. Maybe I'd find a generator here. Maybe I could figure out how to start it. My uncle had showed me how both systems worked all those years ago. Maybe it would make the radio work.

The logical place for the generator was in the room where I'd found the tools. I didn't want to go back down into that claustrophobic place, but my other options weren't good. As the waves grew larger, I crawled to the stairs. The cat pranced underneath me like this was some grand game. I slid down the steps and went back into the cabin. I took a long, cloth belt from a plush, purple robe on the floor and used it to tie the open trapdoor to a hook low on the wall.

I tightened the fabric as best I could and dropped back into the dark space. A wave hit the boat and slammed me into the metal table. My breath whooshed out of me and I gasped. The cat cried above me. Its little face peered down.

"I'm okay," I assured her. The cat cocked its head to one side, as if it wasn't sure that was true. "Just stay there." The last thing I needed was to be worried about losing her—if it was a her—down here. She stayed as if she understood my command. Or maybe she was just smart enough to know better.

I got back down on my hands and knees as the boat continued to rock. It wasn't likely that a generator would be up high. I felt around me as I crawled, hoping I wouldn't find any spiders or furry creatures dead or alive. Which made me wonder about the body up above. But no time to think about that now. I'd found a generator to my right.

I squinted at it as if that would help me see better. It didn't. This wasn't some fancy generator that started by flipping a switch. But it wasn't that different from my uncle's. "Please have fuel and oil or whatever else you need." I toggled a switch back and forth, priming the pump. It shuddered, coughed, and my heart felt like it literally leaped in my chest. Then the generator died. "No, no, NO!" I pounded my fist on it. "Ow." Then I went through the routine again.

It belched smoke, but it rattled to life. I pulled myself up out of the pit and ran to the radio. The green light glowed. I grabbed the mic and yelled, "Mayday, Mayday, Mayday. This is Chloe Jackson. I'm adrift on a ghost ship off the coast of Emerald Cove. Mayday, Mayday, Mayday." "Ghost ship" was a term for lost, empty boats, not for ones with paranormal activity.

I finally let loose of the button on the mic.

"Hey, Chloe Jackson, this is Coast Guard Petty Officer Kevin Collier. Are you in imminent danger?"

"No." Maybe that was what Mayday was for and there were other terms for other situations. "Petty Officer Collier, I've never been so happy to hear a voice in my life."

"I feel the same. We've got a copter, planes, and boats out searching for you. I don't know who you are, but the governor sure seems interested in your rescue. We have your coordinates."

"You do?" I asked. I'd never met the governor, but Vivi Slidell, my boss and co-owner of the Sea Glass with me, knew everyone. She was a power to be reckoned with when her dander was up. Which it had been for most of the few short months we'd known each other.

"Yes. Your VHF radio is hooked to a GPS."

"Thank heavens."

"Let's just talk until someone gets to you. I think the whole fleet of boats from Emerald Cove is out looking for you, and half of Destin's fleet."

"There's a body on board." I'd been so caught up in my own drama, I'd forgotten to mention it.

"Say again," Collier said, his voice more urgent.

"There's a dead body. I think it's a woman. And I'm not an expert, but I'd say she's been dead a while." I faced the radio and heard Collier talking to someone else. My nose itched and I turned. Smoke tendrils were curling up out of the hatch where the generator was. A belch of smoke rose as my eyebrows lifted in alarm. I whirled back to the radio.

"Mayday. The boat's on fire. Abandoning ship."

"Chloe—"

I picked up the cat and raced up the stairs onto the deck, I heard a *whunk*, and flames shot up and out. I had no time to look for a lifeboat or life jacket. Flames chased us.

"Sorry about this," I said to the cat. I took a running start and leaped.

CHAPTER 4

We went a few feet under and I kicked away from the boat. I resurfaced holding the sputtering cat with one hand and paddling furiously with the other. The straw hat floated nearby, so I swam over, snagged it, and put it back on my head. I put the cat on top of the stiff crown so I could swim faster. Thank heavens the top of the hat didn't touch my scalp, because the poor cat's claws had to be fully out. The cat yowled in protest. Smoke roiled from the sailboat. The boat would be more visible at least.

I focused on my strokes and kicks, fighting the increasingly large waves. Trying not to panic as thoughts of my almost drowning when I was ten swirled in my head. This was different. I was older and I wasn't in a storm. Yet. I glanced over at the clouds that were swirling closer.

A motor throttled, sounding like a boat was speeding toward me. I hoped it would be able to spot me in the waves. And then I saw it. I waved my hands. The boat slowed. A man threw a life ring toward me. I swam to it, latched on, and kicked while he pulled me to him. He reached down a strong, tanned arm. Deep laugh lines sprouted from the outer corner of his light brown eyes. He had a long, white beard and white, flowing hair. It was like Neptune himself had come to rescue me.

"Take the cat first," I shouted. The man lifted the hat from my head. He turned, placed the hat on the deck, and hauled me out of the water. It was a cigarette boat: built for speed, with a sleek hull and a narrow beam or width. These boats had a long nose and a short rear section for seating. Used by law enforcement, thrill seekers, and drug runners. I hoped he wasn't the latter.

He picked up the cat and gave it a cuddle before handing her over to me. "Are you okay?"

"I think so. Shaken."

"Take a seat." He picked up a handheld radio. "I've got Chloe Jackson." He clicked off the radio. "You are Chloe Jackson, I hope, and not some other random woman stranded at sea . . . with a cat?" I nodded. He hit the radio again. "Yes. I'll meet you." His voice was sharp. He looked at me bemused as I held the cat and cuddled her to me.

Her meows sounded angry. I couldn't blame her. We were both shivering.

"There's a blanket under that seat. Get it and then strap in. It's going to be a bumpy ride." He glanced at the clouds that raced toward us.

So Neptune could quote Bette Davis, who'd been one of my grandmother's favorite actresses. I found the blanket, buckled into the seat next to him, and he pulled the throttle back. The nose of the boat lifted as we jetted across the water. A streak of lightning flashed green across the sky.

"Thank you," I shouted over the roar of the engine.

The cat clung to me like I was a lifesaver, its little claws digging into the shirt I'd taken from the boat. I didn't recognize the man driving the boat. His turquoise T-shirt and khaki shorts all flapped about him in the wind. A baseball cap was tucked in the back of the waistband of his shorts. Strong, tan legs braced against the floor. He glanced at me and gave a quick nod. He took a band from his wrist and tied his flowing hair into a ponytail. He reached over and ran a finger across the cat's back before he turned back to focus on steering.

"How'd you end up out here?" He waved back toward the sailboat.

I shouted my explanation of hearing the cry and getting swept out into the Gulf.

"It seems like you got lucky today," he said. "And the cat did too."

I nodded even though he couldn't see me do it. "I did. Thank you for saving us."

"Where'd you find her?"

"She was in a cabin. I'm not sure how she got on the boat. My best guess is while it was onshore before it washed back to sea. Can you drop me off at the Sea Glass?"

He gave me a sharp look. "Why there? I'd thought . . . you'd want to go to the Coast Guard station in Destin for help and a report."

"I work there. Vivi will be worried." If she'd called the governor, she must be frantic.

"Vivi?"

"Yes. Do you know her?"

"It's an unusual name." He changed the direction the boat was headed and concentrated on steering across the increasingly rough Gulf.

I brought my knees up to my chest and re-tucked the blanket around the cat and me. I turned back to look at the sailboat. Smoke rolled around it like steam above a witch's cauldron. The boat was rocked by a huge gust of wind, then hidden from view by sheets of rain. So far we'd outpaced the rain.

Fifteen minutes later my rescuer slowed. He grabbed the baseball cap out of his waistband and tugged it low on his head. With the nose of the boat down I could see the shore and Emerald Cove. To the west the high-rises of Destin were white against the dark sky. The man entered the harbor and then pulled up to the dock behind the Sea Glass. A crowd stood behind it and they cheered when they saw us. My face heated up. This was unexpected and not exactly welcome. I was exhausted by what I'd gone through and a bit embarrassed at all the trouble I'd caused.

"Thank you," I told him as I undid my seat belt.

Joaquín hurried forward as I stood. He reached out his hand and I grasped it, holding the cat in my other hand. His aquamarine-colored eyes were narrowed with concern and his dark hair was more tousled than usual.

"Get me out of here. Please," I said to Joaquín as the group rushed toward us. I turned to give the man back his blanket, but he was already puttering away. I'd forgotten to ask him his name.

It took me a minute to realize a blond reporter was shoving a microphone in my face. "Tell us about the dead body you found."

Apparently, reporters here listened to VHF radio broadcasts. On some level I'd known questions would come, but I didn't expect them to be from a reporter, or so soon. Joaquín strong-armed us right by her. Vivi waited by the back door to the Sea Glass. As soon as Joaquín and I were in, she slammed the door closed and locked it. Soon I was sitting at the bar with Vivi and Joaquín standing on the other side. Wade Thomas, who owned the Briny Pirate restaurant next door, stood by Vivi's side.

I glanced at the clock. It was eleven thirty-five. It felt like I'd been gone for days, not five hours. Vivi hadn't opened the bar yet, which was unusual for her.

"We didn't know you were back," Vivi and Joaquín said in unison.

"And you already found another body?" Joaquín asked. He crossed himself.

"I got back late last night and didn't want to bother anyone." I'd gone home for two weeks to wrap up my life in Chicago. "At least I think I found a body. The more I've thought about it, the more improbable it seems that actual human remains would stay together like that." In the moment I'd been so scared that I'd made assumptions. The cat mewed.

"Who's this?" Vivi asked. Her face lit up brighter than I'd seen it since we'd first met in June. Vivi wore her hair in a silver bob. She was tall, slender, and rarely missed a day at the gym. She dressed better than anyone I knew and had more designer handbags than the purse department at Belk.

I'd come down here to fulfill the last request of my best friend Boone, who'd died in Afghanistan. I'd promised I'd help his grandmother if anything happened to him. Vivi hadn't been welcoming—she wasn't the frail, needy woman I'd expected either—and of course she was grieving over the loss of her only heir. When she'd found out I'd inherited twenty-five percent of the bar she co-owned with Boone, on top of inheriting his house and boat, things went from bad to worse. However, in the past few months we'd come to an uneasy truce.

Vivi reached for the cat.

I handed her over. "This is Pippi." The name fit, because this was one brave little cat, and of course she had the long, white stockings. Pippi cuddled up against Vivi and started the low throb of a purr. Wade reached over and scratched Pippi's head.

"Are you okay, Chloe?" Wade asked. "We've had boats wash up before, but I don't think anyone's ever been swept back out in one."

"I'm okay. Except for being cold." My teeth wanted to chatter, but I clenched my jaw to keep them from it.

"Coffee or something stronger?" Joaquín asked.

Something stronger was tempting. "Coffee."

Joaquín poured and handed me a cup of coffee. After drinking a bit I gripped it in both hands, trying to warm them.

"Vivi, I need to get over to the restaurant. You call me if you need anything," Wade said. "Chloe, you do the same."

"Thank you," I said as he left.

"What happened?" Joaquín and Vivi spoke in unison for the second time.

I'd opened my mouth to answer when someone pounded on the back door so hard it almost made the many pictures and signs hanging on the walls bounce.

Vivi hurried off and came back with Ralph Harrison,

the owner of the Redneck Rollercoaster, which was actually a trolley.

"Where did you get that hat?" Ralph demanded. His dark face looked shocked—or afraid. His short afro looked like it had more gray in it than when I'd left, which worried me.

The sodden hat sat next to me on a barstool. I glanced at Joaquín, whose perfectly manicured eyebrows raised at me in a what-the-heck look.

I picked up the hat. It was straw, with bright red, now wilted, artificial flowers around the brim. "This hat?" Ralph nodded. "It was on the boat," I said. "I found it in one of the cabins on the sailboat. Why?"

"Because I gave that to my late wife on our twenty-fifth anniversary."

"Your wife who disappeared over a decade ago?" I asked. If I remembered the story right, she'd gone off on a boat with friends and had never been seen again. "The one you had declared dead?"

"It was twelve years ago," Ralph said as he nodded again. He picked up the hat and sank down in its place.

CHAPTER 5

Joaquín poured Ralph a beer, which he took and swigged down a huge gulp.

"I saw you get off the boat in that hat and I had to go sit and catch my breath. That reporter noticed me and ran over to ask what was wrong. I asked her to leave me alone and she did. But it was like she sensed I had a story. She moved off but came back when I walked toward the Sea Glass," Ralph said.

"How do you know it's the same hat?" I asked. "If you were in a tourist spot, there had to be hundreds of the same one."

"We went to a millinery store and custom-designed it." He picked up the hat. "Look at the band inside. They embroidered her initials. RMH—Raquel Meredith Harrison—and 'Happy Twenty-Fifth Anniversary.'"

We all leaned in to look. Another firm knock whacked against the back door.

"I'll get it," I said. Ralph's sorrow came off him in waves, hitting me like little punches. I felt guilty for something I had no control over. But Ralph had become a friend over the past few months and I'd never want to hurt him, even though it was inadvertent.

My body was stiff from my morning's activities. My legs acted as if they didn't really want to hold me up. The knock sounded again before I got to the door. "I'm coming," I yelled before flinging it open.

Two men in suits stood at the door. They were both tall and thin, with close-cropped dark hair. One was a bit older than the other. "We're special agents with the Coast Guard and are looking for Chloe Jackson."

"That's me." Was I in some kind of trouble? I started shivering again, which probably made me look guilty of something.

Vivi came up behind me. "Bill. How are you?" Bill came out as a three-syllable word. Vivi's Southern drawl got stronger when she was angry or worried. They might not realize it, but Vivi wasn't happy.

"Vivi, good to see you. We need to speak to Ms. Jackson."

"She's been through quite an ordeal this morning. A later time would be much better."

I turned back and forth. Everyone looked over my head as if I wasn't even there.

"I understand that, but unfortunately, unless there's a medical reason, this can't wait."

"I called my personal physician and he's on the way

over to check her out. He can determine if she's up to being questioned."

Vivi had been suspected of a murder last June. She'd been questioned at length several times. "I'm fine, Vivi. There's no harm in talking to them."

Vivi looked down at me. She was only a couple of inches taller than me, but she always wore heels that added at least three more inches. She opened her mouth, then snapped it shut.

"This way, then." She turned her back to us, but we all followed her like ducklings after their mother.

We passed the kitchen, bathrooms, and Vivi's office before entering the main part of the bar. The officers noticed Joaquín and Ralph. The one named Bill turned and looked at me.

"We need to speak to you alone."

"That's not necessary," Vivi said.

"Yes. It is," Bill responded.

"Does she need a lawyer?" Joaquín asked. His brow was furrowed with concern.

A lawyer. I hadn't done anything wrong. Unless they thought I was trespassing on the boat, which I guess I was, but for what I'd thought was a good reason. "It's fine," I said. "I'm sure they just want to know what happened this morning."

"Exactly," the other Coast Guard man said.

I led them to the front of the bar by the wall of doors that were usually open. The views of the white sandy beaches were normally stunning, but the rain had unleashed, so everything was obscured to soft grays. We sat at a high top. I took the stool with the best view. That would keep my back to Vivi, Ralph, and Joaquín. I didn't need them distracting me.

The inside of the bar was more tiki hut than saloon. Photos and signs lined the walls, including some of Vivi and her friends from high school and college. This was a fishing community, so there were the requisite photos of smiling men and women holding up whatever fish they'd caught. Many were in black-and-white. Oh, the secrets this place knew.

"I'm Special Agent Bill Topping and this is Special Agent Alex Lowe."

"Did you find the boat?" I asked.

"We had to call off the search because of the weather."

Even though I figured that was the case, I was still disappointed. I glanced back at Ralph, who was staring intently at us. I was sure Bill and Alex would be talking to him soon.

"How did you happen to be on the boat?" Bill asked. His voice was neutral.

I explained to them how I was out for a run and thought I'd heard a baby cry. Bill kept the neutral look on his face, but Alex did half an eye roll. I turned and pointed to Vivi. "I found a cat. I guess the fog distorted the sound."

"That can happen," Bill said.

"Then what happened?" Alex asked.

I ran them through the events of the morning, pausing just before I got to the part about finding the skeleton.

"You found a body," Bill said. "That must have been difficult."

Alex leaned back a little.

I nodded and described the scene.

"You're sure there was a body onboard?" Alex asked. "Stress, fog, physical exhaustion can lead to hallucinations."

"Yes." It came out louder than necessary. I needed to stay calm. But I was exhausted and Alex was stressing me out. "That wasn't any hallucination."

"Go on," Bill said.

I explained about finding the ring, which I hadn't thought of until that moment.

"What happened to the ring?" Alex asked.

"I stuck it in my sports bra. It has a small hidden pocket. I'll just go to the bathroom and dig it out."

"Can you retrieve it here, Chloe?" Alex asked.

I turned slightly away from them. Yeesh, this was embarrassing. But I managed to fish in the little pocket, find the ring, and pull it out without flashing anyone. "Here." The ring was magnificent. It was the first time I'd had time to look at it closely. It had a huge center diamond with clusters of other diamonds around it, set on a narrow gold band. It looked old.

"Let me see it," Ralph said. He strode across the room, even as Bill and Alex shook their heads.

I glanced at Alex and Bill. Bill reached for the ring. I turned to Ralph and held it out to him. Ralph stared at it, then slumped onto the stool next to me.

"Ralph?" I asked gently. "Was this Raquel's?"

"It was a family heirloom. She never took it off."

The Coast Guard officers started another flurry of questions.

Ralph held up a hand. "Raquel, my former wife, went out with friends on a boat twelve years ago last August. Two men. Two women."

"And you didn't mind your wife running around with other men?" Alex asked.

Ralph froze for the tiniest second. "They were friends." His voice was firm.

But I wasn't sure he was telling the truth about that. I focused on the ring I was still holding. Had Raquel wedged the ring in the corner hoping someday it would be found?

"The last time I talked to Raquel—" Ralph's voice cracked. He cleared his throat. "She called from the tennis club. It was around six p.m. Everyone was hot and decided boating would be the fastest way to cool down. They were only supposed to be gone a couple of hours, but never returned."

We all sat for a minute. I think the grief in Ralph's voice even got to Alex.

A commotion broke out at the back of the bar. I turned to see Delores, Ralph's current wife, dashing across the room. Delores had bright red hair, a curvy figure, and a steel magnolia attitude. She flung herself into Ralph's arms and they clung to each other. She leaned back and put her hands on either side of his head. She studied him as if he was the most precious thing she'd ever seen.

"I'm okay," Ralph said.

"Is what I heard true?" Delores was in the uniform she wore at The Diner. She must have gone from her job as a dispatcher straight to The Diner. People here worked hard to make ends meet. In the few short months I'd lived here I'd quickly realized that many people were one disaster away from being homeless. "Did Chloe find Raquel?"

"It looks that way. At the very least some of her things," Ralph said. He took her hands and kissed each one. "Just give us a minute."

Delores looked the rest of us over. Her eyes burned like lasers and she made eye contact with each of us. Alex even leaned back a little. "Ralph had nothing to do with Raquel's disappearance."

Up to that moment I never thought he had.

CHAPTER 6

I could tell by the surprised look on Bill's face that he'd had the same thought.

"Mr. Harrison, would you please wait over there?" Bill asked. He pointed to a table on the other side of the bar, midway between where we sat and where Joaquín and Vivi stood.

And although he formed it as a question, there was no doubt in my mind that it was a command. Ralph pushed himself up and followed his instructions. Ralph had served in the Air Force and an order must still sound like an order to him. Delores swept her glare over all of us once more and then went to join Ralph.

I walked Bill and Alex through the rest of my time on the boat, jumping in the water, and being rescued.

"What was the name of the man who rescued you?" Alex asked.

"Don't you know?" I asked.

Alex barely managed not to roll his eyes again. "If I knew I wouldn't have asked."

"Well, I don't know either," I said.

"How can that be?" Alex asked.

"He knew who I was and I wasn't in the best of shape, so we didn't talk much."

"Did you get the name of his boat?"

"I didn't. He hauled me in from the side. He radioed that he had me, so your dispatcher should know who he is, right?"

"They don't," Alex said.

That didn't make sense. "Is there some way to trace the call back to him?"

"There's no record of someone calling and saying they had you," Bill said. "We would have asked that you be brought to us."

What? "But I heard him."

"Like you said, you weren't in the best of shape," Alex said.

"I know what I heard." He'd radioed someone. I'd assumed it was the Coast Guard. "How did you know I was here and not still out on the Gulf if he didn't call?"

"We got a call once you were back onshore from someone with the fire department," Bill explained. His voice was gentle. Almost too gentle, as if he was beginning to think I'd made the whole thing up.

"Then maybe someone onshore saw who dropped me off." A lot of people had gathered behind the Sea Glass; surely someone knew the man or knew his boat. I turned to where Joaquín and Vivi stood and called over, "Joaquín, do you know the name of the man who rescued me?"

Joaquín shook his head. "I was so relieved to see you, I barely looked at him."

"Ralph was outside, but the rest of the crowd were a bit of a blur," I said. "Maybe the reporter got his name." I looked back and forth between Bill and Alex hopefully.

"We'll check into it," Bill said.

"Why was the crowd out there if they didn't know I'd been found?"

"My understanding was they were setting up search parties."

"Do you have any other questions? I'm exhausted. I got in late last night and woke up early."

"No more for now," Bill said.

"Will you let me know if you find the boat?" I asked.

"Yes," Bill said as Alex said, "No."

I stood and so did they. I handed over the ring to them. As I headed back to the bar, they peeled off and went over to Ralph.

As much as I wanted to go home and go to bed, I settled on a barstool. I wanted to talk to Ralph when the Coast Guard was done with him.

"More coffee?" Joaquín asked.

I held out my cup, grateful to him. "Yes, please."

Joaquín poured another cup for me and pushed the white mug with the turquoise Sea Glass Saloon logo across the bar. Wisps of steam spiraled up from the coffee.

"What did they ask you?" Vivi asked.

I filled them in as I let the coffee cool.

"We didn't even know you were back," Joaquín said again.

"I'm sorry. I got back late last night and didn't want to wake anyone." Joaquín fished at the crack of dawn every morning the weather was good. Calling Vivi would have been awkward. We had a complicated relationship, but I think she was getting used to me and me to her.

I drank some of the coffee. When I'd first arrived in June she hadn't wanted me here, but after I solved a murder she'd been accused of, she'd thawed a bit. I'd spent the rest of the summer working my butt off, too busy to worry about what the future held or to be sad that I'd been downsized from my job as a children's librarian in Chicago. I'd taken a break and gone home to collect my belongings. While I was in Chicago, I threw an engagement party for my former roommate and made the rounds saying goodbye to family, friends, and former colleagues. I'd even managed to go to Trivia Night with my librarian friends. Now, I was here to settle into my new life.

"How did you know I was out on the boat?" I asked.

"Delores called me," Vivi said. "Someone from the Sheriff's Department found your shoes and key chain sitting on the beach. I confirmed they were yours." She paused. "It was a terrible moment."

That punched me in the gut. "I'm sorry."

"And Vivi called me. We were about to set out on our own search, along with half the boat owners from Emerald Cove," Joaquín said.

"Did you recognize the man who dropped me off?" I asked.

"Like I said, I didn't pay him no never mind."

Sometimes I thought Joaquín had an inner Southern granny in him.

"I knew that reporter was lurking and I wanted to get

you in the Sea Glass before she could bother you,"
Joaquín said.

"I don't know who he was and would like to thank him
again." And ask him who he called if it wasn't the Coast
Guard. "Hopefully, someone in that crowd recognized
him and will let me know." I drank more coffee. "Bill
said no one called in saying they had me. But the man
called someone. I wonder who?"

Vivi looked over my shoulder, so I turned on my barstool. The two Coast Guard officers, Ralph, and Delores
all stood and then headed our way. The Coast Guard officers passed with curt nods and "We'll be in touch" statements. Ralph and Delores stopped at the bar. Ralph's
brow was creased with deep lines and his eyes looked
pained with sorrow. Delores, on the other hand, looked as
fiery as her red hair.

"Are you okay?" I asked. Stupid, stupid question.
How could he be?

"I will be. Hate reliving this again."

Delores took Ralph's arm. "Come on. Let's get you
fed before your blood sugar drops." She looked us over.
"Y'all take care."

None of us spoke until we heard the heavy back door
close.

"What's he talking about?" I asked.

"When his wife disappeared, Ralph was a suspect,"
Vivi said. "And when he filed to have her declared dead,
it came up again."

"He was cleared both times," Joaquín said.

"Let's hope the third time isn't the charm," I murmured. I didn't want Ralph to be arrested.

CHAPTER 7

I stood on the screened porch of Boone's house, *my* house—I was still adjusting to it being mine—looking out at the Gulf. The storms had passed, the sky dazzled a showy blue, the water its trademark emerald green—the reason this area was called the Emerald Coast. The house was made of cement blocks and was as sturdy as could be. It was a two-bedroom, two-bath with an open floor plan. I hadn't made many changes to it. So the walls and furniture were still all beige. I'd added a few throw pillows, but other than that, it was all Boone's style.

Vivi had insisted that I take the rest of the day off even though I'd protested. She had also insisted on taking care of Pippi. She said so I didn't have to go buy pet supplies, but I think Vivi had an ulterior-motive/love-at-first-sight thing going on. I didn't have it in me to argue . . . for once.

I'd already gone to Destin to buy a new phone—good grief I was dependent on that thing—and carried in the rest of my belongings from my car, those acts alone making me realize how tired and overwhelmed I was. My muscles all ached. I wanted to nap, but I was too keyed up. So I selected a beer, took it back out to the porch, and sat on a cushioned wicker chair. Hard to believe this was my house, my view. The house was isolated down a long drive with stands of tall loblolly pines and coastal forest made up of scrub oak and magnolia trees on either side.

I thought about Pippi and put up some posts describing her on local Emerald Cove social media pages in case she was lost. For Vivi's sake I kind of hoped no one would claim her. After I finished I popped open the beer, toasted skyward to Boone, and took a sip. A wooden walkway led from the porch over the sea oats waving on the dunes to the white, sandy beach. I was restless and thought about grabbing one of the paddleboards under the porch. A knock on my front-porch door came just in time to save me from heading out.

I trotted to the door and opened it. Rhett Barnett stood there with his dark, wavy hair, deep, green eyes, and long, enviable lashes. Here I was, sunburned, sweaty, covered in dried saltwater, and looking near my worst. I ran a hand through my short hair, which was plastered to my head. I'm pretty sure I smelled like a fish left out on the beach for a few days.

"Hot stuff," Rhett said.

"Hi." I blushed, knowing that wasn't true. At least not right now.

He held up a bag. "I brought a late lunch. Two Hot Stuff burritos."

Oh, he wasn't talking about me. I pushed aside the disappointment. My stomach rumbled loudly as I smelled spicy chorizo and hot sauce. Rhett just grinned. It's nothing he hadn't heard before. I'd gotten over being embarrassed about the rumbles long ago. "It's so good to see you. Come in." *So good to see you?* I sounded like some lovesick protagonist in a Victorian novel. Next thing you know I'd need smelling salts and a fainting couch.

"Is that from Maria's?" I asked.

"It is."

Maria and her husband, Arturo, ran a food truck in Emerald Cove with the best Mexican food in the Panhandle according to Rhett. "Let's eat on the porch. Want a beer?" Wow, I'd actually put coherent sentences together.

"A beer sounds great." Rhett flashed a smile before he walked toward the porch.

I opened the refrigerator and stuck my whole head in, hoping to cool it off.

"You okay?" Rhett called.

I jerked my head up, hit the shelf, and bottles of water tumbled out. I picked out a beer. "Just looking for this." I backed out of the refrigerator and held it up. Not that there was much else in the refrigerator, because I'd cleaned it out before I left. I shoved the water bottles to the side with my foot. I'd pick them up later. I gathered plates, utensils, and paper towels to use as napkins.

As I headed to the porch, I realized I hadn't seen Rhett for almost four months. Right after I'd solved a murder, he'd left town. I'd heard he'd bought a new, bigger boat and was traveling around the Caribbean. Before he left I'd thought there were some sparks between us. But I might have killed them when he'd heard my original plan was to return to my job in Chicago.

Once on the porch I handed Rhett the beer and set

down the plates, utensils, and napkins on the wicker coffee table. He looked comfortable sitting out here, but he'd probably been here often when Boone was still alive. Rhett was a year older than him, but they'd gone to the same public schools here.

"Excuse me for just a minute. Go ahead and start." I turned to my right and went through the sliding glass doors that led to my bedroom. I went to the bathroom, quickly stripped, and took a fast shower. A cold one. I threw on some leggings and a tunic and went back out after running my hands through my hair. This wasn't ideal, but at least I didn't stink.

Rhett had put an aluminum-wrapped burrito on both plates. He'd also taken out a paper basket full of tortilla chips and containers of salsa and guacamole.

"You could have started," I said as I sat in a wicker chair adjacent to the love seat he sat on.

"My granny would knock the grits out of me if I did something so uncouth." Rhett grinned as he unwrapped his burrito.

I'd met his grandmother once and I was pretty sure she would knock the grits out of Rhett if he ever called her "Granny" to her face. She was a lady, and an intimidating one, as tiny as she was. I knew Rhett was from a wealthy, well-known family, but I didn't know much more than that.

"What's your family like?" I asked right before I took a big bite of my burrito.

Rhett had picked up his burrito, but now set it back down. "Hard to capture them in one or two sentences. You'd probably have to meet them."

Meet his family? Too soon, way too soon. And if his

grandmother was an example of what to expect, no, thank you.

"Some of them think they're Southern aristocracy and cling to how things used to be." He used air quotes around "used to be." "That group loves a good cotillion and debutante ball. Some are lawyers or doctors. Some live in the backwoods, off the grid."

"So they're complicated, like most big families." I could relate to that with my large extended family.

"They are."

"I heard you bought a new boat and spent the summer cruising." I hoped I'd kept my tone light and breezy instead of needy and hurt because he'd left without a goodbye. Rhett had been a criminal defense lawyer in Birmingham, but had left for some reason and returned to Emerald Cove, where he was a volunteer fireman.

"I did."

"Was it fun?" I asked.

"Parts of it were." Rhett stared down at his burrito and didn't elaborate.

I almost inhaled my food—I guess being swept out to sea on a ghost ship and finding a skeleton gave me an appetite. I only took breaks to sip a beer and glance at Rhett as he ate. When I finished, I licked a bit of hot sauce from my pinkie and looked up to find Rhett watching me with a look I couldn't interpret. Want? Desire? Disgust? I'm guessing no one licked their fingers at Rhett's family's house. My whole body heated up. Maybe I needed to go stick my head back in the refrigerator.

"Are you feeling okay? You looked flushed," Rhett said.

"Hot sauce," I managed to get out while simultaneously wishing I'd just combust and disappear. "I'm going to get a glass of water. You want another beer?"

"Water sounds great. I could get it for you."

"Nope. You just stay put. Moving keeps my muscles loose."

In the kitchen I stuffed the water bottles I'd knocked out back into the refrigerator. I took a pitcher of cold water and set it on the counter. After I grabbed two Mason jars I used for glasses, I poured the water and carried it out to the porch. Even though Rhett reached out for his glass I set it on the coffee table. I didn't want to risk our fingers brushing against each other and me blushing again.

"What are you doing here?" I asked. Might as well clear the air and the awkwardness that hung between us.

Rhett laughed. "Chloe Jackson, you are unlike anyone I've ever met."

Last June he'd told me that I intrigued him. Now I was unlike anyone he'd met. I hoped that was a good thing. But I'm guessing between my snoring—it's how we'd met—the stomach rumbles, and finger licking, it probably wasn't. Not that it mattered, because I wasn't looking for a relationship. I was still sorting out things with past relationships. Until I did that, I wasn't in the mood for anything more than some friendly banter, even though the flushing and heating up said otherwise.

"I came to check on you. I was still out searching when I heard you'd returned."

Rhett had been out searching? For me? Well, that just gave my heart an arrhythmia. I did my best to ignore it.

"They notified the volunteer fire department once a deputy found your sneakers and key chain on the beach with no sign of you or the boat you called in about."

Ah, so he was out there in an official capacity, but he didn't have to bring me food or keep me company. "Thank you for searching for me. As you can see, I'm fine." Mostly fine, except for being achy and a bit emotional after everything that I'd been through. "And thank you for the food. It was delicious." I looked down at the empty wrappings.

"I should probably head out," Rhett said. He stood, so I did too.

We walked to the front door in an awkward silence. I didn't want to ask when I'd see him again. "Thanks again," I said.

"Anytime," he said as he headed to his car.

"Hey, Rhett," I called. He stopped and turned back toward me. "Did you see a red speedboat while you were out on the Gulf?"

He thought for a moment. I liked that he took his time.

"No. Why do you ask?"

"It's probably nothing, but I thought I saw a red boat heading toward me. I shot off a flare and they turned around and headed west. It was probably nothing. I'd been pretty shaken both physically and mentally by then."

Rhett frowned. "It might not be nothing. Besides the skeleton was there anything strange on the boat?"

Word about the skeleton had spread quickly. "No. Not that I remember." Maybe I'd take out Boone's boat and do a little searching myself. The people on the red boat must be up to something and I wanted to know what.

CHAPTER 8

Rhett had reached his car—a BMW convertible—when I called out again, "Wait. Do you want to go on an adventure with me?"

He turned and squinted at me. "You're going whether I say yes or no, aren't you?"

I shrugged. He had me there. "Yes."

"Do you want me to drive?"

I was tired. "That would be lovely."

"Get what you need and hop in."

I ran into the house and gathered up my purse, the keys to Boone's boat—it was still so hard to think of it as mine—a couple of beach towels, sunscreen, and several bottles of water. I tossed it all in a big, hot-pink tote. I made sure the doors were locked and headed out. Rhett was texting away on his phone, but when he looked up, he tossed it on the car seat. He took the tote from me, put it on the back seat, and rounded the car to open the door for me. I slid in and he shut it firmly.

"What do you have planned?" Rhett asked once he got in the car.

"A search for the boat I was on this morning."

Rhett gave me a long look before he started his car. He drove us to the Sea Glass and parked without asking any more questions. I almost dozed off on the ten-minute drive and yawned more than once. To keep myself awake, I'd dug around in my purse and found my sunglasses. We walked down the marina past the Sea Glass. I stopped by Boone's boat. It was a twenty-footer, center console boat. Nothing fancy, but sturdy and dependable. I'd never taken it out on the Gulf before and only a few times on Choctawhatchee Bay. Emerald Cove was on a peninsula that separated the Bay from the Gulf.

"Why don't we take my boat?" Rhett asked.

I had to admit I was curious about his brand-new cabin cruiser. And not piloting would be a relief. I didn't want to admit how tired I was. "Thanks. Sounds good."

We walked behind Wade Thomas's restaurant, the Briny Pirate. Wade provided all the food for the Sea Glass. We had a tiny kitchen, so if people were hungry for more than peanuts, they could order and someone would run the food over to them. It was a win-win for both places. We continued on past a low-slung condominium building and took a right onto a dock. After passing several boats Rhett jumped onto the deck of a beauty. At least forty-five feet long, with a cabin and onboard engines.

"It's amazing," I said.

Rhett grinned at me and held out his hand to help me onboard. "Wait until you see the inside."

He gave me a tour. Every detail was top-notch: king size bed, bathroom with a tub, chef's kitchen, a guest cabin, and a comfy living area with a wall of shelves full of books. I lingered in front of them, astounded to see everything from the Hardy Boys to law books. Rhett had moved back here almost a year and a half ago.

We came back out on the deck and climbed a ladder to the wheel. Rhett fired up the engines. The initial rumble shot up through my legs all the way to the top of my head. *Whoa!* Rhett backed the boat out of its slip with ease. We putted down the harbor heading toward the Gulf.

"Which way, oh fair one?" Rhett's voice was playful, but his look was serious.

Don't blush. *Don't blush.* "We came back to the harbor from the south, but I wasn't tracking how far east or west we were." I sighed. "The Gulf's a big place. I'm not sure we'll have any luck finding her."

"The Coast Guard haven't had any luck yet. They have the same coordinates I do from your Mayday call," Rhett said.

Odd to think of Rhett and other boaters hearing my call. My desperation. It was a private moment heard all too widely.

"The time between your call and hearing you were at the Sea Glass seemed like a thousand days."

"I'm sure you've had a lot of moments like that as a firefighter." Why did he make me so uncomfortable? In a good way, but still uncomfortable.

Rhett gave a brief nod. "I have, but this time it was different."

Last summer, before Rhett had left on his trip, a mutual friend of ours had told me that Rhett liked me. I knew I was interested, but at the time I hadn't planned to move down here permanently. When I said I was leaving, Rhett hadn't said a word. Part of me had been hoping he'd ask me to stay, but that thought had been ridiculous because we hadn't known each other very long.

"You said in your call that the boat was on fire." Rhett glanced over at me. "It may have sunk."

"It's possible. It's also possible the storm doused the flames and the boat's still drifting around out in the Gulf." We hit the open water, and as soon as it was safe, Rhett opened the throttle. The bow lifted and the wind tossed my hair. If I wouldn't have looked like an idiot, I would have spread out my arms like Kate Winslet did in *Titanic*. With the calm seas, it was like we were flying. I refrained and instead opened a weather app on my phone. I found a radar view of the storm track. "The storm went from the southwest to the northeast. Peak winds were sixty miles an hour." I kept my voice calm. I shuddered a little, thinking of what would have happened to Pippi and me if we hadn't been found before the storm hit.

"You're safe," Rhett said. He typed some figures into a computer near the steering wheel. A few moments later he frowned at the screen. "We'll head northeast of where you radioed from." He glanced over at me again. "We might as well sit. It will take us about thirty minutes to get to the spot."

The chair was like a luxury recliner—lots of padding, wide arms. After I sat I pulled two water bottles out of my tote and handed one to Rhett. I heard the jet engine of a Coast Guard helicopter. Over the summer I'd learned to tell the different sounds of the Coast Guard, Air Force, and tourist helicopters. I shaded my eyes and looked up. The helicopter flew over us heading west, back toward Destin.

"Do you think they're giving up the search?" I asked.

"I doubt it. Might be something more pressing going on, or they found her. I'll flip on the radio and see if we can hear any chatter." Rhett switched from channel to channel but didn't find out anything.

My eyes started drooping. I curled up on the chair and gave up fighting the need to sleep.

"Chloe?"

A warm hand touched my arm and I bolted up, face-to-face with Rhett. His green eyes sparkled against his deep tan.

"Didn't mean to scare you."

"Did I snore?"

"You sounded just like Chewbacca. It was cute."

Thank heavens he thought Chewbacca noises were cute, because I'd dated a few guys that made all kinds of suggestions on how to cure snoring. One guy actually taped a rock to my back so if I rolled over on it, I'd wake up. That was the end of that relationship.

He took my hands and pulled me up. "Look, is that her?"

Fifty yards in front of us the boat drifted along, listing a bit to one side.

"That is. That's her. You found her. How long was I out?" Now, all of the sudden, I was calling the boat her too.

"Thirty minutes."

"How did the Coast Guard not find her?"

"It was a gamble. I didn't think we'd have any luck."

"So you just came out here to humor me?"

Rhett glanced down at his brown deck shoes. "Pretty much."

"Thank you."

He raised his eyebrows in an expression that made me think my answer wasn't the one he was expecting. I meant it. I was grateful for his company and his expertise.

"I need to radio the Coast Guard that we found her."

"Absolutely." I waited while he made the call. "Any sign of a red boat?" Red boats were unusual down here. White reflected light and heat away. White also stood out more against the water if a boat was disabled or the passengers needed help.

My uncle taught me as much about boats as he could after I'd nearly drowned, so I'd feel safe out on the water. Combine that with my natural curiosity and I'd learned a lot. It's one of the reasons I'd become a librarian—I was always asking questions. Librarians had access to databases not everyone did.

"None. I haven't seen many boats out here."

"Can we get any closer?"

"Yes," he said as he pulled back the throttle.

In a few minutes we were just feet away from the boat. Rhett cut the engine and all we could hear was the gentle slap of the waves and the creaks from the other boat. I don't think Rhett's boat would dare to creak. The cabin windows were blackened—probably from the smoke— but the rain must have extinguished the fire.

"I wish we could get back on and take another look around. But it's apparently a crime scene, so I guess we shouldn't."

"Definitely not."

Part of me was hoping he'd have a different answer. I know if I'd come out here by myself, I would have climbed aboard. Rhett started up the engine and drove a circle around the boat. We heard the whine of a high-speed engine. I looked over my shoulder.

"Rhett, it's the red boat I told you about." They were a couple of football fields away. "What's it doing out here?"

"Its timing is strange."

"Do you think they were following us?"

"I didn't see them if they were. They might have heard my call to the Coast Guard."

Crack. The sound was followed by a thud and fiberglass splintering from the boat. Someone on the red boat had shot at us.

CHAPTER 9

Rhett started the engine and tossed me the radio. "Call the Coast Guard."

It took a second for my brain to catch up to what I'd heard and seen. As Rhett pulled back the throttle, I called the Coast Guard and explained the situation. The boat surged forward and I was thrown back in the chair. No other shots sounded, but Rhett didn't let up.

The red boat chased us. Speeding closer. "It's chasing us," I shouted, as if Rhett wouldn't hear me.

He glanced over his shoulder. "We can't go any faster." His face was grim. "There's a flare gun in the compartment between the seats. Use it if you have to."

A flare gun against what had sounded like a high-powered rifle. But I opened the compartment, grabbed the gun, and steadied it over the back of the seat. "They've peeled off and are circling back to the boat."

If they monitored channel 16 on their radio, they would know I'd called the Coast Guard.

Rhett slowed and turned so we were facing them.

"Do you have any binoculars?" I asked.

Rhett reached back into the compartment between the seats, dug out binoculars, and handed them to me. I looked at the boat.

"They've boarded. It looks like two people are on the deck. They're carrying something, but it's too small to see what."

I handed Rhett the binoculars. He stood, feet braced. "It might be a duffel bag. Did you see one when you were on the boat?"

"No, but I didn't do a thorough search of the whole boat. There were closets and compartments I didn't look in."

Rhett continued to watch. "They're back on the red boat." He handed me the binoculars. "Keep an eye on them." He stood with his hand on the throttle.

"They're heading south." Thank heavens. "I wonder why they aren't coming after us. We must be witnesses to something."

Rhett was back on the radio with the Coast Guard, updating them on what had just taken place. I could hear the Coast Guard telling Rhett that the helicopter had headed back to its home base in New Orleans for a rescue mission there, but they had a boat in the area. We were to wait for its arrival.

"That's probably why they took off," Rhett said. "They knew the Coast Guard was coming."

Thirty minutes later we'd been dismissed. We showed them the bullet hole and told them what we knew. They didn't allow us on to the boat, so we headed back to Emerald Cove.

"The Coast Guard certainly doesn't like to share," I said.

Rhett smiled. "Most law enforcement types don't. It doesn't matter if they're military or civilian."

"Why in the world would bad people use a red boat? Don't you think that makes them stand out in a world of mostly white boats?"

"I don't know. Maybe they stole it at the last minute and will ditch it somewhere."

That made sense. "Have you heard anything about the man who rescued me? I didn't find out his name and I'd like to thank him." I was determined to find him. Who had he radioed if it wasn't the Coast Guard? Could he have something to do with the people in the red boat? Something about him felt off to me because of the way he took off so quickly. Also, after I'd mentioned Vivi, he changed directions for some reason.

"I haven't."

Another strike-out. "Lots of people were milling around behind the Sea Glass, but I haven't had time to ask anyone else. And, actually, I didn't pay that much attention to who was there." I thought about the reporter from the TV station. She might have caught something on film.

"What'd he look like?"

I described him, but I could have been describing a lot of older boaters. "However, he had a cigarette boat." I hadn't seen many of them in this area.

"You should check with Ann Williams. She knows a lot of people too."

Ah, the enigmatic Ann. I'd thought she had a thing for Rhett, but she was the one who said he was interested in me. It was a good idea to talk to her. Plus, I'd ask her about the red boat. Ann lived on the edge of society and was known to "fix things" for people. I'd originally misinterpreted that to mean she was a handywoman, but I'd finally realized she fixed—or tried to fix—problems for people. She looked into bigger issues, like people smuggling liquor. Not that she was a private investigator. More like she was someone with special skills who anyone would want on their side.

"Great idea."

"Want to drive?" Rhett asked.

"It's not like I haven't driven a boat before."

"You might enjoy something with more thrust."

I didn't dare look at him for fear of turning redder than the mysterious speedboat. I could never tell if he was making innuendos or not. I was being ridiculous. How often did I get a chance to pilot a boat like this? Never; that's how often. I finally managed to look at him and grinned. "Sure."

Rhett gave me a quick lesson on the control panel and then stepped aside so I could take over. I slowly pulled back the throttle until we were flying. I loved the feeling of power it gave me. Rhett stood close by. Aside from getting swept out to sea and getting shot at, I liked living down here. I glanced at Rhett. I liked the people too. All too soon we were at the no-wake zone that led to the harbor.

I turned it back over to Rhett to let him dock her. He drove me home and walked me to my door. I'd barely managed to keep my eyes open on the ten-minute drive over.

After I unlocked my door I turned to him. "You sure

do know how to show a girl a good time. It's not every day I get shot at."

He looked bemused. "I'd like to show you a better time."

I couldn't hold back the blush that seemed to start in my chest and headed upward as I thought about his earlier comment about thrust. "Today would be hard to top." I turned to go in, but Rhett caught my hand.

"Would you like to go out to dinner?"

"Dinner?"

"Yes. It's something most people do in the evening. You have food at home or a restaurant. You eat."

"I know what dinner is." I didn't know how to handle the emotions that swirled through me. I was definitely attracted to Rhett, but I had to sort out my feelings about Boone and my failed engagement before I jumped into anything new.

"Not tonight," Rhett said. "You've had a long day. But sometime soon?"

His face was hard to read. It was set to neutral, with a hint of interest. "Sure. It would be my pleasure."

A slow smile spread across his face. One that made me want to grasp him by the collar and pull him to me.

"I hope so, Chloe Jackson." He brushed a kiss across my knuckles, dropped my hand, and strolled back to his car.

He waited until I went inside. I closed and locked the door. Then I leaned against it. "It would be my pleasure?" I muttered. Why the hell had I said that? I could only chalk it up to being almost asleep on my feet.

*   *   *

I jerked awake and looked around, unable to figure out where I was. Boone's. The memories of my day washed over me like a rogue wave. I was still in the clothes I'd worn out on the boat with Rhett. My stomach rumbled— the burritos a distant memory. I found my phone. Nine p.m. I needed food and didn't have any in the house. I wasn't about to go grocery shopping and then fix a meal now even though I liked to cook. A trip to The Diner appeared to be in order.

I took another quick shower, threw on some clean clothes, and drove into Emerald Cove. I'd come to love this little town. It was an oasis from the bigger crowds and bigger buildings of Destin. In the middle of town was a circle of grass with a gazebo for concerts, picnic tables, and a tot lot. It was lined by palm trees and magnolias. Various businesses surrounded it, including the kiosk for Ralph's trolley, aka the Redneck Rollercoaster, a coffee shop, a nail salon, a beauty parlor, and The Diner.

A van with the logo of the local TV station pulled away from the curb in front of The Diner as I came around the circle. I got a glimpse of blond hair in the passenger seat. Was the reporter here eating or was she bothering Ralph and Delores? I immediately got huffy at that thought. I parked a few spaces down from The Diner. It was easy to find parking this time of night.

Delores looked surprised when she saw me walk in. Ralph sat near the back in a corner booth. Delores pointed to it, so I went and sat down across from him. Only one other family was still eating.

Ralph's face was drawn with worry lines, but he smiled when I sat down across from him. Delores brought over a glass of water and a plastic-coated menu.

"Are you waitressing and running the place tonight?" I asked.

"I let the other waitress go because it's so slow, and the cook is still here. You want anything else to drink?"

"Water's fine," I said.

"So I'll bring you a chocolate shake," Delores said. She didn't wait for me to answer. Delores had told me once she thought I was too skinny, which made me laugh because no one had ever said that to me before. I was short, sturdy, and my lanky brothers had teased me growing up. People were always surprised when they found out I liked to run.

"Was that blond reporter in here?" I asked.

"She tried to come in, but Delores told her she was trespassing on private property and to get out. It didn't stop her from filming in front, though. I'm sure it will be on the ten o'clock news."

"What did she want?" I asked.

"I'm not sure." Ralph shook his head. "Maybe Raquel's family has been dredging up dirt again."

I reached across the table and patted Ralph's arm. "It's been a day."

"It's just such a shock after all this time. What could she have been doing on that boat?" His anguish was palpable. "I heard you and Rhett went out searching this afternoon. That you found the boat. Did you learn anything new?"

"I didn't." I decided not to say anything about the red boat and getting shot at.

Delores came back with the chocolate shake in a tall, clear pedestal glass with a scalloped edge. "What do you want, hon?"

"One of everything," I said. My stomach rumbled, as if it approved. Delores and Ralph laughed as I said, "Excuse me."

"How about a shrimp po'boy with a side of fries?" Delores said.

"Sounds good. Thank you." I was too tired to make a decision right now. I spooned in some of the icy goodness of the milkshake. I knew by now that Delores's shakes were way too thick to try using a straw.

"Do you want that dressed?"

I'd learned since I'd moved down here that "dressed" meant it came with lettuce, tomatoes, pickles, and mayonnaise. Lettuce and tomatoes were almost a salad, so I wouldn't feel so guilty about the fried shrimp. "Yes, please."

"I'll get the cook right on it," Delores said.

"You look tired," I said to Ralph.

"Back at you. My mother would have said you look droopier than a wilted magnolia blossom."

I knew he was right. I'd brushed my hair and teeth before I came over. My brown eyes had looked glazed. "I feel pretty droopy too. I took a long nap. When I woke up I realized I was hungry, and I hadn't gone grocery shopping yet. That's what I was supposed to do today. Get organized. Settled in and, tomorrow, start my new life."

"The universe has a way of laughing at our plans."

"It does." I ate some more of my shake while I pondered that. I'd never thought I'd move away from Chicago. It was where I'd gone to college, worked, and my brothers lived there. My parents lived there when they weren't out touring the United States in their RV. It wasn't that I didn't enjoy traveling, it was just that Chicago always drew me back.

"I'm sorry anyone ever suspected you of having a hand in your wife's disappearance." I'd spent many a happy evening here with him and Delores. Ralph had told me in June that they had been high school sweethearts. Both of their families disapproved of the interracial couple. They'd broken up, and Ralph married Raquel. They'd had a boy and a girl, both of whom worked with Ralph at the Redneck Rollercoaster.

Seven years after Raquel had gone missing, Ralph had had her declared legally dead. A year after that he and Delores had married. They would be celebrating their fourth anniversary in a couple of weeks.

Ralph gave me an intent look. "It wasn't just me. It was Delores." He glanced toward the kitchen and leaned in. "She got into some trouble when she was young."

CHAPTER 10

I leaned back in surprise. The Delores I knew was straighter than a level. "What kind of trouble?"

Delores brought over my po'boy and slid in the booth next to Ralph. So I was going to have to wait to hear more.

"This looks delicious." The sandwich was on a piece of crisp French bread roll. The shrimp was piled high and drizzled with Delores's secret sauce. I took a bite while they looked on. The coating on the fried shrimp was crisp, the shrimp still tender and not greasy. Delores had brought a side of coleslaw, which wasn't too sweet or too vinegary, along with the French fries. "This is so good." I knew it wasn't just because I was so hungry.

"What do they think happened to the boat that disappeared with Raquel on it?" I asked between bites of food.

"A little bit of everything," Delores said.

I lifted my eyebrows, hoping they'd add more.

"There are rumors about a Bermuda Triangle–type area in the Gulf where things disappear," Ralph said. "Some people thought they got caught up in that."

"What's disappeared?" I asked.

"A couple of big boats. Forty-five footers. One was called *The Flying Dutchman* and one was the *Pirate's Lady*. Back in the seventies," Ralph said.

"Who names their boat after a sea captain condemned to roam the seas for defying God?" I asked. *The Flying Dutchman* was a Wagner opera—his first great masterpiece.

"There are a lot of bizarre boat names," Ralph said.

"They eventually found bits of the *Pirate's Lady*," Delores added.

"Bits?" I asked.

"It was incinerated," Delores replied.

"Burned at way hotter temperatures than normal," Ralph said.

"What do they think happened?" I asked.

"Smugglers. They probably boarded, stole what they needed, killed the passengers, and then burned the ship. And they used some kind of accelerant to make it burn hotter and faster." Ralph shook his head. "It was a bad time."

"That's awful. The Gulf looks so innocent." I said it knowing how fast bodies of water could change from placid to furious.

"We heard lots of rumors about the *Pirate's Lady* being spotted everywhere from the Caribbean to Honduras," Delores said. "But they found what was left of her not too far from her home port."

"Between forty and fifty yachts disappeared in a three-year period," Ralph continued. "They think the owners inadvertently hired crewmen who were actually drug smugglers."

"But that was way before Raquel and the others disappeared," I said after I finished my po'boy.

"There's always smugglers around," Delores said. "They might not be smuggling drugs now. It could be people, or even fish."

"Small planes have vanished too," Ralph said.

"But couldn't that just be normal engine problems?" I asked.

"Everyone down here loves a good conspiracy theory," Delores said.

Ralph put his arm around Delores and pulled her closer. They had the kind of love my parents had, deep, meaningful. They could rely on each other. I hope I had that someday, but not yet. As far as I was concerned, twenty-eight was the perfect age for adventure; the rest could come later. I'd been engaged once and wasn't eager to dip my toe back in that pool.

"That was delicious, Delores," I said when I finished.

"Ready for dessert?" Delores stood up. She snatched up my plate and took it off to the kitchen before I could answer.

Moments later Delores came back with two pieces of her famous Mile High Pie. This time it was key lime. There was a saying about big Southern hair—the higher the hair, the closer to God. Delores applied that philosophy not only to her red hair but to her pie.

"Pie!" Ralph's eyes lit up.

"We'll share our piece, Ralph," Delores said.

"I don't care," Ralph replied. He looked at me. "All she's been letting me eat is salad and salmon. I've eaten so much salmon, one of these days someone is going to find me swimming upstream in Alabama."

I laughed, and Delores rolled her eyes but laughed too. Ralph and I dug in. When I was stuffed I put down my fork to take a break. "Did either of you hear anything about the man who dropped me off at the Sea Glass this morning?"

Ralph and Delores looked at each other. "I didn't," Delores said.

"I didn't see him either," Ralph said.

"You have a good Samaritan you need to find?" Delores asked.

"Yes," I said. I gave them the same description I'd given Rhett earlier.

"You should call the newspaper. They'd love a good human-interest story," Delores said.

The paper was a local weekly. "It seems to me it's mostly human interest."

"Too many fools around here," Delores said. "Most with good hearts, though."

"Did you hear about the guy who didn't want to leave his alligator in his hot car, so he took it into the convenience store with him?" Ralph asked, a big smile breaking across his face. "I know the clerk, and she just about fainted."

"No fools better think about bringing an alligator in here." Delores looked over at the door, as if she expected someone to do that at any moment. "It will end up on the menu."

I was laughing at this point. I wouldn't mess with Delores when she was riled up. But then I thought about Ralph saying she'd been in trouble. I wondered what that was about. I put some money on the table to cover my meal and a generous tip and stood up. "Thanks for the company."

"Ralph, you walk Chloe to her car. It's dark and late."

It was only ten thirty. If Delores knew how many times I'd walked alone in my Chicago neighborhood after dark, she'd probably faint. "It's fine. Don't get up."

Delores was already out of the booth and pulling on Ralph's arm. "It might be fine up north for a young woman to be roaming around on her own after dark, but that's not how we do things down here."

I knew enough of Delores to know I needed to give in gracefully. Besides, maybe Ralph and I could finish our conversation. "Thank you, then. The dinner was excellent."

"You needed it after all you've been through today."

I couldn't argue with that either, so Ralph and I headed outside. The air was still warm, but not as humid as it had been this morning. No fog tonight, thank heavens.

My car was only three buildings down from The Diner. During the summer I'd often had to park in the municipal lot a block away. "Getting back to our earlier conversation, what kind of trouble did Delores get into when you were younger?" Maybe I was pushing the bounds of our friendship by asking, but Delores getting in trouble was so out of character for the woman I knew.

Ralph sighed. "She harassed Raquel when we started dating. Back in the sixties it was pretty mild stuff compared to what goes on today. Phone calls and egging her car and house. Not enough to get arrested, but enough to get the attention of the police."

We arrived at my car. "So when Raquel disappeared people remembered, even though it was more than thirty years later?" That was ridiculous.

"Yes."

"You're both good people. I'm sorry." I patted Ralph's arm for a moment. "What about the people who were with Raquel on the boat that evening?" The big neon sign The Diner winked out.

"That's my signal. Delores knows how I can ramble on. That story will have to wait until another time."

Ralph stood by my car until I locked the doors, started it up, and pulled away from the curb. I waved and Ralph lifted his arm as if it took all his power to wave back. That made me sad.

I was jittery and at loose ends. Maybe from the pie and the shake, or maybe from the nap. I decided to see if I could find Ann Williams. She hung out at a bar on the harbor not too far from the Sea Glass, so I drove over, parked nearby, and hurried along the walkway past the turn off to Boone's boat.

I glanced down the dock at Rhett's boat as I walked. He had a light on. I might have missed dinner with him tonight, but there was always dessert. I let that thought swirl around for a minute before forcing myself on toward Two Bobs. Unlike the Sea Glass, this bar was two stories and had decks facing both the harbor and the Gulf. It had an upper deck that faced the harbor that was strung with lights. Laughter and music drifted down to me.

Two Bobs was the last building before the waterway

between the harbor and the Gulf, so the views from the decks were amazing. A lot of people came for sunset and stayed. Unlike the Sea Glass, which closed at nine, Two Bobs stayed open until the wee hours. The crowd was thinner than the last time I'd been here, at the height of the summer, but there were still a lot of people. The age range varied widely from people who barely looked old enough to be legal to sixty-year-olds partying it up.

I made my way to the bar and ordered a local pale ale. It just didn't seem fair to come in and not order anything. I noticed their drink prices had gone up. Last June it was rumored that they'd been buying alcohol smuggled in from Cuba and Mexico. I'd never heard whether that rumor was true or not. After I paid I surveyed the crowd but didn't see Ann.

I slipped around people to the staircase on the west side of the room and climbed the stairs to the rooftop bar and deck. The bar had lots of sleek, stainless-steel tables and stools. The main colors were red, silver, and black. The décor was what I called industrial chic and out of place for a beach bar. People of all ages were dancing away to music playing through speakers. However, I didn't spot Ann.

I went back downstairs and out onto the deck that faced the Gulf. Ann sat at a corner table with her back to the building. She had long, wavy hair that hung halfway down her back in enviable waves that were sultry instead of frizzy. Her light-brown eyes were big, with thick lashes. Although I couldn't see it, I knew she had a tattoo on her inner ankle that I'd found out was a pirate flag. She went by the name Ann Williams, but Joaquín had told me that she was related to the pirate and war hero

Jean Lafitte. As usual, she wore black, this time a light, clingy sweater and shorts.

She waved me over as soon as she spotted me. A man who was sitting with her turned to look at me. Ann said something to him. He leaned in, saying something back. She shook her head and he leaped up and left. In a huff, if the way the scowl he tossed at me was any indication.

"I didn't mean to interrupt," I said when I reached her.

She flicked her hand, as if dismissing my concern. "You did me a favor. Things were going south quickly. It was getting awkward."

Probably doing a favor for Ann was a good thing. I pulled out the recently evacuated barstool and sat on the edge.

"I heard you had an interesting morning," Ann said.

Of course Ann knew. Ann knew a lot of things. "I did. I wanted to pick your brain about a couple of things."

"I don't know what happened to Raquel Harrison."

Interesting to know, but not what I'd planned to ask. "I'm interested in finding the man who rescued me this morning. He left so quickly I didn't have a chance to thank him." I gave her my standard description of the man and his boat. I left out that I was curious about why he'd radioed someone other than the Coast Guard that I'd been found.

"Interesting. Cigarette boats are very expensive. I priced used ones recently. They ran from two hundred thousand to almost a million."

I could picture Ann owning a cigarette boat. "That much?"

"Yes. That's why you don't see many of them around

here. If you want to find the man, have you checked the security cameras at the Sea Glass or the Briny Pirate?"

Duh. "I haven't. I'll do that tomorrow." After a man had been killed behind the restaurant, Vivi had upgraded our security system. Hopefully, it would give me the answer no one else had.

"I saw you on the evening news. It looked like you'd had a rough time. Perhaps the reporter has some footage that they didn't show on TV."

I'd had a similar thought about the reporter. It was disconcerting hearing I was on the news. It also made me realize that I hadn't told my family any of this. I'd better make some calls on my way home. I didn't want my brothers or my parents, who'd taken their RV to Northern California, to think they had to show up here.

"Did you want something else?" she asked.

Hmmm, that was interesting. Ann was always direct, but now she seemed almost antsy, which was unusual for her. Was she meeting someone? But the need to stay on her good side won over the need to linger to see what she was up to. "A red boat. I spotted it this morning while I was on the boat. And then again this afternoon, when Rhett and I were out on his boat." I described it the best I could, having only ever seen it from a distance.

She perked up at the mention of Rhett. Oh, it was subtle. The slight lift of an eyebrow. But for Ann, she might as well have leaped up and shouted his name. She had told me last June she wasn't interested in him, but maybe that wasn't true.

"A red boat?" she asked. I nodded. "I might know a guy. Let me do some checking and I'll get back to you."

If anything, Ann was a woman who kept her word. Every time I'd asked her for help with something she was on it. So I trusted her now to do what she said. I stood. "Thank you."

I walked back through the bar to leave. I saw a man who resembled the one who had rescued me. The beard was shorter, though. He stood against the wall, looking out over the crowd. The lighting was dim, so I might have been wrong, but I headed toward him anyway. When I was about ten feet away, he spotted me. I waved. His eyes widened and he took off. Out the door, beer mug in hand.

CHAPTER 11

What was that about? I hurried after him, but by the time I got to the walkway that ran along the harbor he was gone. I twirled in a circle, but nope. I didn't even see anyone hurrying away. Then I heard the low rumble of a boat and noticed one of the slips designated for Two Bobs boat parking was empty. I know there wasn't a cigarette boat parked there when I arrived, but boats came and went. I ran east along the walkway toward the waterway between the harbor and the Gulf.

There it was. The cigarette boat zooming faster than it should in the no-wake zone. But at this time of night it didn't matter so much. There was little boat traffic. I darted to my left, running in the sand, trying to catch him. I didn't see the boat's name on the side or back, which was unusual in itself.

"Hey," I yelled. "I just want to thank you." But either

he didn't hear me or he ignored me. I ran to the edge of the water and stood, hands on hips, wondering what was up. It was then that I realized Ann never said if she knew the man I'd described or not.

I walked into the Sea Glass at eleven on Wednesday morning. By that time I'd slept well, taken a run, unpacked, shopped for groceries, and put things away. I'd even talked to my brothers and parents. I'd also checked the local newspaper and TV to see if there were any stories about the ghost ship, its contents, the red boat, or the man who rescued me. I didn't find any new information, which was frustrating.

The Sea Glass was quiet now, but I bet by this afternoon a good crowd would be in here and out on the beach. It was a glorious day, in the eighties with low humidity.

Vivi looked me over. "I thought we agreed you'd take today off."

"I didn't agree." I didn't want to start a fight on my first day back. Vivi and I were still prickly around each other on occasion. Joaquín had gotten better at stepping out of the middle. He'd throw up his hands and mutter in Spanish if it wasn't important. Sometimes, though, he'd weigh in when we each pleaded our case to him.

Joaquín, dressed in his usual Hawaiian shirt—this one pink with sailboats and swordfish—threw his arms around me and hugged me until I thought he would crack a rib.

"Joaquín, you just saw me yesterday," I said, hugging him back.

"We have to celebrate every day." He twirled me in a

dance move I could never pull off on my own. He finished by dipping me dramatically. Enough so that Vivi laughed and he'd postponed any argument.

"I'm heading out to talk with a liquor distributor. They're doing a sampling of a new tequila some celebrity is promoting," Vivi said. "I'll be back this afternoon."

Not long after she left, a group of five men came in and swarmed over to a high top near the doors that opened to the deck. They were all laughing and nudging one another. I was surprised to see Rhett and Ralph with them. Rhett rarely came in because of what everyone down here called a feud between Vivi's family and Rhett's. Personally, I thought the whole thing was ridiculous, but what did I know?

I ran my hand through my hair and tugged down my shorts.

"Are you going to wait on them or just stare like they're your next meal?" Joaquín asked.

I snapped my mouth—which I didn't know was open—closed. "Wait on them."

"You look cute, Chloe. Like you always do."

I smiled at Joaquín. He was the best, because I know cute wasn't how I looked yesterday.

"Go." Joaquín shooed his hands at me. "Rhett won't bite. Unless you want him to."

I tried to give Joaquín an evil glare, but I couldn't ever stay mad at him for more than ten seconds. Especially when he was teasing me and what he was saying was absolutely true. I laughed.

"Be quiet," I said. "Rhett will hear you." I picked up a pad to write down orders.

"Not over the noise that group is making. I wonder what they're up to."

I shrugged.

"Chloe, you're still standing here, a single woman, and that's one good-looking group of men. Get over there."

Thanks for rubbing the status of my love life in. I headed over. When I took drink orders I usually identified the people I waited on by what they wore, or some physical attribute. With these guys it might just be hot, hotter, and hottest. I wondered if they were firemen. Both Ralph and Rhett volunteered with Emerald Cove's fire department.

"Hey, Chloe," Rhett said when I got to the table. "Ignore these guys. I think they've inhaled too much smoke over the years."

They all laughed.

"You wish," one of them said.

"You know Rip?" another asked.

"Rip?" I asked.

Ralph pointed at Rhett with a half smile on his face. It was good to see after what he'd gone through yesterday.

"We'd like a couple of pitchers of beer, please," Rhett said.

"And water," Ralph added.

Even I didn't have to write down this order, and I could fill it without help. I picked up the first pitcher and angled it under the tap. My father had taught me how to pour a beer when I was fourteen. Most of my friends were being taught algebra by their fathers. Mine thought I needed other life skills too.

I filled the second pitcher and put both on a tray. Then I filled another pitcher with water.

"What are they up to?" Joaquín asked.

"I'm not sure. One of them called Rhett 'Rip.'" I lifted

the tray, thanking the powers that be I'd spent so much time swimming and paddleboarding that I had strong arms. Over the summer I'd learned how to balance things on a tray too.

"Rip? I'll bring the water and the glasses," Joaquín said, "because I want to know what's going on."

We carried everything over. I poured glasses of beer and passed them around, listening to them talk about the fire they'd put out this morning. Joaquín poured the glasses of water.

"And then Rip here had to save a cat from a tree," one of the guys said. He winked at me. "That's how the rookie got his nickname."

I set the two pitchers on the table. "The rookie?"

They all pointed at Rhett. "Newest guy in the department."

"And he didn't have a nickname until today?"

Rhett turned to me. "I'm sure you have better things to do." He sounded a little desperate.

I glanced around the bar. "Nope. It's pretty slow right now." I looked back at the table full of men. "Tell me about this nickname."

"Last night a cat ran up a tree over on Palm Court, and his owner was frantic when it still hadn't come down by this morning," Ralph said. "Rookies are on cat duty."

"So Rip here uses the ladder."

"But he makes a rookie error by taking off his jacket."

"Because it's hot out."

"Poor, poor rookie."

They were all talking over one another.

"He climbs the ladder up to the cat."

"The cat was black as night."

"Only the cat didn't want to come down."

I looked over at Rhett. He was looking down at his beer as if he'd like to disappear into it.

"It ripped his shirt to shreds."

"Thus the nickname 'Rip.'"

"He finally calmed the cat and brought him down."

"Rip is a cat whisperer."

"And that cat stuck to him like Rip was catnip."

I could understand the cat's feelings.

"Rip finally managed to give the cat back to the owner."

"Who had to be eighty."

"She catches a glimpse of Rip's abs through the shredded shirt."

"And says, 'Oh, wow, you're ripped.'"

I was laughing at this point, imagining the whole thing playing out. Rhett looked up at me and grinned.

They all laughed again. Then they raised their glasses.

"To our brother, Rip."

There was a round of "hear, hears," followed by long drinks. Rhett's cheeks were pink.

Joaquín put a hand on Rhett's shoulder. "Drinks are on the house in honor of Rip."

I guess Rhett had just become Rip.

"Chloe, please tell me there's a what-happens-in-the-Sea-Glass-stays-in-the-Sea-Glass rule," Rip said. "Otherwise, by tonight everyone in town will be calling me Rip."

"Sorry. That's never going to happen," I said, shaking my head. "Besides," I swung my hand around at the other people in the bar, who included a couple of regulars, "everyone in here already heard."

The firefighters whooped it up and did another round of toasts.

"Do the rest of you have nicknames?" I asked.

"You bet they do," Rip said. He pointed at the guy next to him. "That's Bull, because he's full of it."

"That's Ax, because he can throw one." Bull pointed at the man across from him. "He just can't hit anything with it."

Ax pointed to the man sitting beside him. "That's Smoke, because the ladies think he's so hot."

Smoke shrugged a self-deprecating shrug.

I turned to Ralph. "What's your nickname?"

He gave the men around the table a look. "It's not to be repeated in polite society."

I laughed again. "I'm not that polite. Let's hear it."

Everyone shook their heads.

"No one messes with Ralph," Ax said.

"That's right," Ralph said. "If they know what's good for them."

A man cleared his throat. I turned to see Bill and Alex from the Coast Guard standing there.

CHAPTER 12

From the looks on their faces and the way they were looking at Ralph, I knew they'd overheard that last bit. Their timing couldn't have been worse.

"Can I help you?" I asked, glancing back at Ralph, worried what they'd think about him after his comment. I knew Ralph was joking, but they might not.

The rowdy firemen settled down when they noticed Ralph's face. It had gone from laughing to serious in seconds. Eyebrows rose, glances were exchanged, and uneasy quiet settled over them. Alex was staring at Ralph, arms crossed, chin lifted.

"We had some follow-up questions for you," Bill said.

"Did you find anything on the boat that will help you figure out how Raquel ended up there?" I asked. I wanted to put a hand on Ralph's shoulder so he would relax. But the gesture would be noticed and might make things worse.

"We need a few minutes of your time," Bill said.

"Joaquín?" I asked. *Throw me a bone so I can get out of this. There must be something pressing I should do.*

"Go ahead. I'll cover," Joaquín said.

Thanks.

I reluctantly led Bill and Alex to Vivi's office. I sat in her chair and gestured to the chairs across the desk.

"It was very foolish of you to go out looking for the boat yesterday," Alex said.

"We'd just like to know exactly what you saw," Bill said.

I told them the same story I'd told the Coast Guard officers yesterday. Alex took lots of notes, scowling the whole time. Bill nodded sympathetically.

"Did they find anything on the boat?" I asked.

"A skeleton," Alex said.

"Yes. I told you that yesterday."

"Chloe," Bill said, "we confirmed the one you found wasn't real. Like you said, bones don't hold together like that."

I closed my eyes for a moment and pictured the scene, felt the rocking of the boat and the creaking it caused. This was excellent news. It wasn't Raquel. Ralph wouldn't be in trouble. "That's good news."

"But we did find a skull and some bones in the other cabin."

"Is that why I couldn't get the door open all the way?" The thought made my stomach roil.

"Yes," Alex said.

"So the people who boarded the boat left them there?"

"Yes. They must have realized you'd radioed that you'd found the boat and that they didn't have much time before someone from the Coast Guard would show up," Alex said.

"Do you have any idea who it is on the boat?"

"A female. That's all we know right now," Bill said.

If it was a female, it could be Raquel. "There wasn't anything else that gave you any clues as to why they were there or what the people who were on the red boat wanted?"

"We have forensic experts going over it," Alex said.

"Other than the remains, we didn't find anything out of the ordinary that one wouldn't find on a pleasure craft," Bill added.

"No drugs or guns?" I asked. "There must have been something of value on the boat if it was worth shooting at people for."

"Agreed," Alex said, "because you led the bad guys right to the boat we may never know what."

He had a point, but if Rip—I smiled inwardly at the nickname—and I could find the boat why couldn't the Coast Guard or the people on the red boat? "Do you have any idea how long the remains were there?"

"A long time, because of the condition."

"So the boat was drifting around for years?" I asked.

"It's possible, but things don't add up," Bill said.

"What things?" I asked.

"The condition of the boat was too good," Bill said.

I was surprised they'd shared this much information.

"How well do you know Ralph Harrison?" Alex asked.

If they were asking this and the remains on the boat were female, they must have considered him a prime suspect. How well did I know him? "Well enough to know he's a good man who has suffered incredible losses."

"How long have you known him?" Alex asked.

"Four months. We met last June when I first came down here."

"So you don't know him well," Alex said.

"He's become a friend. I have good instincts about people. I'm a former librarian, and we are used to assessing people and situations quickly." The library I'd worked for in Chicago was in an urban setting. All kinds of people, from CEOs to the homeless, came in. All were welcome as long as they complied with our rules.

"Is there anything else you want to tell us?" Bill asked.

Both Bill and Alex leaned forward. It was as if they knew I knew something and just wanted to hear it from me. I had nothing for them. I'd told them everything I'd seen. So their expectant expressions worried me.

"I've told you everything I know." They both sat back but didn't look surprised. Maybe this was just some kind of intimidation technique the Coast Guard used to get people to confess things. However, when you have nothing to confess, it doesn't work.

"We've discovered the boat you were on is actually the *Fair Winds*."

"What's the *Fair Winds*?" I asked. Then it hit me. "The boat that disappeared twelve years ago?" My voice quivered as I said it.

"Yes," Bill said.

"How did you figure that out?" I asked.

"We just did," Alex said.

Apparently, they didn't want to share that information with me. I wasn't sure why. "Where's it been all these years?"

"The name was no longer on the back, so it could have been almost anywhere," Bill said. "Although I'm guessing not in this area, because someone might have recognized her."

Alex and Bill stood, so I did too. I followed them back out to the bar.

"Ralph Harrison," Alex said, "we'd like you to come with us."

Oh no. I watched them walk out and then sent Delores a quick text letting her know what had happened. This was bad.

The next couple of hours I went through the motions of my job, my mind a constant whirl of speculation about the *Fair Winds* reappearing. In the afternoon I turned to Vivi. "Do you mind if I take a look at the security camera's video? I want to see if I can figure out who the man was who dropped me off." I told them what happened with him last night at Two Bobs.

"You were at Two Bobs last night?" Vivi's tone suggested she didn't approve.

I wasn't sure if the disapproval was because I was out late when she thought I should be home or if she just didn't like Two Bobs. "I went to find Ann Williams." Not that I had to justify my actions to Vivi, but I would for the sake of keeping the peace.

"Oh, and after all you'd been through yesterday, that's what you thought you should do instead of resting?" Vivi pressed her lips together as if she was holding back a lot of things she had to say. "Yes, you can look at the security camera footage. Use my office and take your time."

That was an interesting turn of events. She sounded worried about me. It made me happy. I hurried over to Vivi's office, which was just off the bar, and settled in her chair before she could change her mind. With the new system all I had to do was type in the day and hour I needed. No scrolling back through hours of footage. The pictures were now high-resolution color too.

I watched as we pulled into an empty slip behind the Sea Glass. A small crowd stood outside with their backs to the camera. I could pick out a few people I knew, like Ralph and Joaquín. I watched Joaquín hurry forward. I stopped the recording and zoomed in on the man in the boat with me. His head was down and he wore a baseball cap, so the camera didn't capture his face. As if he didn't want his face to be captured. What was that about?

As soon as I was off the boat, he backed it out and in seconds was out of sight. Darn, that was frustrating. I watched until Joaquín and I entered the Sea Glass and were off camera. What was with this guy? And why did it bug me so much? It didn't seem like it would help much to watch any video Wade might have. The angle of his cameras would be worse than ours.

I printed a photo that had the best angle of him, where a lot of beard and a bit of nose showed. Not much to go on, but this was a small town, so someone should recognize him or his boat. And if they didn't? What then?

I took the picture back out into the bar. Joaquín was mixing something in the blender. We didn't have any pre-made mixes like lots of beach bars did. Everything here was made from scratch with no artificial flavors. It was one of the reasons the bar was so popular. Vivi was checking on customers. She smiled and laughed. I had noticed over the summer that she never wrote down any orders, but never got anything wrong either. Maybe someday I'd be able to do that too.

I took an apron from the small kitchen area behind the bar and tied it around my waist. I scooped up a pad and pen and went out to relieve Vivi. She could help Joaquín make drinks and do a better job than I ever could. It was something I needed to start working on.

"I've got this," I said. Vivi and I still had a lot to work out with me owning a quarter of the bar. We'd never discussed division of duties, but every month she deposited a quarter of our profits, along with my salary and tips, in my bank account. It was a lot more money than I'd ever made as a children's librarian, but the summer was the busiest time of year here.

Vivi headed back toward the bar as a man walked in from the beach. He was very definition of a silver fox with his thick, silver hair, expensive-looking, pink short-sleeved shirt, and khaki shorts. My head wasn't the only one that swiveled to look at him. He was tall and fit. He paused in the doorway, as if he knew how to make an entrance. He pushed up his sunglasses up on his head to reveal light-gray eyes. He looked familiar to me. Maybe he'd been in over the summer, but honestly, I thought I'd remember someone this striking.

The man scanned the room and then noticed Vivi.

He walked halfway across the bar until he was almost even with me.

"Vivi," he called. He swept his arms open in a grand gesture.

It made me wonder if he was an actor. Vivi glanced over her shoulder, froze, and pivoted toward the man. The whole bar went quiet.

"Get out," she said. Her voice was low and mean.

CHAPTER 13

Usually when Vivi was angry her drawl became prominent. Not this time. I'd never heard her speak to anyone like that. Not even me when I'd first arrived and she hadn't wanted me here. Vivi had tried to buy me out almost as soon as she found out that Boone had left me part of the bar. However, I was stubborn and had promised Boone I'd be here, so Vivi was stuck with me. She turned on her heel and walked toward the back of the building. Seconds later the back door slammed so hard the whole building shook a little.

Joaquín stood behind the bar, holding a glass. Our eyes met, and I'm sure mine were as wide as his. I had no idea why Vivi didn't want this man here, but if she didn't, he was out of here.

The man threw back his head and barked out a laugh. "I guess she wasn't happy to see me."

I stepped in front of him struck by his familiarity again. "Sir, you need to leave." He tried to step around me, but I blocked him. I'd dealt with a lot of ornery people in my years as a children's librarian, so I wasn't afraid. Well, not much anyway.

"I just want to have a drink and wait for Vivi. We both know that she'll be back."

"That's not going to happen." I took a step closer. Expensive cologne and sea salt wafted off him.

Joaquín came and stood beside me. "The lady told you to leave."

I wasn't sure if he was talking about me or Vivi.

The man put up his hands. "Okay, but you tell my partner Vivi, I'll be back." He turned and sauntered out.

Joaquín and I looked at each other, eyebrows up. We were in the middle of the bar, so we didn't want to make a big deal about it.

"Anybody need anything?" I asked, smiling as if we kicked unknown men out of there every day.

A table full of women waved to me. I went over to take their orders while Joaquín went back to making drinks. I checked with the people seated out on the deck before heading back inside. I was still using descriptors to help make sure I got the drinks to the right person. Woman, fluffy gray hair, lemonade and vodka. Woman in flamingo print dress, Riesling. Woman, silver hoop earrings, Bloody Mary.

I took the drink orders to Joaquín. I could handle the Riesling and lemonade and vodka while he made the Bloody Mary. None of the heritage business owners were in here, so I couldn't ask them who the man was and why Vivi had reacted that way. The heritage business owners were people whose families had opened businesses in

Emerald Cove in the fifties or before, when all that led to the town were dirt roads. They were a tight-knit group of friends, for the most part.

After I delivered the next round of drinks I went back behind the bar with Joaquín. Fortunately, no one was sitting at the stools that faced us right then. Usually, women perched on the barstools, admiring Joaquín. He danced his days away, having once been a professional backup dancer for people like Ricky Martin, Beyoncé, and Justin Timberlake out in California. The ladies loved him, and he flirted, even though he was married and devoted to his husband, Michael.

"Who was that man?" I asked Joaquín.

He lifted and dropped his shoulder. "No idea. I was hoping you knew him."

"Do you think Vivi will tell us when she gets back?"

"You know Vivi. Pulling things out of her is harder than digging for clams in cement."

"Did he look familiar to you?"

"No. Why? Do you know him?"

I shrugged. "He must look like someone I know. You know how that is." I'd always called it "the familiars."

"I do."

"Did you hear how he called her 'partner?'" Joaquín nodded. "What do you think that was about?" I took a glass from a shelf and polished it, even though it looked perfectly fine.

"I did and I don't know. But I don't like it."

Neither did I. Not one bit.

By six I was just about dead on my feet. Vivi hadn't returned and the crowd from the afternoon had thinned.

Oddly enough, none of the heritage business owners ever showed up. Most days at least one of them wandered in here. I wondered if they were gathered together somewhere else.

"Go on home," Joaquín said. "I can handle this place blindfolded."

"And one arm tied behind your back?"

"Both. If things pick back up, I'll call Michael and ask him to run down here to help." Joaquín and Michael lived on a boat not too far from where Rip's boat was docked. Joaquín's fishing boat was in the slip next to the one they lived on.

"Okay, thanks."

"You're not even going to argue with me? You must be tired."

"If you hear from Vivi, please let me know."

"Will do. Now, get out of here. I'm sick of seeing you already." Joaquín winked to show he was joking.

I gave him a hug, but instead of driving home I decided to call the reporter, as Ann had suggested last night. Before I did I decided to do a little research.

The reporter's profile on the station's website said her name was Mary Moore. I wondered if her middle name was Tyler. Mary was all over social media sites, but the more I scrolled through her posts, the more I realized there wasn't anything about her personal life.

According to her bio, she graduated from University of Florida a couple of years ago. It was pretty impressive that she was already on TV. I'd watched some clips of her on air. Mary had a natural charm and sincerity that made me think she'd be moving to a bigger market station soon. I sent her a DM through social media asking to meet off the record and didn't mention why I wanted to talk to her.

I heard back right away. We decided to meet at the Crab Trap in Destin. It was a beach restaurant, but also had lots of picnic tables, restrooms, and showers to rinse off sand for the public to use. There was plenty of parking and, even better, it was unlikely that anyone from Emerald Cove would see us there.

Thirty minutes later I sat at one of the picnic tables on the far west side of the Crab Trap. The air was warm, the beach expansive, and the water dazzled. Mary pulled up in a television van, with someone I assumed was a cameraman in the driver's seat. I stood as she approached.

"I said off the record."

"We're on our way to cover another story." She stuck out her hand. "I'm Mary Moore."

She might be on the way to cover another story, but I'd bet anything she hoped I'd talk on camera. "As in Mary Tyler Moore?"

Mary smiled a perky on-camera smile. "My parents were big fans."

"You must get sick of that question."

She did a self-deprecating shrug. "I'm used to it. So, Chloe, I'd love to hear about what happened when you were swept out to sea."

I'm sure you would. "I would love to see any footage you shot of my return." I'd watched the brief clip on the news but was sure they'd shot more than they showed. I also didn't want to tell her why I wanted to see it—so I could identify my rescuer and ask him who he'd called. Unfortunately, Mary had excellent radar and perked up.

"Why?" she asked.

"Because it feels intrusive that you have footage of me at a very vulnerable time in my life that I didn't give you permission to film." I had honed my lying skills on hundreds of small children who asked questions I wouldn't answer truthfully, from *Do you believe in Santa Claus?* to *Where do babies come from?*

Mary's eyes narrowed for the briefest of seconds. Sadly, she didn't seem to buy what I was trying to sell her. Just my luck that she was an astute reader of people instead of the vapid blond teleprompter reader I was hoping she'd be.

"I can give you a copy of what was on TV, but not the additional footage."

"Why not?"

She gave me an earnest look that I didn't think was put on.

"It's just not done. It's the property of the studio. We don't give unused footage to anyone."

"If you help me out, maybe I'll go on record." I wouldn't.

She laughed. "Maybe if you go on record, I'll show you the footage."

"It looks like we're at a standoff," I said.

"Why don't you tell me why you really want it?" Mary thought for a moment, then snapped her fingers. "It's the man who drove the boat. You don't know who he is."

"Of course I do." I shook my head, like *how could you be so wrong?* "As I explained," I used my patient voice, "that was a very vulnerable moment for me. I don't want it to be used." Did that sound like a threat? Like I'd sue the station? I hoped it did.

"Who is he?" she asked.

"I don't see how that's any of your business."

She looked me straight in the eye and nodded. Though the nod wasn't one of agreement, but one that looked like Mary was thinking there's-a-story-to-pursue. None of this was going as planned, so I would have to change direction. Sometimes honesty really was the best policy, just not as often as people would like to think.

"Would you be willing to meet me halfway?" I asked, not knowing if I could trust her.

"What do you have in mind?"

"You let me see more of the footage and I'll tell you when I find my rescuer. He'd make a great human-interest story. Why was he out there? Why take time to help a stranger? The man's a local hero." I shut up before I laid it on too thick. I needed to pique her interest, not bash her over the head.

"You're going to a lot of trouble to find this man just to thank him. Why do you really want to find him?"

Wow, she was a hard sell. "I just do." Okay, fine. I'd give her a partially honest answer. "He saved me. He's just some guy who went out of his way to help a stranger. I want to thank him. I was too flustered to do it in the moment, and it's been bothering me."

She took some time to mull this over. "Okay, I agree to your terms with a stipulation."

"What?"

"You don't meet with him without me. I want to get it on camera. And if I find him first, I'll let you know who he is and arrange a meeting we can film. Everyone loves a good reunion story."

"They do." I didn't exactly agree to her terms, but I'm guessing she was savvy enough to pick up on that.

She looked at me with a thoughtful expression on her face. "I can help you find him, Chloe. If you go on camera, you'll have people all across the Panhandle searching for the man and his boat. It will be a lot faster than you asking one person at a time if they know him. Here's my card. Call me if you change your mind."

I took the card and watched her walk away. She had a point.

As I drove up my long driveway, I noticed a black car parked near my house. At first I thought it was Rip, but realized it wasn't a convertible or a BMW. It was a Cadillac with Texas plates. I wasn't expecting anyone. A man swung around the corner of the house, then. I gripped the wheel. It was the man from the bar. It hit me why he looked familiar because he looked like Boone. He must have been Boone's mysterious father.

CHAPTER 14

No wonder Vivi had reacted the way she had. Boone would never talk about his dad except to say that he'd never been in his life and that he wasn't even listed on his birth certificate. I didn't bug him about it because the look of pain on his face the few times I'd brought it up made my heart hurt.

I pulled up and parked to the side of the house. My Beetle looked tiny next to the Cadillac. It took me a moment to gather my purse because I wasn't ready to confront this man and find out what he was doing here. He smiled and waved, so I climbed out of the car while wondering if I should back down my driveway and leave.

"Hey there, you're the little gal who was at the Sea Glass this afternoon. Feisty little thing, aren't you?"

I'd like to feisty him right into next year. I put on a smile. "Yes. I am the feisty little gal."

"Now, don't take any offense," he said with a charming smile.

The smile was so similar to Boone's, it almost knocked me backward. But Boone had had dark-brown eyes and a broader build than this man. Boone's features tended toward Vivi's side of the family from the pictures I'd seen of his grandfather and uncles.

"May I help you?" I asked.

"I have lost all my manners. I'm Steve Kincheloe."

He stuck out his hand as he strode toward me. We shook. I wasn't about to say "Nice to meet you" because I had a very empty feeling in my stomach. And for once it wasn't hunger.

"Chloe Jackson. You're Boone's father."

"Aren't you a smart little thing too."

I wasn't normally a violent person, but this guy made me want to punch something. Probably him. I arranged my face in my go-to, neutral librarian expression as my brothers had called it. A hint of friendliness mixed with a pinch of don't-push-me warning. Boone might have looked a bit like this man, but from my brief observations, that was the only thing they shared.

"I was thinking of knocking the place down and building something grander." He gestured toward Boone's house. My house.

"Pardon me?"

"I grew up in one of those tiny, concrete block houses with five siblings." He gave a dramatic shudder. "No way I'd live in one again."

"It's not for sale." The house was part of Boone, but even if it wasn't, I would never consider knocking it down. I'd come to love it in the months I'd lived here over the summer. We had a small tropical storm in late

August. The house held steady and didn't even shake in the wind.

He looked at me like he pitied me. "Of course it's not for sale. Boone left the place to me, along with his boat and half the Sea Glass." Steve took a step closer to me.

"Boone would never do that." I held my ground as I had in the Sea Glass, even though inside I was wavering more than the sea oats in a stiff breeze. "You were nothing to him. A sperm donor at best. A negligent, absent father at worst. He left everything to me." I almost clapped my hands to my mouth. I wasn't usually mean.

Steve didn't look surprised. It was like he already knew. He flicked out his hand, as if he was flicking my comment away. "We'll see about that, missy. I have a will."

Did he really? "So do I."

"Boone had a chance to rethink things over in Afghanistan. He rewrote his will and I'm here to claim what's mine." He stepped around me—close enough that he almost touched me, but far enough away that I couldn't file a police report like I wanted to. For what I don't know. I don't think you can file one when someone is a jerk. I watched, arms crossed, as he drove off. When Steve was out of sight I went into my house. I walked through it out onto the porch and collapsed on the wicker loveseat. What should I do now? I had to do something.

Rip showed up forty-five minutes later, a bottle of red wine in his hand. He couldn't have been more surprised when I'd called and asked him to come. I'd debated who to call. Vivi? Joaquín? I needed to talk to someone who didn't have a stake in what Steve had told me. And wouldn't run to Vivi with the news once they heard it. My hands had shaken as I made the Bolognese sauce and pasta. The Caesar salad came from a bagged mix. I'd put butter out to soften for the baguette I'd bought yesterday.

Rip's smile disappeared when he took one look at my face. "You're pale. Do you need to sit?"

"Probably." My voice wobbled a little in a way I wished it wouldn't have. "Help me carry all this out to the porch." We needed to eat no matter my predicament. It took us a couple of trips to get everything out on the porch and onto the coffee table. "Let's eat. Then talk."

Rip nodded his agreement, but a little line formed between his brows. He wore a light-blue T-shirt and tan shorts. His forearms and legs tan from his months of boating. Our conversation centered around "Would you like some Parmesan?" "More wine?" and "This is good."

"Has your nickname caught on, or did you manage to squelch it?" I asked.

"That bit of information spread through town faster than a wildfire. When I stopped in Russo's to buy wine, everyone was calling me Rip."

"It suits you."

"My grandmother doesn't think so. She called."

I'll bet that was one heck of a conversation. When I was sure Rip was full I set down my fork on my plate and patted my mouth with my napkin, hoping there wasn't a stray bit of lettuce or pepper in my teeth.

I tucked myself in the corner of the love seat we'd shared during dinner. Our legs so close that I could feel the heat of his body. Rip stretched an arm along the back of the love seat and leaned into the other corner. He put an ankle on his knee.

"How was your day?" I asked.

"Other than my new nickname, it was good. We did a controlled burn of some forest over near the bay."

"I'm surprised you can still do that."

"Why don't you tell me what has you pale and cooking dinner for me?"

I started with Steve showing up in the bar and Vivi's reaction. How I'd come home, found him here, and recognized who he was.

"Boone's dad?" he asked. "You're sure?" Rip ran his hand across the back of his neck for a moment.

"There's a resemblance." Later I would ask him what he knew about Steve, but for now I'd stick to my story. Then I blurted out the rest, almost without taking a breath.

"Does he have a will?"

"I don't know. He left before my brain could catch up enough to ask him sensible questions." I looked down and realized my hands were clasped together. "Do you think it's true?" I looked around the porch before looking at Rip. I didn't want to move. I was already spoiled by the luxury of being on the beach. Of being able to run on it, watch it, hear it, smell the salty air, carry a paddleboard or kayak down to it with ease. Without Boone leaving the place to me, I could never have afforded this.

Rip's face was serious. "It's hard to believe. I think Steve only showed up here a few times during Boone's childhood. Usually long enough to stir up trouble and ill will. I suspect Vivi paid him to go away again. Maybe that's what he's after now."

Rip and Boone had gone to school together. "You're right. Boone would never do that to Vivi. Never." Would he? Was he hoping to reconcile with his father? Maybe deploying to Afghanistan had changed his perspective on life more than I had realized. More than he ever said. "Should I contact a lawyer?"

"You should definitely get hold of the lawyer in Chicago and let him know what has happened."

I stood up. "Thank you for coming."

Rip stood up too. "Anytime. I'll help you clean up."

We carried the food and plates back into the kitchen. "I'll worry about the dishes later," I said after I put the leftover food away. "I need to go see Vivi. I need to get to her before Steve does." Vivi couldn't hear this news from him. "She was livid when she found out Boone left so much to me. I can't imagine how this is going to go over."

"Do you want me to go with you?"

It was a lovely offer. A heart-softening offer. I gave him a little smile. "You probably aren't the best candidate to go with me. But I appreciate it."

"I kind of figured that was what you'd say." Rip walked over to the door, opened it, and paused. "This wasn't exactly what I had in mind when I mentioned having dinner together, but thanks for having me. Thanks for trusting me."

"Thanks for coming." I stared at the door for a few moments after he left.

CHAPTER 15

Vivi's face was pale after I told her the news. It made her look older than normal. We sat across from each other in matching love seats. A low coffee table between us. Vivi wore an ankle-length sundress in pale pink with a white sweater over it, her feet in gold sandals with nails painted the same shade as the dress. Her lipstick a shade darker. I was still in my work T-shirt, shorts, and flats. I always felt like a mess around Vivi.

"I'll get us some water," I said, "unless you want something stronger."

"Water's fine." Vivi stared out her front window toward her palm trees, palmettos, and magnolias. All artfully arranged with hibiscus, camellias, and other native plants. No lush lawn that was hard to maintain and required lots of water. Because it was dark, she could only see her reflection.

I'd only been in Vivi's house a few times. It was a big Victorian and sat on the beach, like mine. As the crow flies or the runner runs, our houses weren't that far apart. The road between our two places meandered around coastal lakes and forests. I passed a huge family room that faced the ocean and a dining room on the way to the kitchen. All three levels of Vivi's house had deep verandas that spanned the width of the house. Only the one on the first floor was screened in.

Vivi's kitchen was bright white, with marble countertops and an island. A *Coastal Living* magazine and a coffee cup sat out on the island. The coffee was only partially drunk and the smell lingered in the kitchen. Some of the cupboards were glass-fronted, so it was easy to find glasses and fill them with ice and water from dispensers on the front of the refrigerator. I waited another minute to give Vivi some privacy before taking the glasses back out to the living room. I set one in front of her on a coaster with sandpipers on it and took mine around to the other love seat.

Vivi was leaning back, focusing on some far-off spot, the index finger of her right hand up against her lip. A large diamond sparkled on her ring finger. Pippi came trotting in. She looked from me to Vivi, as if she had to make a choice. Then she sprung up on the love seat and curled up in Vivi's lap. Smart choice. Vivi needed comforting more than I did. Vivi started stroking her back.

After I sat Vivi looked at me and took a sip of her water. "Bringing that man into this house was the worst and the best thing I ever did."

I nodded for lack of anything to say. I knew Vivi well enough by now not to push her. Maybe older, dearer friends could do that, but with me, she would just shut down.

"I met him gambling in an illegal game in Biloxi, Mississippi. He was handsome, charming, smart." A smile flickered across her face. "Apparently he's still all those things."

Joaquín had told me last June that Vivi had had a gambling problem in the past. "I wouldn't say charming. Unless you think a pigsty is charming."

The smile flickered again. "I decided he was perfect for my daughter and invited him to our Sunday dinner. By the time the meal was over, my daughter was besotted. Soon after pregnant. And then, of course, Steve took off. He came sniffing back around about the time my daughter was due. A hefty check sent him on his way and out of our lives for a while." Vivi stared at Pippi, who was purring contentedly. She looked up at me. "Perhaps I do need something stronger. There's a bottle of bourbon in the back of the cupboard above the sink. Would you be a dear and get it?"

Calling me "dear" was new. I hustled back to the kitchen. I couldn't reach the bottle, but found a step stool in the pantry. Once I retrieved the bottle and put everything away, I found a rocks glass for Vivi. I wasn't a bourbon drinker, not even when it was the good stuff like this bottle of Blanton's. I poured some into the glass and left the bottle in the kitchen before heading back to Vivi.

"Thank you, dear," Vivi said when I handed her the glass. "Any time Steve needed money, he swung into town with some lavish gift for Boone, flowers and jewelry for my daughter. I always suspected all of it was stolen, or won gambling at the very least, because it was the one thing he was good at." She laughed a cynical-sounding noise. "Probably he was cheating. That's something else he was good at." She took a sip of the bourbon and set the glass back down on the coffee table.

I was relieved she didn't knock it back and ask me to get her more. Vivi didn't drink often, especially for someone who owned a bar. Maybe because alcohol was always around, it somehow lost its appeal.

"Me slipping him a check always made sure he'd leave town again. Once, when I decided I was fed up with paying him, he moved in with my daughter and Boone. Made them both promises about being a changed man. But he was a lying son of a moonshine maker. He cheated on her the second night he was in town. Didn't bother to hide it. My punishment for not paying him off as soon as he showed up. My daughter put up with it because she thought Boone needed his daddy." Vivi took another drink. "He didn't attend my daughter's funeral, or Boone's. But he gave us Boone, and for that I'll always be grateful."

"Boone was an amazing man." My voice choked up as I said it. My best friend, and he'd been in love with me, only I didn't find out until after he was gone. I'd loved him as a friend and now would always wonder if it could have been more. It's the reason, even though I was attracted to Rip, that I tried—not always successfully given the past couple of days—to keep an emotional distance. "So you did something right, Vivi."

She smiled a real smile then. "When Steve wasn't around, my daughter was a fabulous mother and woman. The heritage business owners became Boone's fathers. Ralph especially. He was so good to him."

Ralph. I hadn't given him a thought, or thought about what had happened yesterday since Steve showed up.

"I'll call the lawyer in Chicago who wrote Boone's will," Vivi said.

"I sent him an email before I came over."

"A follow-up call won't hurt."

"You're right of course." Vivi was good at bending people to her will.

"And then we'll wait for Steve to show back up with his will."

I stood up. Vivi might be willing to wait for Steve to show his hand, but I wasn't. Not that I knew what I could do. "I'll see you in the morning."

I called Joaquín on the way home and filled him in on Steve's appearance at my house. I told him that I'd gone to Vivi's but didn't tell him what she'd said about Steve. They'd known each other long enough that he probably knew how badly Vivi would react to this news.

"Come stay with us tonight," Joaquín said. "Michael's nodding. I'll make you happy drinks."

I laughed. Happy drinks involved fruit and paper umbrellas. "I could use a happy drink, but I'm tired and want to sleep in my own bed." Boone's bed.

"Then I'm staying on the phone with you until you get home, just in case Steve is waiting for you again. Something is off about that man."

"That I would appreciate."

"Do you really think he has a will?" Joaquín asked.

"I'm hoping it's just a threat to get Vivi riled up and writing checks."

"Boone wouldn't do that to Vivi."

It was the same thing Rip had said. "I just pulled into the drive. There aren't any cars parked by the house."

"I'm staying on the line until you're inside."

"You're the best." We chatted as I climbed out, hurried to the door, unlocked it, got in, and set the security alarm. "I'm all set."

"No, you aren't. You walk through the house. Don't miss the closets or under the beds."

I thought about protesting but gave in and did as he asked, filling him in as I went. "No boogeymen and no Steve. I do need to use the dust mop under the beds. Thank you, Joaquín."

"You sleep well."

"You too. Hugs to Michael." I hung up. The reality of being so alone settled into my bones. I got a glass of water and took it out to the porch. A thin line of moonlight shone on the Gulf. The air smelled of the wood of the porch, salt, and pine from the trees around the house. The water whooshed and subsided, as if to say, *Don't worry. All is well.* If only it were.

Thursday morning I set out for an early jog. The water had small waves, the beach was fairly empty. A couple of men were out fishing. I had to run farther up on the beach so I wouldn't accidentally run through one of their lines. The sand was softer up there, and harder to run on. I wasn't making much progress, which was exactly how I felt about finding out anything about Raquel and helping Ralph. I jogged back down to the firmer sand, waving to a woman I often saw running. We'd never talked and usually were heading the opposite way from each other.

While I'd like to make more friends here, especially some female ones, I didn't really like to run with other people. I was content on my own, pushing myself or holding back as the mood struck. Running was my thinking time, or my mind-clearing time. Whichever I needed in the moment. In Chicago I had often listened to music when I ran, but here I loved listening to the sound of the water on the sand and the gulls' cries.

I turned around after thirty minutes, ran back home, and got ready for the day. It was still early, so I made a big breakfast, with a veggie-loaded omelet, bacon, toast, fresh squeezed orange juice, and coffee.

I flipped on the local news and there stood Mary Moore on the beach, in front of the Sea Glass. She rehashed the story of my rescue, then the camera cut in close on her face.

"The identity of the Good Samaritan who saved Chloe Jackson remains a mystery. So far, no one we've talked to has been able to identify him. If any of you recognize this man," they showed a shot of the man as he pulled away from the dock behind the Sea Glass, "or his boat, please contact me. We'd love to give him the hero's welcome he deserves."

The weatherman came on and I flipped off the TV, but continued to stare at it. Mary hadn't exactly violated our agreement, but seeing that on the air didn't make me happy. After I finished my breakfast I checked to see if I'd heard back from Boone's lawyer—nothing.

Next I did a search for the *Fair Winds*. There were several articles about the disappearance of the boat on various anniversaries. I blinked and reread the names of the four people who had been on the boat. Raquel, of course, and Susan Harrington. Never heard that name before. Blake Farwell. He might be related to Jed. But the shocker was Cartland Barnett. Was he related to Rip? I did a quick search and found out that Cartland was Rip's father. Cartland was much younger than the others on the boat.

Why had no one mentioned this? How odd that Boone and Rip had both had absentee fathers—though for very different reasons. I did the math in my head. Rip would have been around sixteen when the *Fair Winds* disappeared. Maybe that was one of the reasons they'd become friends. Rip had told me in June that Boone had talked about me a lot. I glanced at the clock. I didn't have time to search more right now. I needed to get to work.

I took a quick shower, then drove over to the Sea Glass. It was ten o'clock, and I was the first one in. I didn't want Vivi here alone in case Steve showed up and I'd grown to like being here by myself in the morning. I got the barstools down from the tables, and dusted, looking at all the pictures and signs hanging around the bar. After working here for three months I was starting to recognize younger versions of some of our patrons.

After that was done I sliced lemons, oranges, and limes for the drinks we'd serve today. Joaquín sailed in a few minutes later in a navy-blue Hawaiian shirt dotted with pink, cheeky-looking flamingos.

"You're early," I said.

"I didn't want Vivi to be here alone if Steve came in."

"Me either. She's not in yet."

"Should we be worried?" Joaquín asked.

"I already got a start on that, but it's not doing any good." Vivi was usually here before our eleven o'clock opening.

He looked around. "You're spoiling me by doing all the grunt work before I arrive."

"Are you calling me a grunt?" I asked.

"Never, darling. It's just that you will tackle any job. No one else who's worked here ever did that. If they did, it was usually accompanied by a lot of complaining."

"I'm not good at sitting around."

"I've noticed."

Vivi came in a little after we opened at eleven. Even though she wore a bright blue, short-sleeved dress, silver heels, had make up on, and her hair was in its usual sleek bob, she looked tired, which made me feel bad for her. She tossed her silver designer bag in her office before she came over to Joaquín and me.

"Any sign of Steve?" she asked.

"Not yet. Did you talk to the lawyer?" I asked.

Vivi glanced at Joaquín.

"I filled him in last night. He needed to know in case Steve showed up."

"Of course," Vivi said. "I'm glad you did."

Whew.

"I spoke to Boone's lawyer about an hour ago. If Steve has a will dated after the one he drew up, it will be up to the court to decide which one is valid. All we can do right now is wait for Steve to show up and see what he has to say. He might not even have a will. Maybe he's bluffing."

"I hope you're right," I said. Maybe this was just another of Steve's schemes to get money from Vivi.

Two groups of people came in off the beach, so we didn't have time to discuss it further. That was a good thing, because the whole topic was just too depressing. While I had a selfish interest in wanting Steve to be lying,

I was more worried for Vivi. I couldn't imagine her having to turn half ownership over to Steve. Vivi and my butting heads would look like Little League to their major-league issues.

The phone rang. "Sea Glass Saloon, how can I help you?"

"Is this Chloe Jackson?" a man's voice asked.

"Yes." Maybe this was my rescuer. Maybe the reporter's piece on TV this morning had worked. It didn't sound exactly like him, but we'd had to talk loudly because of the engine noise.

"I just wanted to tell you that I saw you on TV and I'd rescue you anytime."

My eyes got wide. "Who is this?"

He started a list of ways he thought he could rescue me. All of it had to do with us being naked.

"Go to hell," I said and pressed the Off button to end the call.

Vivi and Joaquín were staring at me.

"What was that about?" Vivi asked.

"Someone who volunteered to rescue me. You don't want to know the rest. Let's just get back to work."

Vivi put a Reserved sign on the high-top table where the heritage business owners usually sat. I hoped some of them showed up, because they had Vivi's back in a way no one else did. Their parents had all known each other—sometimes even their grandparents. They'd all gone to school together, and even if they left to go off to college or serve in the military, they all returned to run the businesses their families had started.

I took care of the people at the two tables. Every time

someone came in Joaquín and I jerked up our heads, but Steve hadn't shown up. Various heritage business owners came in and out, and the table was never empty. By one thirty I was someplace between being on high alert and trying to convince myself that Steve had lied. That he was just hoping for another payout from Vivi.

CHAPTER 16

At two I was back in the kitchen, unloading the dishwasher. Joaquín stuck his head around the corner of the door.

"Chloe, a man is in the bar who wants to talk to you about the cigarette boat."

My heart accelerated. Maybe Mary Moore's report had made the Good Samaritan realize I was looking for him. I hustled out to the bar. The man who stood there wasn't the man who'd rescued me. He was shorter, less tanned, and didn't look like the pictures of Neptune I'd seen. But maybe he knew my rescuer. He awkwardly held a box that was about twelve by twelve inches under one arm.

"I'm Chloe," I said. "I'm looking for the cigarette boat and its owner."

"I don't know nothin' about the owner, but I got something for you." He put down the box on a barstool and opened it up. He pulled out a boat in a glass case and set it on the bar. It was in the shape of a cigarette boat and was made of cigarettes. "I thought this would commemorate your adventure."

It was intricately detailed. I didn't know what to say, so I just stared at it and then the man. "It's amazing. Thank you."

"I'll give you a bargain price of fifty dollars, and if the next time you talk to that reporter you mention my work, I'd appreciate it."

I went around the back of the bar, not knowing whether to laugh or cry. I got my purse, found fifty dollars, and handed it over to the man. He left whistling as he went.

"Why'd you buy that, Chloe?" Joaquín asked.

"I didn't want to hurt his feelings, and it is kind of cool."

We both studied it.

Joaquín laughed. "It is."

Business had been steady. Joaquín turned up the cheery island music. He danced and swayed his hips even more than usual, and that was saying something, because he was usually moving around. He winked and flirted with the women who sat in the row of seats at the bar to watch him. Joaquín even twirled me around and dipped me once when I brought him an order.

Vivi sat with Ralph, Wade, Edith Hickle, who owned the Glass Bottom Boat along with her father and daughter, Frank Russo, who owned Russo's Grocery Store, and Jed Farwell, who owned Emerald Cove Fishing Charters.

Wade brought over a selection of raw oysters—yuck—
and jambalaya. I ate a bowl of jambalaya that had just
enough spice to tingle my tongue, but not overwhelm it
so I couldn't taste the shrimp, chicken, and Andouille
sausage.

Wade sat next to Vivi, as he always did when he was
here. The man was madly in love with her. While I could
tell Vivi was fond of him, I wasn't sure she was in love
with him. However, the summer tourist season kept
everyone so busy that no one had much time for personal
relationships. It had been all work and then fall into bed
exhausted.

I finished delivering drinks to a table out on the deck.
The beach wasn't nearly as crowded as it was during the
summer, but there were still plenty of people enjoying the
late-afternoon sun. As I carried the now-empty tray back
in, I saw Vivi sit bolt upright. Wade stood and crossed his
arms over his chest while the rest of the crew turned to
look in my direction. I turned too.

Steve stood next to a man close to my age in a pin-
striped business suit. His wavy, dark hair was slicked
back and gelled into place. He wore a pristine white shirt,
with a purple tie the only thing that didn't scream power.

Steve sauntered by me over to the heritage business
owners. I wanted to whack him with the tray I was holding, but didn't really think that would help the situation. I
pictured a headline: "Waitress beats man to death in a be-
tray-al." I loosened my grip on the tray. The man in the
suit stood next to me, and his floral aftershave made my
nose itch. He had thick lips and deep-set eyes under a
prominent brow. He was attractive in a smarmy way.

"Well, well, the gang's all here. Did you miss me?" He
stood next to Jed Farwell, who leaned away from him.

Steve stuck out his hand to shake, but everyone just left it out there. He laughed, then stuck his hand in the pocket of his red-plaid shorts. "What a welcome home."

"You're not welcome here," Vivi said. Her drawl, pronounced, was a cue to most people to run.

"Well now, Vivi, you are going to have to get used to me being here as half owner of the bar." Steve turned to look at me. "I'm sure we can keep you on as a waitress with a little work on your looks and clothes." He then turned to Joaquín. "And with some additional training, perhaps you."

I wasn't going to let Steve's comment about my appearance get to me. I looked just fine. However, I was worried about Vivi. Her face had gone from white to pink to scarlet. I went and stood beside her. My tray ready if I needed to use it on someone. Joaquín came and stood behind us. I smelled mint and noticed Joaquín gripped the stone pestle he used to muddle herbs and fruit in his right hand. Tiny bits of mint clung to it. The rest of the heritage business owners crowded around us.

"Oh, look at that intimidating group, will you, Ted?" Steve said.

I assumed Ted was the guy in the suit. "If you have a will, let's see it," I said. I noticed the people in the bar had mostly gone quiet. Except for the people out on the deck, who didn't have a clue as to what was happening in here.

"You all remember Ted Barnett," Steve said.

Barnett? That was Rip's last name. I could see a slight resemblance. Although Ted looked like the used-car salesman version of Rip. Where Rip was muscled, Ted was soft. Ted had the pale looks of someone who was rarely outdoors, while Rip was tanned.

"I remember him," said an older man who sat at a table

next to us. The man was a local curmudgeon who usually drank whiskey sours, but had the occasional old fashioned. "I was his high school math teacher. Always caught him cheating."

Ted turned a bit red at that. "People change."

"Oh, let's not keep them in suspense any longer," Steve said. He motioned to Ted with his hand.

Ted reached into an inner pocket of his suit jacket and pulled out a thick, legal-size envelope. He handed it to Steve. Steve smiled and extended it to Vivi. I wanted to snatch it out of his hand and read it.

"Here you go." When she didn't reach for it Steve dropped it in front of her. He looked at me. "We'll give you a week to pack up and move." He turned to Ted. "Let's go."

"Round of drinks on the house," Vivi called out after they left. "Chloe, after you help Joaquín with the drinks, please come to my office." She slipped off her barstool and looked at the heritage business owners. "Thanks to all of you for being here. I hope you'll understand if I need a moment alone." She patted Wade's arm.

The heritage owners all murmured things like "Let us know what we can do" and "We have your back" as they left the bar. Wade stayed behind. Vivi picked up the envelope and walked back to her office, back stiff, head high. I wanted to go after her. I wanted to find out what was in that envelope, but I started taking orders instead.

An hour later I knocked on Vivi's office door. Joaquín and I hadn't seen her since she went in.

"Come in." Vivi's voice sounded strong, firm.

I slipped in, closing the door behind me. Vivi had documents sprawled across her desk. The envelope they came in lay empty, pushed off to one side.

"What do you think?" I asked, sitting across from her and gesturing to the papers.

She gathered them up, tapping them lightly on the desk to align their edges. "It must be a scam, but they look legitimate to me." Her lips settled in a tight line. An expression I hadn't seen since June, when I'd shown up. "I made an appointment with a lawyer I know for eight o'clock tomorrow morning. I'd like you to come with me."

"Of course," I said. "May I?" I pointed to the documents.

"Yes, I made a copy for you," Vivi said. "But let me warn you, he has an alleged email exchange between him and Boone. It's not easy to read them. But they sound like Boone, and I'm not sure Steve could pull that off." She folded the documents, put them back in the envelope, and gave it to me.

That didn't sound good. "I'll read them at home tonight. It's still busy out there." I stood. "What do you know about Ted Barnett?"

"I don't trust him," Vivi said. "He takes after his grandmother."

I nodded, but maybe Vivi wasn't the most reliable source on the topic of the Barnett family.

"Chloe," Vivi said as I headed toward the door, "if the worst happens and this somehow turns out to be true, you can come live with me at the big house."

Vivi called her home "the big house." Before Boone died she had dreamed of a future when Boone's family would live in it and she'd move to the house I lived in now. I was shocked. I'd thought if things turned out to go Steve's way that Vivi wouldn't be sad to see the last of me. "Thank you." I could feel the pull of tears behind my eyes. "That means a lot to me. I'll get back to work and see you later."

Vivi stood. "I think I'll go home. I'm a bit tired after all Steve's drama."

"Okay, I'll see you in the morning, then." I glanced at my copies of the will and emails, wishing I had time to read them now, but they would have to wait.

At nine thirty I was finally sitting on my back porch with a beer. The weather had cooled off enough that I'd thrown on a sweater over my T-shirt and shorts. Maybe I did need to up my wardrobe a bit for work. Vivi always looked like she'd walked off the pages of a magazine. But I also didn't want to give Steve the satisfaction of knowing he was right. So shorts and T-shirts it was for now.

Wade had left jambalaya for Joaquín and me, so I'd eaten more of it before I came home. The water sparkled and swooshed gently. I took a sip of my beer. If I didn't get some exercise, I wouldn't get any sleep tonight. And I wasn't ready to face the documents Vivi had given me yet. I needed a clear head for them.

After I changed into a one-piece swimsuit and board shorts, I went outside. Boone had stashed toys—boogie boards, surfboards, a kayak, paddleboards, and oars— under the porch. I'd started to drag out a paddleboard when I heard footsteps coming up the walkway. I dropped the board and grabbed a paddle. It made a better weapon.

CHAPTER 17

"It's only me, Chloe," Rip said as I turned.

I relaxed the paddle, which I held like a baseball bat. Rip wore a T-shirt and running shorts. "I guess I'm a little on edge."

"I heard what happened at the bar today."

Not surprising. The good people of Emerald Cove loved to talk. "I'm sure you did, and you know my propensity to want to work off my worries, so you showed up here to either stop me or save me." I turned my back to him and pulled out a paddleboard. "I don't need to be stopped or saved."

"Actually, I just thought you might want some company."

My shoulders slumped. Some days I could be such a witch. I turned to Rip. "I'm sorry. It's been a bad few days."

"Apology accepted. I'll go."

"Or you can come paddleboarding with me." When I went on my own at night I stayed on this side of the first sandbar, where the water was only inches deep.

"I'd like that, if you really want me to."

I didn't answer. Of course I wanted him to. I just tossed him a paddle and dragged out a second paddleboard. We carried them down to the Gulf. The water was dark, and the half-moon was playing hide-and-go-seek with the clouds. I confess I was glad for the company. We didn't talk, but stood on the paddleboards next to each other, paddling west along the shore. I snuck glances at Rip. If I didn't have the paddle in my hands, I'd probably be fanning myself, because he looked really good on a paddleboard. Really good.

The third time he caught me staring, I figured I had to say something. "Race you until we're even with that tall pine." I pointed to a tree that was about thirty feet ahead and then took off. Ugh. I couldn't believe I'd said, "race you," like I would have to one of my brothers when I was eight. But it was too late to take it back. Rip chuckled, and while I'd shot out ahead of him at first, he caught up easily.

When we were almost even with the tree I used my paddle to splash him, trying to throw him off, but he just laughed and worked harder, winning the race.

"You're a cheater, Chloe," Rip said, laughing. "Haven't you heard that cheaters never win?"

"That so isn't true." I shrugged. "If you grew up with brothers like mine, you would cheat too."

"I hear you about the brothers," Rip said.

We turned our paddleboards back toward my house. I still didn't know much about Rip's family. I didn't quite know how to bring up his father disappearing on the *Fair Winds*. "Are you related to Ted Barnett?" Maybe the name Barnett was common down here.

Rip continued to paddle. One stroke, two, three. I kept up with him, waiting for an answer.

"He's my cousin. We practiced law at the same firm in Birmingham. Green and Long."

That was interesting.

"He's a year older than me. His family moved to Birmingham after he graduated. We saw each other a lot, growing up at my grandmother's house."

"Did you hear he's Steve's lawyer?"

Rip nodded. Now I wished we were in a well-lit room so I could see his expressions more easily.

"Is he a good person?"

Rip went back to paddling. I worked my arms hard, trying to keep up.

"I want to believe he is," Rip finally said. "He was always good to me. He's the reason I ended up at the firm after law school. Ted got me the job."

"But you left. Why?"

"Did you ever see that Tom Cruise movie, *The Firm*?"

"Yes. Of course. I read the book too. John Grisham wrote it."

"I don't think this firm was too far off from the one in the movie."

As I recalled, when Tom Cruise left his firm they went after him to kill him. I resisted the urge to look over my shoulder to see if gunmen were on the shore waiting for Rip.

"It took me a few years to figure out that wasn't the place for me. That being a criminal defense lawyer wasn't for me."

We had something in common with drastic changes in our lives—children's librarian to waitress and lawyer to volunteer firefighter. It made me wonder how he could have such a fancy new boat without a job. But his family came from money, so maybe he had a trust fund. It really wasn't my business.

"That being said, I can't imagine Ted taking Steve's case. The firm usually only deals with very wealthy clients. The five percenters."

So something was up, but how to find out what? My body was physically tired, but my head didn't feel any clearer. I paddled back to shore.

"I read that your father was on the *Fair Winds* when it disappeared. I'm sorry. That must have been very difficult."

"It was. The not knowing what happened has always been the worse part. People were cruel in their speculating that the four of them ran off together. I never believed that."

"That's awful."

"It's why I left for Alabama when I was eighteen, and why my mom moved to Tampa."

We carried the boards and paddles back up to the house, and Rip helped me stash them under the porch.

"Thanks for keeping me company," I said as I walked to the door to the screened porch. It was hard to see his expression.

"Any time, Chloe Jackson."

His voice was soft, deep, caressing. The slight drawl caused tingles to zap around my nervous system. Why did he have this effect on me? I wanted to invite him in, to find out what those firm lips would feel like against mine. But the timing was terrible. I had to get ready for the meeting with Vivi and her lawyer in the morning. For once, good sense won out. This must be what it felt like to be a grown-up. I waved a goodbye, went into the porch, locked the screen, and watched Rip walk off with a sigh.

I clicked on a lamp, picked up the papers, and read. The will itself was straightforward, brief, and unemotional, as one would expect a legal document to be. It was dated three months after mine. Everything Steve had said was here in black and white. I bolted up when I read the emails.

CHAPTER 18

They got to me. The papers shook in my hand. The first one was written right after Boone had arrived in Afghanistan. The language sort of sounded like Boone, but they also felt a bit off to me. That could be wishful thinking on my part. I looked out at the ocean. Leaving this slice of paradise would be difficult, but if this will was legal, Vivi would be destroyed by Boone's betrayal.

In that case I might have to move in with her just to make sure she was okay. The letter Boone had sent to me with his original will had said I'd figure out why he wanted me down here. Was all this what he'd been alluding too? No, he never would have manipulated us so cruelly.

I stared back down at the papers. The emails started with Steve writing about what a lousy father he'd been and apologizing. Steve wrote that a couple of health issues had made him rethink his life. I wondered if that was true, because Steve looked like a photo you'd see next to a definition of good health. Was there any way to check that out? I made a note on my phone to follow up.

Boone's first few replies sounded stiff. A quick *glad you're okay.* As Steve's emotional pleas for a reunion got longer and more intense, Boone—if it was Boone—started writing back longer messages. I knew Boone's time in Afghanistan had been rough. I could see how he might want to settle things in his life. But the email that bolted me up was when Boone wrote Steve and started talking about them reuniting and running the Sea Glass together when Vivi retired. He said he'd been rethinking his life too, and that it was time to leave Chicago and return to Florida.

The following emails were them discussing their plans. Boone had never told me any of this in all the times we'd video chatted while he was in Afghanistan or in any of our email exchanges. But then again, Boone had never told me he was in love with me, or that he was leaving me anything. I found out in the letter he'd written before he left for Afghanistan. The one that was with his will. However, not telling me he was in contact with his father was a stretch.

Although, when I thought about it, Boone never talked much about his life down here—that Vivi had left him a house and he was part owner of the bar. The boat I knew about, but not much else. I'd never pressed him because he'd clam up or change the subject. I always figured he'd talk when he was ready to, though that chance had been snatched away.

In the end I didn't know what to make of all this. I wanted it to be a scam. For Vivi's sake. For mine. And so Boone would remain the same man I thought he was.

At eight fifteen Friday morning I sat next to Vivi in her lawyer's office. George Colton's desk was larger than most kitchen islands and, like kitchen islands, had a massive slab of marble as its top. The only things on the desk were a mahogany pen holder with an expensive-looking pen in it, a closed laptop, and the papers Vivi had handed him when we had arrived at eight.

The office had the usual shelves of law books, but instead of vanity photos of him posing with people, there was a massive oil painting of the Gulf. Vivi wore a Lilly Pulitzer, long-sleeved dress and I'd worn a blue, polka-dot sundress. Maybe Steve's remark about my looks had gotten to me more than I realized.

George looked over his reading glasses at us, holding the will in his hand. He had thick, gray eyebrows and a pleasant, rounded face, and his tie was covered with sailboats. Vivi and I took turns filling him in on the original will and Boone's background with his father. How unlikely it was that Boone would do something like this to Vivi.

George shook his head. "I don't like this. Green and Long has a reputation for shady dealings."

I knew more than I wanted to about shady lawyers from an experience last summer. What was with the lawyers down here?

"They've been sued more than once," Vivi said. "Nothing ever sticks, though. They pay people off to make things go away."

"They don't make people go away, do they?" I asked, thinking back to Rip comparing the place to the lawyers in *The Firm*.

George and Vivi looked at me as if I was daft.

"I'm sure they've paid off their share of people," George said.

That was better than making them disappear.

"Our problem is proving this isn't legal," George added.

"What about the emails?" I asked. "I think they might be fake."

"The emails won't have any bearing on whether the court declares this will to be the legally binding one." George leaned back in his chair.

"I can't figure out why Green and Long would help someone like Steve," Vivi said.

"He doesn't sound like the kind of man they usually represent," George replied.

"Maybe he has something on them," I said.

Vivi and George looked at each other.

He started nodding. "Now, that makes sense." He made a note on the legal pad in front of him. "I'll have someone start digging into the emails to see if they are legitimate. I can hire a private detective to look into Steve."

"No need to hire a private detective. I have someone I trust."

I assumed Vivi was talking about Ann Williams, who had helped her out before. How many times, I had no idea.

"The good news is that military lawyers aren't experts in the law in every state. The military just spends vast amounts of money on software that makes it possible for their lawyers to do wills in a number of different states. Still, the tiny details are important in a will, so maybe we can find something."

I reached over and squeezed Vivi's hand. "What kinds of mistakes could be made in a will?" I asked.

"Lots of things, but I'll give you a couple of examples. State of residence is important. While Boone's property was here in Florida, I believe he was a resident of Illinois."

"He was," I said.

"Different states have different requirements for the number of witnesses. If that wasn't done correctly, the will would be invalid."

My grandmother had a saying about grasping at straws. I feared that was exactly what George was doing, but if that made Vivi feel better, I was all for it. I glanced at her, and she looked a little less tense than she had when she walked in.

"Okay, then," George said, "I'll take extra care reading through this and I'll be in touch when I have news."

Vivi and I stood outside by her Mercedes. The sun was warm, with a gentle breeze. The palm tree leaves rustled against one another and the humidity was low, which was a relief after the long, hot summer.

"I'm going to go see Ann," Vivi said. "I told her I'd probably be by this morning."

"I can go with you. There's time before we open."

Vivi opened her car door and got in. "I'd rather go alone."

"Where does Ann live?"

"You can ask her." Vivi closed the door, started the car, and left.

I stared after the car. Vivi was so prickly sometimes. What did she want to say to Ann that she didn't want me to hear? I could try to follow her, but my vintage red Beetle wasn't really a stealth mobile. I'd track Ann down later.

CHAPTER 19

Twenty minutes later I was sitting on the deck of the Sea Glass reading the last chapter of *Pride and Prejudice* by Jane Austen. I should say rereading it, because I'd read it several times, but the last time had been years ago. Tonight was the first Spines and Wines Book Club event at the Sea Glass. I'd told Vivi and Joaquín in June that I wanted to make some changes. This was an easy one that everyone had agreed to. I'd thought I'd take baby steps before rolling out any bigger plans.

I sighed as I closed the book. I liked it because Darcy and Elizabeth didn't have an easy path to love, which made the book more believable. Oh, but that ending. My love life had more or less been a disaster, with a broken engagement and then finding out about Boone's feelings for me. Rip was intriguing, but I wasn't sure I was in a good place emotionally to get involved with anyone. A fictional romance on the other hand . . . I'd also always had a book crush on Colonel Fitzwilliam, Darcy's cousin. He was always kind and compassionate, where Darcy wasn't. Even though Elizabeth Bennett forgave Darcy for what he did to her sister Jane, I'm not sure I could be as forgiving

I'd like to laze around out here in the sun dreaming of finding my own Darcy or Fitzwilliam, but I had work to do. I went back into the bar and locked the doors behind me. Joaquín came in a few minutes later, and I filled him in about the papers I'd read last night and what the lawyer said this morning as we took the barstools down from the tables.

"Then Vivi took off to find Ann on her own and just left me standing in the parking lot."

Joaquín chuckled. "I gave up trying to figure out Vivi a long time ago. And the stress of Boone's death changed her. She's quieter than she used to be and doesn't laugh as much."

"That's understandable, and I guess I'm a poor substitute for Boone."

"You're not a substitute for anyone, Chloe. We love you just as you are."

"Did you just quote *Bridget Jones's Diary*?"

Joaquín laughed. "I did. You aren't the only one who reads."

"I love that book and how it's a modern retelling of *Pride and Prejudice*."

"The movie isn't bad either."

"It's hard not to like a movie with Colin Firth and Hugh Grant."

"Agreed. But back to Vivi. A lot of her dreams, whether they were realistic or not, died with Boone."

"Like him moving back here and running the bar?" I asked.

"I don't think he planned to stray far from your side. So if you'd stayed in Chicago, so would Boone."

I sighed. I'd lost a lot of nights' sleep wondering about Boone and me. "Do you think Michael would be willing to help out with the will? He's been in the military, so he might pick up on something George Colton wouldn't." Michael was former Navy intelligence and good with computers. Not to mention he still had contacts in the military world.

"I'm sure if you asked him, he would."

I called Michael right then, even though I should have been chopping fruit. "I have a favor to ask you," I said after we greeted each other. I explained what I needed. "Also, I'm suspicious of the emails that Steve claims are from Boone. Although they aren't as important as proving that the will is flawed and invalid."

"Sure. It might take a few days," Michael said.

"That's fine."

"Do you have the emails?"

"I have hard copies that either Ted Barnett or Steve printed out."

"Send them home with Joaquín. But don't get your hopes up. They might have scrubbed any information that would show where the emails really came from."

Ugh. I hadn't thought of that. "Okay, thank you." I guessed if this battle went to court that the originals would have to be provided at some point.

After we hung up I chopped fruit while Joaquín inventoried the liquor or spirits supply, as he called it.

"Have you heard anything about your rescuer?"

"I've barely thought of him since Steve showed up." I hadn't thought of Ralph or the remains on the ship much either. Each dilemma had taken a back seat to losing Boone's house and my share of the bar. I hated it when I turned into an "all about me" type.

Vivi walked in a few minutes later. She motioned for Joaquín and me to come into the office.

"George Colton just called and said Steve's will does have a cancel-previous-wills clause. He was hoping it wouldn't have one, because then we'd have better legal standing."

"Has he found anything else?"

"Not yet," Vivi said.

"The wheels of justice turn slowly, right?" Joaquín said.

Vivi nodded. "Let's get back out to work."

At nine that night I was walking the ten women who'd showed up to the book club out to the parking lot. We'd had a lively discussion about the book. I was pretty sure one of the women had only watched the BBC version with Colin Firth, because she kept talking about Darcy coming out of the lake. It was a fantastic scene in the film, but it wasn't in the book. Fortunately, no one called her out on it.

I was standing talking with two of the women when someone called my name. I looked up to see Rip and another man walking toward us.

The two women looked at me.

"Oh, he is handsome," one of them said, tugging my arm.

"Is he your Darcy?" the other woman asked.

"If he's Darcy, the other one is Colonel Fitzwilliam." They both giggled.

"Just imagine them in those tight pants like Colin Firth wore." This time they faked fanning themselves. Then they climbed into their car and drove off with a wave.

Where was a sinkhole when I needed one? Or an alien spaceship that would beam me up? I didn't think either of the two women had had that much to drink, but they were a lot louder than they thought they were and I was pretty sure Rip and his friend had heard every word. Good thing I wasn't standing directly under the lights in the parking lot because my face grew warm. I was probably a nice shade of fire-engine red.

Rip and his friend stopped beside me. I recognized his friend as one of the firefighters who had been with Rip at the Sea Glass. He was the one called Smoke because women thought he was hot. I couldn't disagree with that.

"Did they just call me Darcy?" Rip asked. "And Smoke, Fitzwilliam?"

"I'm not sure what they said," I replied, lying my butt off. Rip's friend Smoke wore a white linen shirt that accentuated his broad shoulders, making Rip's almost look slim. It was tucked into dark, fitted slacks, and I confess I started picturing the two of them riding horses in tight pants like Darcy and Fitzwilliam did in the BBC production of *Pride and Prejudice*. I mentally smacked my face so I didn't start drooling.

"Chloe this is my friend Smoke. He was at the Sea Glass with me."

Smoke reached out and shook my hand. His big hand made mine feel almost dainty, and trust me, there was nothing about me that one would call dainty. My brothers had always teased me about my stubby fingers. I'd finally realized my fingers weren't that stubby. Theirs were just longer and leaner than mine. Oh, boy, I was still holding Smoke's hand. I dropped it quickly. Rip didn't look amused.

"It's nice to see you again, Smoke." I hoped my voice covered my inner embarrassment. "What are you two up to?"

"Hopefully, no good." Smoke laughed.

"So you're a volunteer fireman too, Smoke?" I asked.

"Fitzwilliam here is full-time instead of a volunteer like I am," Rip said. This time they both laughed.

It sounded like Rip was trying to change the subject. If they wanted to go out and do whatever *no good* entailed, it shouldn't bother me. But it did. Ugh. How to get out of this gracefully? "How do you two even know who Darcy and Fitzwilliam are?"

"Any man with a mother, sister, or who has had a girl-friend knows the standard for all men is Darcy," Smoke said.

"I've heard from many a woman that Fitzwilliam here looks quite dashing in a wet linen shirt," Rip said.

I bet he did.

Smoke bowed toward Rip with a hand flourish. "Ah, but not as many as have said that about you."

They both laughed again. I laughed too. It was hard not to around Smoke and Rip.

Even eighty-year-old women liked to see Rip without a shirt, and who could argue?

"It was nice meeting you, Fitzwilliam and Darcy. I'll see you around." I headed back to the bar to help finish closing.

"It seems like your book club was a success, Chloe," Vivi said. "Well done."

I still wasn't used to getting praise from Vivi and it always made me a bit suspicious. I had to remind myself that I'd met Vivi at one of the lowest points in her life. The woman I met then and the woman I'd heard about from her friends over the past few months were two very different people.

I'd seen peeks of the old Vivi during the summer, but most of the time we'd been so busy there wasn't much time to think about it. I'd been shocked when she offered me a place to live if Steve's will turned out to be legal. It was a generous offer, but I couldn't imagine that happening. What would I do if I didn't own part of the bar? Stay here and find another job, or head back to Chicago, or move somewhere new?

"Thank you," I said. Vivi didn't usually stay to help close, but we'd both seen how tired Joaquín was and sent him home early. "I was wondering if we could put up some shelves and add some books, like a lending library or take-a-book, leave-a-book kind of arrangement."

"This is a bar, not a library, Chloe."

It was worth a try, and I'd bring it up later or just start bringing in books. I'd moved more books than clothes down here and more were being shipped to me. I'd lived with Rachel, and her apartment had been filled with books. I'd never realized that most of them were mine.

"That reminds me. I'm volunteering at the Emerald Cove Library tomorrow morning at ten, so I'll be a bit late."

"You can take the librarian out of the library . . ." Vivi said.

She wasn't too unhappy about it. In fact, when I first told her I wanted to start volunteering at the library, she'd said, "Fine. Whatever. I hope you worked it out with Joaquín." But she'd said it with a hint of a smile, so I thought she was pleased. I'd overheard her telling Joaquín about my volunteering, and Vivi had said something about being happy I was putting down roots.

"How did your talk with Ann Williams go?" I asked. Vivi hadn't shown up to the bar until noon. And although Ann often made an appearance in the bar, she hadn't come in today.

"She's willing to help."

I was surprised. First that Vivi had actually told me and second that there was a possibility Ann would have said no.

"Vivi, I can finish up so you can go." I had an ulterior motive for wanting her out of here.

"Thank you, I'll take you up on that." Vivi swept into her office, came out with one of her trademark designer handbags—pink this time—and went out the back door.

After I finished cleaning I would track Ann down. Hopefully, she'd be at her usual spot at Two Bobs.

CHAPTER 20

The air was nippier than I was used to it being; for now the humidity was almost nonexistent. I wished I had a sweater and almost laughed out loud. It was over seventy. In Chicago I'd never think of wearing a sweater in this weather. I must be going native already. I loved hearing the gentle slap of the water against the boats and dock as I walked toward Two Bobs.

I went in, ordered a beer, and started the hunt for Ann. She wasn't in her usual spot. A plump man with long, blond hair was out there, smoking away. I wondered if Ann would kick him out if she showed up, or if he was a placeholder for her. He looked a little shady to me.

I walked through the bar and up to the outdoor rooftop deck. Music was playing, and the white fairy lights danced in the breeze. It was mostly couples up here. A few were dancing in the middle of the space. High-top tables lined the perimeter. Window boxes filled with flowers topped the deck rails.

As I scanned the deck, I noticed a man waving to me. Smoke. I smiled and waved back. He gestured for me to come over. I did an inner shrug and decided *why not*. Ann wasn't here. Sticking around waiting for her would be a lot more fun with company.

"We meet again," Smoke said.

It might have sounded cheesy from anyone else, but he sounded happy to see me. I slid onto the barstool across from him. Well, slid would be a stretch. It was more of a hop and a wriggle. Smoke had deep blue eyes that were almost violet. His thick lashes were blond at the tips.

"If you're looking for Rip, he decided to call it a night."

"No. I was looking for someone else." That sounded odd, but not as odd as calling Ann Williams a friend. "She's not here."

Smoke held up his beer and said, "Well then, here's to us."

We clinked the necks of our beer bottles.

"And to new friends," Smoke said.

I nodded, wondering why no words were coming out. It was so unlike me. "Are you from Emerald Cove?" Whew, finally I'd remembered how to talk. But talk about cheesy lines. If I wasn't careful, I'd be asking him what his sign was, the way my mom said people did when she was young.

"Nope. I'm from Minnesota. My parents vacationed down here after they retired. I came to visit a couple of times and decided I'd had enough of the cold. I've been here two years."

"I just moved here from Chicago. I'm afraid I'll miss the cold. And the snow." I liked snow. It was frozen water and gave me whole new ways to be out on the lake. If I was careful—and I always was—there was much less chance of drowning when things were frozen solid.

"If you're like me, like most people down here, you'll soon think fifty is chilly. Kids don't get to go out to recess here if the temperature drops below forty. In Minnesota we went out unless the windchill dropped below minus twenty."

"I'm already adjusting. I had actual goose bumps earlier." We both looked down at my arms. I was still covered with them.

"Want to dance? That should keep you warm."

I loved to dance. I wasn't good at it, but I still thought it was fun. "Sure." We made our way out to the dance floor. Smoke was a good dancer. He didn't just shuffle his feet back and forth. A couple of times he took my hand and give me a twirl. By the time the song was over the goose bumps were gone.

A slow song came on. Smoke lifted an eyebrow in a do-you-want-to-dance-to-this look.

"Sure," I said again. I was glad he didn't just assume I would want to.

He pulled me to him, leaving a few inches between us. I closed my eyes and followed his lead. When the song was over I stepped back.

"Thanks for the dance. I need to get going." I needed to look for Ann. "I'm volunteering at the library tomorrow before work."

"No problem. Thanks for the company."

"Anytime." Ugh, that came out wrong. "See you around." I walked off. Did I hear him say, "I hope so?"

I walked around the bar again. Still no sign of Ann. Did her not being here mean something? I was being ridiculous. It wasn't as if she'd ever said, *If you need me, you can find me at Two Bobs.* It might have only been a coincidence that I'd found her here the other times. Although that would be a big coincidence. I had only been here a few months, so the locals like Ann didn't really trust me yet. I'd earned a bit of respect when I'd helped Vivi out in June, but only a bit.

I left through the back door and walked along the harbor toward the Sea Glass. I turned up the dock that led to Rip's boat. It was three boats up on my left. Lights were on, so maybe I'd stop to say hi. It was only ten thirty. As I drew closer, though, the shy side of me kicked it. What was I thinking, stopping by an attractive man's place at this time at night? I might as well scream, *Booty call.*

I heard low laughter. First Rip's and then, if I wasn't mistaken, Ann's. All my old insecurities came screaming back. I loved my brothers now, but our growing-up years had been difficult for me. They called it teasing when they commented on my chubby thighs or told me I was dumb. But I remembered a story our minister had told about words being like nails. You can pound a nail in a fence and you can take it out, but the hole is still there.

However, I could thank them for my love of running and reading. I ran to get away from them and I read to escape them. Now, when they reverted to teasing me, their wives jumped down their throats. I backed away from Rip's boat, knocked over a tin pail, and used the noise to cover me running back down the walkway. I ran all the way to my car without looking back. After berating myself, I shook off the insecurities and refocused on the larger problems at hand. Hopefully, at the library tomorrow I'd find some answers.

At five after ten Saturday morning I was sitting on the floor of the children's section of the Emerald Cove Library with an eight-year-old named Dash and six other kids. The library used to be a one-room schoolhouse. It looked like it from the outside, with its white-clapboard siding and bell tower. It wasn't hard to imagine a woman in long skirts with an apron tugging the bell chord, letting kids know it was time for school to start. Inside was cozy, with old wooden bookshelves and the smell of much-loved books. It was one block off the town circle. I felt at home here. Maybe they'd let me move in if Steve's will was legal.

"I was named for Dashiell Hammett," he informed me. "My parents are both crime fiction writers."

Dashiell Hammett was the author who'd created iconic characters including Sam Spade and Nick and Nora Charles. "That is an awesome name," I said.

Dash and the other kids had come to hear me read. We were reading *Upside-Down Magic*, the first book in the *Upside-Down Magic* series. The story was about Nory, Elliott, Andres, and Bax, who went to a magic school, and things didn't always go as planned. Boy, did that sound like my life. They find out that they need to learn a different way from their peers, but that didn't mean they were less intelligent than their classmates. I loved this book and was thrilled to share it with the kids.

After I read part of the book I explained that the library only had one copy and it wasn't available to be checked out until I read them the whole story. Parents rushed forward anyway. One parent tried to snatch the book out of my hand. Fortunately—or maybe unfortunately—I was ready for this. I'd seen it time and again. I explained as patiently as I could that this was the only copy. Then I pointed to a cart, where I'd set up books about magic and similar themes. Everyone rushed over to them. Thank heavens I had come in early and done that.

Dash, on the other hand, asked me if we had *The Mystery of the Whispering Mummy*. It was the third book in The Three Investigators series. The books were originally written in the mid-1960s but had been rereleased in the 1990s. I'd read them even though they had scared me.

"Let's go see if any are on the shelf," I said. Amazingly, we found one. Dash and I high-fived.

"Are there any more?" he asked.

We searched along the shelf. I knew the children's librarians at most libraries had to spend a lot of time reshelving books because things got moved around a lot. My library in Chicago had carts out for people to put books back on, but not everyone used them.

"I don't see any," I said. "I'll see if we can do an interlibrary loan, okay?"

"That would be great. Thanks, Miss Chloe."

I watched Dash walk off with his book tucked under his arm. He turned and waved. This was what I'd loved about working at the library—that smile was a reward for a job well done. If only the rest of my life was as simple.

I had a few minutes before I had to leave, so I decided to go through the microfilms of the *Emerald Cove Daily*. Because of the high cost of digitization and the labor associated with indexing and scanning newspapers, most historic newspapers and documents were available in just one format: microfilm. I wanted to check news-paper articles from the sixties to see what more I could find about the problems Delores had when she was young. And I wanted to find out more about the people who'd disappeared on the *Fair Winds*.

Maybe there was some connection between Delores's troubles and Raquel's disappearance all those years later. As much as I didn't want Delores to be a bad person, if she had problems, they were worth looking in to. People who'd lived here a long time might not be willing or able to see that.

I found the appropriate film and ran it to the place where I thought any articles might be. I wasn't getting much new information, just a confirmation of what Ralph had said. There were calls about a house being egged, one minor female was questioned but not taken into custody. Then I found a more serious allegation. Delores had been caught tampering with the engine of the boat Raquel's family owned. I sat back in shock.

That Raquel had later died on a boat that might have been tampered with didn't bode well for Delores. The family didn't end up filing charges, but Delores had had to pay for the damage. I took that film back, still shaken by what I'd read, but the Delores I knew would never do something like that now. It made it more urgent that I help her and Ralph.

I sat down at one of the library's computers and started another search. This time using Raquel's name. I kept glancing at the clock as it ticked nearer to eleven. I decided a few more minutes wouldn't hurt.

Again I wasn't finding much I didn't already know. Until I did.

CHAPTER 21

Each one of the people who'd disappeared that night had had some brush with the law. The information was part of a follow-up article about them from about five years ago. Raquel had been caught shoplifting at Dillard's in Fort Walton Beach. Cartland had a DUI on a boat on Choctawhatchee Bay. Susan trespassed and Blake wrote a bad check. It was all a long time ago. I couldn't find anything else on any of the incidents, so I reluctantly left. I needed to find out more about each of these people, but first I had to work.

I scurried into the Sea Glass at eleven fifteen. Thankfully, things were slow and Joaquín had things under control.

"Oh, you did all the grunt work," I said when I realized the fruit was cut and the barstools were all down.

"Believe it or not, this place ran even before you showed up. And in the bartending profession we actually call that the barback work."

"Unless I do it? Then it's grunt work?" But I smiled to show I was teasing. "I guess I'll just put my feet up and read, then."

"Right after you help that group that just settled out on the deck," Joaquín said.

I went out and took orders, trying to pay close attention while my mind worked on the sticky knot of the four people who disappeared on the *Fair Winds*. I handed the order to Joaquín to fill. It seemed likely to me that maybe their family members had some motive for wanting one of them to disappear. The others might just have been in the wrong place at the wrong time.

"Chloe?" Joaquín asked. "Are you here with me?"

I snapped back to the real world. "Of course. Right here."

"I told you a few seconds ago that the order was ready, and normally you fill the beer and wine orders."

I looked at the tray of drinks Joaquín pointed at. Two beers, two glasses of Pinot Grigio, and a boxcar—whatever that was. "Oh, sorry. I'm just a bit distracted. I'll tell you about it in a minute." I picked up the tray and hurried out to our customers. I set two of the drinks in front of the wrong people, which wasn't something I usually did. I apologized and admonished myself to get my head in the game. Joaquín and I shared tips and I didn't want my being distracted to hurt his income.

I went back in, poured some peanuts in the shell into a

bowl, and carried them out. "These are on the house." We usually only handed out peanuts if someone asked for them. Sometimes they were in the shell and sometimes they weren't. I guess it depended on what was on sale. "You can just toss the shells on the deck." It would be a mess to clean up, but if it made this group happy, I wouldn't mind the extra sweeping. I also put an empty bowl on the table. "Or you can put the shells in here."

We were so busy that I didn't have a chance to tell Joaquin anything. Ann Williams came in for a bit before noon.

Thank heavens. I had questions. "What can I get you?"

"Iced tea, please." She pulled a book out of her large black bag and started reading.

After I poured her tea and put it at her elbow, I finally got to talk to her. "Did you find out anything about the red boat?"

She closed her book. "I found five people who own red boats between Emerald Cove and Destin. None of them were out on the water that day because of the weather. They all said no one else had access to their boats and I double-checked their stories. So that was a dead end. It doesn't mean I've given up on the search, though."

Darn.

"The other night I asked you if you knew the man who rescued me. You never answered."

"Didn't I? I would have told you if I knew who he was."

"Excuse me, miss, we'd like a refill," a man said.

"Be right with you." I left Ann reading. Business picked up, and Ann left when the bar filled up. She usually did that. I'm not sure if it was because she didn't like crowds or if she was being considerate and leaving so the table was available. No matter; I was frustrated that I hadn't had time to question her further. I mean *talk to her*.

Smoke came in for a beer, but other than taking his order I didn't have time to talk to him. At four I finally had time to eat an apple I'd brought with me, wishing I'd brought a sandwich along too. I took it out to the back and walked down the harbor a couple of slips until I came to Boone's boat. My boat for now, maybe Steve's boat. I unsnapped part of the tarp and went and sat on the bow. I heard a motor thrum in the distance and stood up. A red boat puttered down near the pass to the Gulf.

The door of the Sea Glass flung open and Joaquín stuck his head out. "We're slammed again."

I looked from Joaquín to the red boat. Was someone on it watching me? I wanted to go after it, but by the time I finished taking off the tarp, started the boat, and untied it, the red boat would probably be long gone. Not to mention Joaquín needed me.

"Chloe?" Joaquín called.

"Coming." It probably wasn't even the same boat, but the hairs on my arm all stood up. I climbed off the boat, snapped the tarp back on, and dashed back inside, tossing the apple core in the trash as I got back to it.

"Dinner with Michael and me tonight?" Joaquín asked as I picked up an order pad from the counter.

"Absolutely. I can ask him if he learned anything from the will." Michael was a fabulous cook and I didn't feel like eating alone again. While my family in Chicago sometimes drove me crazy, I missed dinners with them. After I'd left home I'd either had college roommates or Rachel. Living in Emerald Cove was my first time living alone, and while I enjoyed it most of the time, some days were just lonely.

The next few hours flew by. I didn't have time to think—not too much anyway—about red boats and rescuers, or about the three people who disappeared with Raquel. What thoughts I did have yielded nothing. Soon it was eight thirty and last call. By nine fifteen the last customers had left, getting the hint when we dimmed the lights and started putting up barstools.

At 9:35 Michael placed a tray of endive stuffed with shrimp on the table in front of us. Michael was tall and broad. His hair was graying and he had blue eyes that seemed to look right into my heart. We stood on the back of the boat where he had a gas grill going. The lid was shut so I couldn't see what was cooking, but it smelled wonderful.

"I have a bottle of stainless-steel-aged Chardonnay," Michael said.

"I'm making you all martinis," I said. I pointed at my bag. "I brought the ingredients." I'd never been big on cocktails and had usually stuck to drinking wine or beer. But now that I worked at a bar, I'd decided I needed to expand my drinks repertoire.

"I could make it," Joaquín said.

"Nope. I need to practice, and martinis seem simple because they're only gin, vermouth, and a lemon twist." I was so excited to surprise Joaquín and Michael with my new know-how. "You just sit. Where are your martini glasses?"

Joaquín's eyebrows had a little furrow between them. "To the right of the sink."

I patted his shoulder. "Don't worry." I went into the kitchen, found the glasses, and got the gin and vermouth from my tote bag. I'd even remembered to bring a shaker. After putting ice in the shaker I added the gin and vermouth and gave it a good shake. Before I poured the martinis into the glasses, I took the lemon twists I'd brought and ran them around the lip of the glass. I poured the drinks, dropped a lemon twist in each, found a tray, and carried the drinks out to Joaquín and Michael.

"Cheers," we said, lifting our glasses.

CHAPTER 22

I took a big sip, as did Michael and Joaquín. *Ick.* Maybe martinis were an acquired taste. I looked at Michael and Joaquín. They both had funny expressions on their faces. I wasn't sure Joaquín had even swallowed his. I tried another sip.

"This is awful," I said. "This is a disgustatini, not a martini. It's swill."

Michael and Joaquín burst out laughing.

"It's really bad, Chloe," Michael said. "But I'll give you points for trying."

"Let's go in and you can show me what you did," Joaquín said.

"Eat some appetizers first," Michael said.

"Yeah," I said, "we all need a palate cleanser."

Joaquín poured us all a glass of wine.

I ate two of the endive appetizers and sipped some of my wine. "Those are delicious."

"Great. I hope you like the smoked oysters Rockefeller that's next." Michael gestured toward the grill.

I cringed. I didn't like oysters in any form. They looked so slimy. Even cooked I just couldn't get over the texture. I repressed a shudder. "I just remembered I have—"

"I'm kidding," Michael said. "I know you hate oysters. Joaquín told me about the lengths you go to avoid them."

Sometimes our customers would order them from the Briny Pirate. Their waitstaff delivered them, but I hated even seeing them. Smelling them almost made me gag. So when someone ordered them, I'd taken to having a leg cramp that I "had" to walk off, or getting an important call, or needing a bathroom break.

"I didn't realize I was that obvious." I looked at Joaquín, who was laughing.

"You aren't. I've worked in bars long enough to know when I'm being conned," he said.

"I'll try to do better." I crossed my fingers under the table like I was five instead of twenty-eight.

"Come on," Joaquín said, "let's go see what went wrong with your martini."

I followed him to their kitchen. He picked up the bottles of gin and vermouth and shook his head.

"What?" I asked.

"Cheap gin," he said. "And where did you find this vermouth?"

"In the kitchen at the Sea Glass, back in a corner. It looked aged." Vermouth isn't a spirit, like gin or vodka, but a fortified wine. It's spiked with brandy and infused with herbs.

"First, I think this is bad—not like make-you-sick bad, just old, so the taste will be off," Joaquín said. "Second, you brought sweet vermouth instead of dry vermouth. You always use the dry version in a martini. Plus, I think your proportions were off. I tasted more vermouth than gin."

"Got it," I said.

"Now I'll make you one. It's two parts gin to one part vermouth."

"Whoops. I think I got that backward."

"It could happen to anyone." Joaquín selected a bottle of gin and vermouth from their bar. "Different gins will give you different tastes. As an example, some people like a gin with more juniper flavor, while others like a gin with more of a citrus flavor."

"It's so complicated."

"And while James Bond said he wanted his martini shaken not stirred, shaking the gin can bruise it."

Bruised? "You've got to be kidding me," I said.

"Nope. And a chilled glass is best, so the martini will be the right temperature."

I had so much to learn. It definitely was a lot more complicated that it looked when I'd gone to bars in Chicago or watched Joaquín at the Sea Glass. "It's almost like you have to be a chemist or a tasteologist."

Joaquín laughed. "A good palate helps if you care about the quality of the product." He handed me the drink he'd been making. "Give it a taste."

I did. "It's so much better than mine, but I'm not sure I'll ever be a big fan."

"That's okay. Not everyone is."

"Have you had a chance to look at the will, Michael?" I asked when Joaquín and I went back out.

"I have." He opened the grill, moved some things around, and closed the lid. "A couple of things struck me right away."

That gave me hope.

"First, it's very unusual to write out a will in the field. Usually all of that is taken care of pre-deployment."

"But Steve is claiming that he and Boone reconciled after Boone deployed. Does that mean a will couldn't have been done?" I asked.

"It's unlikely, but not impossible."

That was disappointing. "Oh."

"I'll check into a few things, but it will take a while," Michael said.

"What's that?" Joaquín asked.

"If he was out on an operation, it would be improbable that a will would be prepared, signed, witnessed, scanned, and sent off."

"Why?" I asked.

"They wouldn't have the time or equipment with them, or a lawyer available."

"That's great," I said.

"But finding out will be tricky," Michael said.

"Why?" I asked again.

"Because most likely the operation and thus Boone's whereabouts will be classified. Trying to get access to classified information will be difficult."

"Impossible?" Joaquín asked.

"No, but it might have to be done in a judge's chambers, in camera as they say, with only the judge having access to the information."

I felt as if I'd been on a ride the last few minutes, with

hope and despair alternating like the ups and downs of a massive roller coaster. "I'll pass all this on to Vivi's lawyer."

"I'll find out what I can," Michael said. "It won't be easy and, again, it will take some time." Michael opened the grill and put perfectly seared grouper steaks and grilled asparagus onto three plates. He added slices of grilled lemon on the plates too.

I passed the plates around while Joaquín poured more Chardonnay. I took a sip. Wine I understood. This one was crisp up front, with a creamy finish. The stars were bright above us and all seemed well in the world. After everyone had eaten a few bites, I finally asked another question I'd been dying to since I arrived.

"Why didn't anyone tell me that Rip's dad was on the boat with Raquel and the others the night it disappeared?"

Michael and Joaquín looked up in surprise.

"It's not like we're trying to keep things from you," Joaquín said. "We just don't know what you don't know around here."

"You're right." I needed to quit jumping to conclusions or I'd never figure out anything.

"You've seen Rip," Joaquín said after finishing a bit of asparagus, "from what my mom told me, Rip looks a lot like his dad did."

"In other words, incredibly handsome," I said. Ugh. I'd said that out loud.

"Oooohhh, do you have a crush on Rip?" Joaquín asked, wiggling in his seat like an exuberant puppy.

"I'd have to be dead not to notice Rip's looks," I said. I lowered my voice. We were outside on the water. Voices carried, and I'd be mortified if anyone overheard this discussion.

"I have to agree with you," Michael said.

"But the best-looking men in town are right across from me." I was trying to distract them so they wouldn't realize I hadn't denied having a crush on Rip. I'd kept picturing him as Darcy and I had to quit thinking of him like that. It was dangerous. Rip wasn't Darcy, no matter how many times I'd enjoyed picturing him as such over the past twenty-four hours. I'd learned not to put men on pedestals by watching *White Christmas* every year on Christmas Eve with my family. Rosemary Clooney had misunderstood something Bing Crosby was doing and they almost didn't end up together.

"You do have excellent taste in men, Chloe," Joaquín said.

"That's the first time anyone ever said that about me." We all laughed. "How long have you two lived in Emerald Cove?" I asked.

"Seven years for me," Michael said. "I'd been stationed in Pensacola and liked the area. I moved here and met Joaquín when he was home on a visit."

"I wonder what Rip's dad was doing hanging out with Raquel and her friends?"

"He was a tennis pro at the club," Michael said.

Joaquín looked at Michael with his eyebrows up.

"You know me. I was curious about what had happened that night and called your mom," Michael said.

"Did she say anything else?" I asked.

Joaquín put down his fork and patted his mouth with a flamingo-covered cloth napkin. "If you know my mom, you know she said something else."

"I haven't met her yet."

"She doesn't like bars," Joaquín said. "I'll take you to see her sometime, but be prepared. She's a force."

"That doesn't surprise me a bit, knowing you," I said.

"Oh, he's laid-back compared to his mom," Michael said.

"What else did she tell you about Cartland?" I asked.

"She said he wasn't living up to his potential," Michael said.

"That's Mom's way of saying he was lazy. She's a big believer in not saying anything bad about anyone."

I'd never really heard Joaquín say negative things about people either. "How does your mom know what happened?"

"Joaquín's aunt was working as a hostess at the club that night. She overheard part of it, and of course, after the *Fair Winds* didn't come back, everyone was gossiping about it," Michael said. "Cartland always had a job, just not for long. He worked for almost all the heritage business owners at some point. Rip's mom taught school to keep the family afloat."

"I thought the Barnetts were all loaded." It was the impression I'd gotten from Rip's paternal grandmother the one time I'd met her and, of course, from Rip himself. He drove a fancy car, didn't have a real job that I knew about, and bought that big boat and took off on it for several months.

"Rip's mom and his grandmother didn't get along. According to Joaquín's mom, Cartland's country-club lifestyle was subsidized by his mother. But Rip's mom wasn't like that."

"Opposites supposedly attract," I said. It was how I had ended up engaged to a very nice but very dull accountant. I'd set out to find the opposite of the men I'd usually dated, thinking that maybe someone would balance my adventurous side. It hadn't worked out in the end.

"They do, but can they last?" Joaquín said.

"Apparently, Cartland did like his gig at the country club. He was the center of attention and women were always throwing themselves at him," Michael said.

"Even Raquel?" I asked.

"Supposedly it was Susan Harrington who asked Cartland to go along after the four of them had played tennis," Michael said.

That really didn't answer my question about Raquel. I opened my mouth to ask another question.

Michael held up his hand. "People at the club overheard Susan asking Cartland. That came out in the investigation of their disappearance."

"So, they originally thought something went wrong and that the boat sank?"

"That was the official finding," Joaquín said. Michael looked surprised. "Hey, you're not the only one who's curious about all this."

"I've been thinking about it a lot since I was on the boat," I said. "That boat wasn't in bad enough shape to have been drifting around for twelve years."

"What are you saying?" Joaquín asked.

"Someone must have planted the remains on that boat for a reason and sent it back out to sea."

We finished eating while we mulled that over. At least I was mulling, and they seemed to be. I insisted on clearing the dishes and washing them.

"Did you see anything that made you think someone set the boat adrift?" Michael asked as I hung up the towel after drying the dishes. He'd put them away.

"I didn't," I said. "But I've thought about it a lot since. In the moment it was all too scary to even process. Since I've been back I've gone over what I remember, but nothing stands out. The Coast Guard has the boat. Have you heard anything?"

"No. But maybe I'll call a few people. A lot of us vets hang out at a place over in Fort Walton Beach. I'll see if any of them know anything."

I glanced at the clock. It was already ten thirty and I knew Joaquín went fishing at dawn. The man was a machine when it came to work.

"Thanks for dinner," I said. I kissed both Joaquín and Michael on the cheek.

"I can walk you back to the car," Joaquín said.

"Don't be ridiculous. I'll be fine."

Instead of heading to my car I went back to Two Bobs. Still no Ann. The same man I'd seen the night before was sitting at what I thought of as her table. Another man sat across from him and their low voices sounded intense. I couldn't listen in without being obvious. I went up to the rooftop deck; no Ann or Smoke or anyone else I knew. I hurried back to my car and went home.

I woke up around six Sunday morning and dressed for a run. I heard the whine of a high-powered engine. It sounded too close to shore to be going so fast. I opened my sliding glass door and went out on the screened porch. A cigarette boat was barreling toward the shore. It was high tide and the boat made it past the first sandbar. It slowed a bit as it barreled through the second, churning up sand and water.

Why wasn't the driver stopping? It continued on, tearing up the beach toward me, until the sand finally clogged the motors and it shimmied to a stop about ten yards from the dunes. I grabbed my phone and ran down the wooden walkway over the dunes, down the five stairs, and across the sand. The boat still shimmied, so I approached it cautiously.

The man who had rescued me sat in the driver's seat. Rope tied too tightly around his neck to the headrest, his hand tied to the throttle. He was obviously dead.

CHAPTER 23

I stood for a moment staring before I overcame my horror at seeing a dead man and snapped into action. I yanked off my T-shirt, which wasn't a problem because my sports bra was underneath, reached carefully across the side of the boat, and turned off the engine, hoping I hadn't ruined any evidence. I'd briefly weighed the risk of doing so before calling 911, but was worried the engine would burn and spark a fire in the sea oats. Or that the boat would shoot forward, up the dune, and into my house.

I quickly filled the dispatcher in, unable to decide if I was relieved or upset that it wasn't Delores who'd answered. Two fishermen and a woman came over—the same people I often saw on my runs. Their excited chatter washed over me.

"I've never seen anything like that."

"Did you see how the boat flew across that first sand-bar?"

"Darn near ran me down. Scared me near to death."

I listened in, hoping they'd know something about the boat or the driver. "Don't touch anything," I said. "He's dead." That shut them all up. The runner took a few steps back.

They all stared at me. "It's probably a crime scene," I added. We all looked back at the man in the driver's seat. The rope was almost embedded in his throat. I shuddered and looked away. I'd told the dispatcher there was no need to rush, but I heard sirens wailing toward us.

A few minutes later EMTs and sheriff's department personnel swarmed around the side of my house. They told us to move farther down the beach. The EMTs didn't stay long after a woman did a quick check for a pulse, carefully reaching across the side of the boat, and laying her fingers on the man's throat. After a couple of minutes she shook her head.

Deputy Sheriff Biffle showed up and went over to the boat. We'd met last June, when I'd found a body by the dumpster behind the Sea Glass. He was a big, beefy guy with a blond crew cut and a serious demeanor. Ten minutes later he strode over to me as well as one could stride on soft sand in shiny, black laced-up boots. Other deputies pulled the two fishermen and the runner aside, I assumed to interview them. One of the fishermen was gesturing wildly. I imagined most of his fishing outings didn't end like this.

Biffle wore his usual mirrored aviators so I couldn't read his eyes. I hated those things.

"Let's move over there." He pointed toward the steps that led to my house.

"Okay." I led the way.

"Tell me what happened." His voice was calm, as if he saw this kind of thing every day.

I knew he didn't, though. There just wasn't that much violent crime in Walton County. I ran him through hearing the engine, watching the boat, and running down here.

He listened without making a note, nodding the occasional encouragement when my voice trembled. "Do you know him?" He gestured over to the boat.

"He's the man who rescued me."

"Heard about that," Biffle said.

At least that would save some time.

"What's his name?"

"I don't know." I kicked at some sand. "I've been trying to track him down to thank him." I wouldn't mention that I had also wanted to try to find out who the man had called. Now I'd never have the chance. I let that sink in.

"How can you not know his name?"

My hands itched to plant themselves on my hips. I refrained so I wouldn't look obstinate. "I leaped off a burning boat with a cat in my arms after being swept out to sea and finding a skeleton. I'm sorry if I didn't remember my manners when some man pulled me out of the water. We had to hightail it back to shore before we were caught out in a storm." I swished my hand toward the Gulf.

I think Deputy Biffle's lips twitched in an almost smile. "Okay, then. Thanks for the information." He turned to go.

"Wait. I saw him the other night. At least I think it was him." I explained how I'd seen him at Two Bobs. I gestured toward the boat. "Didn't he have some kind of ID on him?"

"No."

"What about the boat? Didn't it have registration papers?"

"The boat's stripped clean of paperwork. Don't share the details of what you saw."

As if I'd want to repeat what I'd seen to anyone. "I won't." I scuffed at the sand with my foot. "Will you let me know who he is? When you find out?"

"I'm sure it will be in the paper." Biffle turned to go.

"Wait," I said. "Don't you think it must mean something that the man who rescued me turned up dead by my house?"

"Yes." Biffle trotted up the stairs and around the side of my house.

I threw up my hands in the air. Now I was gesturing as much as the fisherman had. That thought gave me an idea. I spotted the two fishermen and the runner all standing together down the beach. I jogged over to them.

"How are you all doing?" I asked.

"Quite a start to the morning," the runner said.

"He ran right through some of my equipment," one of the fishermen said.

The other man just shrugged.

"Do any of you know that man or his boat?" I asked.

I heard a round of "No." Darn. Another avenue shut down. "Okay. I hope the rest of your day is better." They all nodded and went their separate ways. I watched the crime scene people for a few minutes and then went back into my house.

I made coffee, no longer in the mood for running. That in itself was highly unusual. It was normally my way of figuring things out. My need to stay in shape stemmed from my almost drowning as a child. I knew that I was a bit obsessive about running and spending so much time on water sports, but I didn't want the water to think it had bested me.

Once the coffee was ready I took it out on the screened porch and settled on the love seat. Hard to believe only a couple of nights ago I was sitting here with Rip. I'd thought my life was complicated enough last night without having my rescuer show up dead on the beach in spectacular style. I sat up a little straighter. Was this some kind of warning? If not, why here? What did someone think I knew? Because as far as I knew, I didn't know anything.

My phone rang. It was the reporter Mary Moore. I thought about not answering, but was curious about what she wanted. I hoped I wasn't opening Pandora's alleged box.

"It looks like there was some excitement near your house."

I didn't like that she knew where I lived, but she was a reporter, so I shouldn't be surprised. "What do you know?" I asked.

"Can we talk in person?"

I weighed the pros and cons. I still didn't know much and hadn't found out much to help Ralph. Maybe we could trade information. "You can come over, but I'm not sure I want to go on camera. And I sure don't want my house filmed." I had enough to worry about without a lot of crackpots showing up. "But you can get some good shots from my walkway to the beach." The closest public beach access was a mile from here. She'd have to walk across the sand with her camera person and equipment if I didn't let them use my house.

"I'll be there in ten minutes."

CHAPTER 24

Mary showed up as promised in ten minutes with her cameraman in tow. Although today it was a scrappy-looking camerawoman. Mary was camera ready, with hair and makeup done. She wore a professional-looking, black short-sleeved dress. I was still in my running clothes, wishing I'd changed because I felt like she had the advantage here.

"Come on in."

Her eyes swept the place as we walked through the house and lighted up when she was on the back porch. The deputies were still out with the boat. At some point I assumed they'd remove it because it was evidence. My rescuer's body had already been taken away.

"We can go out on the porch," I said. "Would you like a cup of coffee?"

"Yes, please."

I escorted her out to the porch, where she stood staring out. I took my cup of coffee and went back to the kitchen. I refilled it and filled a mug for Mary and the camera-woman.

By the time I got back with the coffee, the camera-woman was already outside, filming.

"Do you know who that was?" Mary asked after I set down the coffees.

"Yes and no."

Her eyebrows raised at me over her mug.

"You won't be filming any reunions between my res-cuer and me, because it was him in the boat."

"You're kidding. So he's dead?"

I nodded an affirmation.

"It's an awfully big coincidence that your rescuer ends up dead right outside your house."

I wish she hadn't picked up on that so quickly.

"Who was he?"

"That's where the *no* part of the answer comes in. I still don't know. According to Deputy Biffle he didn't have any ID on him and there wasn't any registration in-formation on the boat." We both drank some coffee look-ing out at the scene.

"Did he die of natural causes?"

"I can't say. I know you want me to go on camera, but I'm only willing to confirm it's the man who rescued me. I won't talk about anything the deputy asked me not to. And if you ask me any gotcha questions, we're done."

Mary nodded. Although I wasn't sure if she'd push or not. She was a reporter and it was her job.

"Give me a minute," I said. "I want to change and then I'll meet you outside."

"Okay," Mary said.

A few minutes later I was out on the beach answering Mary's questions with the boat in the background. Mary stuck to her word and the filming only took a few minutes. I noticed one of the fishermen who was out this morning was still fishing on the beach.

I pointed toward him. "That guy was on the beach when it happened. He might have seen more than I did." Maybe if I helped Mary, she'd be more willing to help me.

"Great. Thanks. Thanks for going on camera."

I wasn't quite sure how to respond. I did it for selfish reasons, not that she'd ended up sharing any information with me.

"I looked through the footage of the day you were rescued," Mary said.

"Find anything interesting?" I asked.

"No. Sorry. The man kept his head down. He didn't want to be recognized."

I thought that over for a minute. "If he didn't want to be recognized, it must mean it was because he thought someone would know him."

"I agree."

"But why would he care?"

"That's what I want to find out," Mary said.

So did I, but for very different reasons. I walked Mary to the door and we both promised to call the other if we heard anything. I'm fairly certain we were both lying.

I arrived at work just before ten thirty and helped Joaquín take the barstools down from tables. He chatted about this and that. By the time we were cutting fruit, I realized Joaquín had no idea what had happened at my house this morning. He would have mentioned it. He usually took out his fishing boat in the wee, predawn hours, fished, took his fish to the market in Destin or over to Russo's, showered, and came to work here. Not an easy life, and he worked harder than I did by a long shot.

"There was, um, an incident at my house this morning."

Joaquín raised his well-sculpted eyebrow. "Did Steve show up again?"

"No."

"Then do tell." He leaned on to the bar and set his chin in hand with a flourish.

By the time I finished my story both of Joaquín's eyebrows were raised and he was shaking his head. He pulled me to him in a hug. Then thrust me back, but held on to my shoulders.

"This is terrible. What are you doing here?"

"What do you think I should be doing?"

"Crying into a mimosa."

I looked at him for a long moment. "What good would that do? It's right up there with worrying."

Joaquín dropped his hands and placed them on his hips. "You are something else, Chloe Jackson."

"Yeah, I've heard that before." If I had the day off, I could go to the library and do some more research. "You know what? Maybe I do need some time off." I sat on a barstool as if I was weak-kneed.

Joaquín's eyebrows raised in alarm and I felt guilty, but not guilty enough to retract my statement.

"Yes," he said. "Go home and rest."

I went around the bar and kissed his cheek. "I'll be

back in later. Four at the latest." I didn't say I'd go home
or rest.

"Take the day if you need it."

"Thanks."

I drove straight to the library. Minutes later I was using
the microfilm again, trying to find background on the
people who went missing with Raquel. I worked on Blake
Farwell first. The Farwell family had been early settlers
here—originally from the Boston area. They moved here
in the late eighteen hundreds so they could fish all year
long. I didn't find anything amiss in his early life. There
was a photo of him at eighteen, when he'd caught the
biggest fish during the Destin Fishing Rodeo.

I knew Jed Farwell, one of the heritage business owners, who ran the Emerald Cove Fishing Charters. It was
busy year round, unlike a lot of businesses, with tourists
and locals who wanted to go deep sea fishing but couldn't
afford their own boats. I wondered if Jed was related to
Blake. I typed a note in my phone reminding me to ask
someone. Then I looked up the disappearance on my
phone. The article about their disappearance said Blake
was a local businessman, not what kind of business he
ran. Apparently, he had enough money to belong to the
country club, unless someone had taken him as a guest. I
made another note on my phone.

Susan Harrington was next on my list. It said that she
owned the *Fair Winds*. Susan had been married to Phillip
Harrington, a defense contractor. An article was almost
completely devoted to a devastated Phillip, pleading for
any news about his wife. It included a picture of an

anguished-looking man in a white suit. The article also echoed similar pleas from Ralph, Mrs. Barnett—it didn't even list her first name—and Samuel Farwell.

Considering what a big deal this must have been at the time and what a small town this was, there wasn't a lot of coverage. Most of the following days rehashed what had happened before. The Coast Guard made official statements, saying they'd gone from search and rescue to search and recovery. There were also articles on anniversaries of the day the boat disappeared, but they didn't offer up any new information.

I found another article. This one was about Frank Russo being rescued by the Coast Guard after he went out searching for the missing foursome. Apparently, on the second day after the *Fair Winds* disappeared something had happened to his boat. He had been stranded out on the Gulf for over twenty-four hours. The article continued, saying his wife, Delores Russo, had reported him missing when he didn't come home by sundown and she couldn't reach him.

I'd forgotten that Frank had been married to Delores. What a scary time that must have been for her. First four people disappearing, and then Frank. I sat tapping my finger on the desk. I was hungry. Maybe I needed to go to Russo's to buy some groceries.

CHAPTER 25

Russo's was almost empty when I arrived at twelve thirty. It was good for me, but bad for Frank. It was hard for a smaller grocery store to compete with the bigger chain supermarkets that lined highway 98 a few miles north of here. The store was a bright, cheery space, with artfully arranged fruit, a small bakery that had amazing scones, a meat market, a deli, and a seafood counter. The canned goods and sauces were high end.

Russo had gotten into trouble last June when I first arrived, but it seemed like the heritage business owners had forgiven him for his transgressions. I wondered if he was earning back their trust—that always took longer. I yanked out a grocery cart from the others and shopped as I looked for Frank. He was a hands-on owner who usually was out interacting with his customers.

I found him in the snack aisle, rearranging bags of

chips. Frank had a big, hook nose and a belly to match. He was always dressed in a nice sports shirt and slacks, but he was just standing there, staring down at a bag of chips as if his mind was elsewhere.

"Hi, Frank."

"Chloe, I heard you were back. It's good to see you," he said when he spotted me. Frank's face wasn't as animated as usual.

"I was in the other day but didn't see you."

"How was your trip home?"

Home was such a weird concept to me right now. Chicago had always been home, but Emerald Cove was my home now. Although Boone's house might not be home for long. I pushed away the wave of sadness at that thought and focused on Frank.

"I am back." I was surprised he hadn't heard about my adventures at sea, or maybe he was just acknowledging I was in the store. "I needed groceries."

"You've come to the right place, then. And I really appreciate you sticking with us." He waved a hand around at the store. "I know groceries are cheaper at the chain stores."

I felt guilty because I did shop at the other stores sometimes. "You have a unique selection and the best produce in town." I pointed to the bag of cheddar and caramel corn popcorn. "Take that, for example. It's the best."

Frank handed it to me and I popped it into my cart.

"Heard you had a rough day when you got back."

I wasn't sure if he was talking about my boating experience or Steve or both, so I just nodded.

"I'm worried about the stress on Ralph with all this being dredged up again." Frank started to shelve bags of various types of flavored popcorns.

I was glad he didn't hand anymore to me because I would have taken them. I'd broken the don't-go-to-the-grocery-store-hungry rule. "I'm worried about him too. And Delores. This has to be terrible for both of them." I grabbed a bag of cheddar and sour cream chips. This might be the start of a theme—cheddar everything. "I was reading about what happened in the *Emerald Cove Daily*."

Frank stopped shelving and turned toward me. "Oh, you have, have you?"

"What happened when you went out to search?" I asked. Might as well be blunt. I often was, whether I wanted to be or not.

"The second day I went out to search, my boat broke down."

"I read that, but did you see anything or find anything?"

"I found some debris. Bits of wood floating. They looked like they might be part of a boat. One that had some kind of catastrophic event."

My eyes kept getting bigger with every sentence. "That must have been awful for you."

"It was."

"Did anyone identify it as being part of the *Fair Winds*?" I went over the timeline in my head. If Frank had found debris on the second day he was out but didn't come home until the third day, that would coincide with the Coast Guard changing from rescue to recovery. They must have believed the debris that Frank found was from the *Fair Winds*.

"Nothing definitive. I picked up what I could. But it was a common make of boat. There were hundreds of them at the time."

"Why wasn't that in the paper?"

Frank looked behind him as if he was checking to see if anyone would overhear our conversation. It was odd, because what would it matter after all these years?

"I also found a scarf. One that belonged to Susan Harrington. One she'd had with her when they disappeared."

"That wasn't in the article I read."

"They decided to hold that bit back in case there was foul play."

I pondered that for a couple of moments. "They thought someone blew up the boat and left the scarf as a clue after the fact?"

"Yes."

So the *Fair Winds* turning up blew that theory out of the water, so to speak. "And people still don't know about it?"

"Just me and the investigators. They swore me to silence. And for once I kept my promise until right now. I can't believe I told you. Chloe, you have to promise to keep this to yourself."

"I will." Something was off here. That no one had ever mentioned this. "I don't get it. Did the Harrington family have some kind of pull to keep this a secret?"

"Not the Harrington family, but Susan's family."

"What was her maiden name?" I asked. Not that I'd know the family, because I was so new here.

"Green."

Green. Green. I lifted my chin. "Was Susan originally from Birmingham?"

"Yes," Frank said.

"Was she part of the family of lawyers? Part of Green and Long?"

"That's the one."

The firm Rip had worked for and his cousin still did. The shady one, according to Rip.

"Why did you go out searching?"

"They were my friends. Lots of people were out searching."

"And if Raquel was found alive, she'd be back with Ralph."

Frank shrugged. "I always knew Ralph was Delores's first love. I didn't mind being second best, and she was good to me." Frank's eyes misted up. "I was right. Delores left. Just not right away."

"I'm sorry." That was a lot to deal with.

"I told her to go, but some part of me hoped she wouldn't."

Poor Frank. He'd lost his friends *and* his wife.

"Frank, you've got a call," a woman called out over the intercom.

"I need to finish my shopping," I said and Frank had given me a lot to follow up on. "Go take your call."

After I put away the groceries I made a quick caprese salad. I pondered Green and Long while I ate. Their fingers were all over the past and the present. I needed to find out more about them. I didn't have time to drive up to Birmingham nor did I know anyone there to ask for help. But Rip might talk to me about it.

I dug through my purse and pulled out my phone, which I'd silenced when I went into the library. There were six calls from Rip and one from Joaquín. What could have happened now?

CHAPTER 26

I called Joaquín first because he might need me to come back in.

"I'm sorry," I said when Joaquín answered. "I silenced my phone." Hopefully, he would think it was so I could take my nap. "Do you need me to come in?"

"No. I need you to call Rip."

I jerked the phone away from my ear in surprise and looked at it for a moment. "You want me to call Rip?" That was just plain old weird.

"He came in looking for you not long after you left. Then, after he left, he started calling every half hour to see if you were back, even though I told him I'd call if you showed up." Joaquín let that hang in the air.

"He was looking for me? Why?"

"He heard about what happened this morning on the beach and was worried. That man has got it bad for you."

I blushed. Thankfully, for once no one was around to see it. "Oh." *That was brilliant, Chloe.*

"I'm surprised he's not camped out on your doorstep."

"He's not." I took the phone and walked through the house to the back. Nope. Not there either. "I'll give him a call, then."

"Hang on."

I waited, thinking about Rip. Maybe I'd been mistaken about what was going on with him and Ann the other night. Why was I so sure a man like him couldn't be interested in a woman like me? Joaquín must have put the phone on mute.

"That was Vivi. She said under no circumstances are you to come back in today. It's slow and we've got things covered." Joaquín lowered his voice. "Fortunately, she wasn't here when Rip came in."

Whew. "Okay, tell her thanks. And thank you, Joaquín. I owe you." I hung up and listened to all the voice mails that Rip had left. He'd sounded increasingly worried with every call. My heart didn't quite know what to do with all the feelings his anxious voice created. My body was singing the "Hallelujah Chorus," but I told it to knock it off. It would be so awful to get involved with Rip and then find out that I didn't own this house or the bar. My life would be a mess and I didn't want anyone else to get caught up in the fallout.

I called Rip back and left a message when he didn't answer. I let him know I was fine and that I was resting. *Ha.* I asked him if he wanted to come over for dinner. I'd bought a nice piece of tuna at Russo's that I intended to grill tonight. Maybe I could get more information about the Green family from him. I ended the call and felt a little guilty, like I was using Rip for information. But so be it. I needed answers. And he was easy on the eyes and maybe on the heart.

I had a new target in mind. The family members of the people who'd disappeared on that boat had a stake in what happened. Phillip Harrington was first on my list, but would be hard to approach. He didn't have a presence on social media except for an old account that he never updated. His last post was three years ago. I'd be suspicious, but not everyone in their seventies was as addicted to social media as someone my age.

I found Phillip Harrington's address. He lived in Seaside, which was about seven miles to the east of Emerald Cove. Showing up at his door would be tricky, but I needed to take a chance. Any other day I would have loved to go walk around Seaside. It was a charming planned community. I'd read that it was the first New Urban community that heralded a return to walkable towns.

Fifteen minutes later I was enjoying the drive along 30A, with its coastal lakes, glimpses of the ocean, and a long bike path. I should get a bike and do some riding. When I arrived in Seaside it wasn't hard to find a parking spot because it was the off-season, if there even was one in this area anymore. Visitors had to park in designated spots and walk to where they wanted to go. The highway split the town in two—one side was the beach, with homes, shops, and restaurants, and the other was the inland side, with more homes, shops, and greenways.

I sent a longing glance at Sundog Books as I wended my way toward Phillip's house. But I wasn't here to wander. I had work to do. I admired the picket fences as I walked along. No two fences on a block could be the same. I loved that the houses had cute names and that some were big and some tiny. Many of the big houses had coach houses or apartments above garages that could be rented out. A stay in Seaside was on my someday list of things I'd like to do.

My phone buzzed with a text as I arrived at Phillip's house. I glanced at it to see that Rip could come to dinner. Great. The house was medium-sized for houses in Seaside. Its modest size belied its price, which would easily be in the millions, like all the other houses here. It was pink, with a deep veranda on the front porch. Potted ferns and white wicker furniture shouted, *Come by and sit a spell.* I just hoped I wouldn't be kicked off of said porch in the next few minutes. I took a deep breath for courage and twisted the bell.

A few moments later the door whisked open. A tall but slightly stooped man with a bushy white mustache and thick, white hair stood there. I'd read that Phillip was a retired program manager for a defense contractor in Fort Walton Beach. He was one of the few people involved in all this who was retired. I didn't think I'd ever seen him in the Sea Glass.

"May I help you?" he asked.

"Mr. Harrington, I'm Chloe Jackson. I work at the Sea Glass." I stuck out my hand, so he opened the screen door that stood between us. His hand was dry and cool. I wished I could say the same for mine. "I wanted to talk to you about the reappearance of the *Fair Winds*."

"Are you a reporter too?"

"No. My interest in the story is somewhat complicated. I'm the one who found her."

"How about some tea, then?"

"Sure," I said.

"You wait out here." He pointed to one of the wicker chairs. "I'll be right back."

So, I wasn't going to be invited in. I can't say that I blamed him. He returned a few minutes later with two tall glasses of iced tea and handed me one. I took a sip because my throat was dry. It was the sweetest sweet tea I'd had yet. It was so sweet I was afraid I would have to stop by the dentist on the way home if I drank it all.

"So, Chloe, why don't you tell me what you want to know? And I'll decide if I can help you out or not."

"Fair enough," I said. "I wanted to ask about Susan's disappearance."

He gave a slight nod, his face sad. "I got used to the idea she wasn't coming back a long time ago. I knew she wouldn't up and leave me. Ours was a great love story." He sighed. "I guess even after all these years a tiny part of me hoped she'd find her way home."

Once again I was leery about saying too much. Choosing my words carefully, I filled him in on my being on the boat. "Did you know Susan was planning on going out on the boat? Did she give you any indication that there might be trouble?"

"Not a thing. She'd been playing tennis with a group of friends and they decided to cool off by taking a quick boat ride. It was a beautiful evening. Not a cloud in the sky. The boat ride should have been a piece of cake."

He confirmed what I already knew. "I've only lived here a few months, but I'm surprised at how quickly storms can blow in."

"You're right about that. Life is like that too. Everything's all calm and then the hammer drops."

I hated making him dredge up all these memories, but I wanted to help Ralph. "Why did you belong to the Emerald Cove Country Club instead of the one in Santa Rosa Beach?" I'd done my homework, and the Santa Rosa Beach Country Club was closer to Seaside than the one in Emerald Cove.

"I moved from Emerald Cove to Seaside about six months after Susan disappeared. I couldn't stand to be around her things. It was a constant reminder of what I'd lost. So I bought this place and all its furnishings. That's when I found out ghosts can follow a person." He looked over at me. "I don't mean an actual ghost like one would need a ghostbuster or priest for. I mean emotions, sentiments. Those don't go away."

I knew that all too well. Boone and I had been so close that sometimes I almost sensed him in the house when I watched TV, as if he'd just left the room or was going to walk in any minute.

"Do you have a theory as to what happened the night they disappeared?"

"I'd always assumed that they had some kind of engine trouble and sank. But with the boat showing back up, I guess I was wrong."

"What about the others who were with her that night? Did any of them cause you any concern? Or did any of them have obvious enemies?"

Phillip leaned back, as if he wanted to distance himself from either me or the question. "'Enemies' is a strong word."

CHAPTER 27

"It is," I agreed.

He looked up at the ceiling of the porch. "I was surprised to hear Cartland was out on the boat that night."

"Why's that?"

"I never thought the Barnetts and Farwells got along."

"Do the Barnetts get along with anyone?" Was family feuds their thing?

Phillip chuckled at that. "I can tell you know Vivi's situation with the Barnetts. But lots of people get along with them just fine."

"Including you?" I was being awfully pushy, but so far Phillip didn't seem to mind.

"Including me."

"No offense," I started to say, then stopped. He seemed like a nice man. I really didn't want to offend him.

"Whenever anyone says that I expect their next words are going to offend me. But please, go on."

I smiled. "You're right. I saw that you were a program manager for a defense contractor. It doesn't seem like that would pay well enough to live in Seaside, or own a boat like the *Fair Winds*."

I expected him to stand up and march back into his very expensive house. He didn't.

"Did you know that the founders of Seaside originally dreamed of this being a place for teachers, artists, and writers? It's become a playground for the wealthy instead." He sipped his tea. "Most of the houses are rentals, with a smattering of permanent residents. But they opened a school that has been wildly successful, and built a non-denominational church. I'm lucky to live here. There's so much to do right outside my door."

"I didn't know that. It sounds like they wanted a planned-out version of what Emerald Cove is."

"You're right on both things. I didn't make enough money to afford this place. Susan had family money. We had plenty in savings and everything was in joint accounts, so I had access to it." He took another drink of tea and almost smacked his lips in satisfaction. "I got more money after she was declared legally dead through trust funds and life insurance policies."

"The police—" I started again.

"Questioned me endlessly, along with Ralph Harrison. They thought I killed them to have Susan's money all to myself. They went so far as to suggest that I must have someone on the side. They accused Ralph of killing them so he could be with Delores. As far as I know, both are false narratives."

The screen door opened, and a woman who looked to be in her late thirties came out. Was this the woman the police accused him of having on the side? "It's almost time for our tennis match." She looked me over and then went back inside.

"My third wife." Phillip stood. "You have the same look on your face the police did when they found out I'd started dating again a year after Susan's disappearance. But I found that a man with a house in Seaside and a fortune who is single is quite the commodity. I didn't stay on the market, so to speak, for very long after Susan was declared legally dead. I had a brief marriage after that and now am married again."

That explained the look the woman gave me—sizing me up as competition. It must not be a fun way to live. I had no interest in being the fourth Mrs. Phillip Harrington, but it made me wonder about Phillip. Was he a womanizer? Did he want to get rid of Susan so he could have her money and move on? He'd said they were a great love match, but it didn't sound like it to me.

"I learned to play tennis and always be at my wife's tennis games. Fool me once and all that." He winked at me and picked up our iced tea glasses. Then he became more somber. "I hope this will somehow help Ralph out and finally find the people who took away my Susan and turned my life upside down."

I watched as Phillip went back into the house, mulling over what he'd said. Phillip had a plausible reason for being able to live here in Seaside while some of his contemporaries were scraping by running businesses. I couldn't stand here pondering. I had other people I wanted to talk to.

*   *   *

I stood on the dock at two and watched as the crew of one of Jed Farwell's charters walked off the boat. They headed to an area where they would clean fish that had been caught and photograph their customers who'd fished if they wanted souvenir pictures. Jed often captained this boat, so I hoped he'd be walking off in a few minutes. I watched the fish get weighed and the excited chatter that followed.

Instead of asking someone if Jed was related to Blake, I decided to ask him myself. Pretty soon Jed trotted down the gangplank to the dock, some kind of paperwork in hand. He was lanky and energetic. On the rare evenings he came to the Sea Glass he had trouble sitting still. Jed would often pull out a bit of rope and tie knots, untie them, and repeat. Although he was in his seventies, like Vivi, he showed no signs of slowing down.

I walked over to him.

"Hey, Chloe. What brings you all the way here?"

I'd noticed lots of people said, "Hey" instead of "Hi" here. And often with a drawl that drew out the word. But not Jed. His *hey* was as brisk as he was. "All the way here" usually meant that I'd made the short walk from the Sea Glass to this side of the harbor. It wasn't a big harbor at the point where it ended. Today I'd parked on this side—the north side—of the harbor, hoping that no one from the Sea Glass would spot me. "I wanted to ask you about something."

He tilted his head toward the building that housed his operation. "Come on in with me. I need to drop off this paperwork." He held up the sheaf of papers in his hand. "Have to file lots of reports these days about our catch."

The building was small, with weathered, red siding. Inside it was only one room, with big windows that looked out over the harbor, the Sea Glass, and, finally, the Gulf. Not a bad place to work. Jed unlocked the door and gestured for me to go in first. Something Southern men did routinely, I'd found out.

"Want some coffee?" Jed asked. He gestured to one of those single-brew coffeepots where you plugged in a little cup.

"Sure. That sounds good." Even though I'd just had iced tea and was jazzed up on sugar and caffeine, coffee felt sociable and might make my questions easier.

I watched as he moved to the machine. His arms were tanned and tattooed with anchors, swordfish, and boats. Jed moved with a certain grace and soon brought back two cups of coffee.

"What can I do for y'all?"

Even after living here for three months, I always felt as if I should look over my shoulder to see who was behind me when someone said, *y'all*. But down here *y'all* was often singular and *all y'all* was the plural, though sometimes *y'all* meant more than one person, so it was very confusing to a Northerner like me.

I wrapped my hands around the cup because they were suddenly icy. Just blurting out personal questions to someone I didn't know well was uncomfortable. *This is for Ralph*, I reminded myself.

"You may have heard about my experience of being swept out to sea and finding the remains," I said.

"'Course I did. Hard to keep something like that a secret. I was out on a party boat with a bunch of passengers when we heard you were missing." Jed blew across the top of his mug and then took a sip. "We called off fishing and joined the search."

"Oh. I had no idea. I'm sorry."

"Don't you think a thing about it. Everyone was pretty durn excited to help out. That storm was comin' up anyways, so we would have had to quit fishing. Yep. People used binoculars they'd brought. Others squinted. More false alarms of sightings of you than fish that day, and we get a lot of false fish sightings." He settled back in his chair and clasped his hands over his stomach.

I squelched the urge to clear my throat, but stalled for another second by taking a sip of my coffee. "Since I found the remains, I've been reading up on what happened. A Blake and a Samuel Farwell were mentioned."

"Samuel was my father, God rest his soul, and Blake my worthless brother. Sorry for speaking ill of the dead." Jed glanced up as he said it, so I wasn't sure if he was addressing me, his brother, or God. "Blake's idea of working was networking at the country club or bars around town." He used air quotes when he said networking. "He'd come in here and lord around every once in a while. But never did any real work." Jed glanced down. "Good thing our mama didn't live to see that."

I'd never realized what a talker Jed could be. I'd thought heading over here that I'd have to pry information out of him. "Was he good friends with the people he went out with that evening?"

"Blake was everyone's buddy and friend to none."

I puzzled over that for a minute. "He acted friendly, but wouldn't help anyone out?"

"Yep. He always ran around saying 'The Lord helps those who help themselves.' The man even twisted God's own words. And that there tells you all you need to know." Jed stood up.

I stayed seated even though it was obvious Jed wanted me to leave. I guess talking about his brother was painful.

"I heard there was some kind of feud between your family and the Barnetts."

Jed laughed. "Who told you that?" He shook his head. "Doesn't matter. If you call Blake being jealous of Cartland's family money, connections, and looks a feud, I guess there was one. Blake once told me Cartland didn't work hard. That from a man who barely worked." Jed moved toward the door. "I'd be stupid to fight with an influential family like the Barnetts."

I stood too. "Did you ever have any dealings with the law firm Green and Long out of Birmingham?" I asked.

Jed pursed his lips for a moment and then shook his head. "Not that I can think of. Always a lot of rumors about them."

Not that I can think of wasn't a no. "Thank you for your time." The door opened just as I was about to reach for it. A younger version of Jed walked in. Only this one was dressed in slacks and a button-down, pale-pink shirt.

"My son," Jed said with a wave toward us.

He gave me a saucy wink as I walked by, even though he was almost old enough to be my dad. I hoped he had more of his father in him than his uncle.

CHAPTER 28

Rip looked tired when he showed up at six. He handed me a bottle of Blanc de Blanc sparkling wine.

I led him out to the screened porch, where I'd set up appetizers of shrimp with my homemade, spicy cocktail sauce and bruschetta on a baguette I'd bought. He opened the wine and poured two glasses.

"Why don't you sit while I get the grill started?" I suggested.

"Do you need any help?"

All kinds, but not with the grill. I was a master from watching my father for years. "No thanks. It will just take me a minute." I'd found an old charcoal grill under the porch during the summer. I'd cleaned it up and cooked out on it several times. I'd dragged the grill away from the house and had already put the charcoal in to light.

"Okay, shout if you need anything. Firemen always love to play with fire." His eyes twinkled.

My face warmed, as did the rest of me. The man was hard to read. I slipped outside while Rip relaxed on the love seat. I was glad he hadn't insisted on helping or trying to take over the "manly" duties. He leaned back his head and closed his eyes. After I started the fire I went to get the tuna. Rip was asleep. His dark lashes rested on those beautiful cheekbones. He breathed deeply. Watching his chest rise and fall made me wonder if I needed to stick my head in the refrigerator to cool off every time he came to visit. I tiptoed past him, got the tuna, tiptoed back, and put the tuna on the grill.

The fish sizzled when it hit the heat, and the fire leaped. Quite the metaphor for how I was feeling. I'd seasoned it with lots of cracked black pepper, a little salt, and lemon. It didn't need anything else. It wouldn't take long to cook. Just a few minutes on each side, because overcooked tuna was tough and tasteless. Rip was still asleep when I came back to the screened porch. I slipped by him again and went to the kitchen. I plated the tuna with some grilled lemon slices and picked up the salad I'd made and carried both back to the porch.

Rip was sitting up, looking around as if he was confused. "Did I fall asleep?"

"Yes. You did." I put the tuna and salad on the small table and moved the untouched appetizers over too. "Let's eat."

"I apologize." He stood and stretched. A tantalizing bit of his abs showed under his T-shirt.

I quickly glanced at the tuna to distract myself. "No need." My voice came out a little wobbly. "Rough day?"

"And night."

I tried to ignore the little prickles of jealousy, thinking about what a rough night meant for him. There was no doubt that legions of women had to be throwing themselves at him.

"We had a fire call at two thirty this morning and didn't leave until seven. Then we were called to help with a fire over in Grayton Beach. It was just one call after the other most of the day."

"You work a lot of hours for them," I said.

"That's part of the deal, being a volunteer. If there's a call, you go," he said.

"You should have told me. We could have postponed dinner."

"I wanted to see you."

Oooohhh.

"I heard about what happened here this morning. But I guess you know that with the number of messages I left on your phone."

That's right. There was a reason he was here. I wanted to grill not only the tuna, but him. Somehow rational thought had left me when Rip walked in. *Focus.* As we ate, I filled him in on what had happened.

"Why here?" he asked, looking out toward the beach as if there'd be some kind of answer.

"I don't know, but it seemed deliberate, right?" I hoped he'd agree and didn't think I was nuts.

"It does. I don't like it."

That was a relief. I wasn't losing my mind. "I'm not thrilled about it either."

"Did you see something on the boat the day you were on it that you haven't told anyone?"

"Nothing. Trust me, I've been thinking about it on and off." I took another bite of tuna and thought while I chewed. "It wasn't as if there were drugs or cash around. Just the remains and Pippi. And neither of them had anything to say."

"How's Pippi?" he asked.

"She's living happily with Vivi. We haven't found her owner, even with all the lost-and-found posts I put up on social media." I put down my fork. "The only thing of value I saw was the ring that Ralph said was from Raquel's family. The Coast Guard have it as part of their investigation."

Rip's phone made a piercing sound. He grabbed it. "I've got to go. That's the signal there's a fire. Sorry I can't stay. That I can't help clean up." He leaped up. "Everything was delicious." He lingered for a moment, looking at me as if he was still hungry.

I almost didn't get my *that's okay* and *thank you* out before he was out the door and climbing into his car. I hadn't even had a chance to ask him more about Green and Long or give him dessert.

At two on Monday afternoon Steve swanned in through the door like he owned the place, and maybe he did. Thankfully, Vivi wasn't there. She was out buying supplies. A woman who was all pointy elbows and knees in a silver, metallic sheath dress came in with him. She carried a large satchel. Her obviously dyed black hair was pulled back in a tight bun that made my scalp hurt just looking at it. She looked down over a razor-sharp nose. Disdain shot from her like a force field from a Romulan ship in *Star Trek*. Shields up, phasers charged.

Steve, on the other hand, looked relaxed in a casual,

beige short-sleeved shirt, one hand tucked into the pocket of his brown slacks. If I had hackles, they'd all be up. I glanced back at Joaquín. He stood stock-still, which was saying something about a man who was a perpetual motion machine.

"Can I help you?" I forced out each word.

"I'm glad to see you took my advice," Steve said, gesturing up and down at me.

He was right. I'd been dressing up a bit more since his comment. Today I had on a one-piece, off-the-shoulder romper. The flowy legs ended just above my ankles. But I'd picked it for comfort, I told myself this morning, not because of Steve.

"We don't need any help," he said. "We're just here to take some measurements for our revamping plans."

Revamping?

"I've heard of shabby chic before," the woman with Steve said, "but this place is just shabby." Her nostrils actually flared.

I'd always thought that was something that only happened in novels. I felt my face go from stone cold to warm to boiling. I loved this place. It had a vintage charm, and sure, maybe a few of the barstools could be upgraded. But the carved initials on the tabletops told a story. The pictures and signs hanging on the walls were the history of Emerald Cove.

"At least the view is stunning," she added. She plopped her satchel on a table and pulled out a book of what looked like wallpaper samples. She flipped through, stopping on a hideous-looking silver-metallic sample. She tapped it with a long, pointy nail. "This should be perfect."

Steve leaned in and looked. "I like it. We'll get rid of all this crap hanging on the walls. Put up the wallpaper and a few abstract paintings."

She looked down at the floor, which was concrete. Not exactly pretty, but it was easy to clean off all the sand that got tracked in every day. "With some stain these would work."

"We can add some industrial lighting and wrap the bar in stainless steel," Steve said.

Perfect. Cold and soulless, just like Steve. "I think you're forgetting that even if the will is legal, Vivi still owns half of the Sea Glass." I looked back and forth between them.

Steve threw back his head and let out a hardy laugh. The kind of laugh that made me think physical violence wasn't such a bad idea. I enjoyed a moment of picturing my fist connecting with that face. I knew it would hurt like heck afterward but it would be worth it.

"Chloe, do you really think Vivi isn't going to sell out, now that the place is half mine?" Steve asked when he finished laughing.

Ah, so that was his plan. "You might like whoever buys it even less than you like Vivi." I wondered if there was a way to raise the money so I could buy it, if it came to that. I'm not sure a GoFundMe would work. Unfortunately, I had no experience in illegal activities that raised cash fast. "I think you may be underestimating Vivi."

Steve's smarmy grin disappeared. He leaned over me. "I think you may be underestimating me."

"I read the emails you wrote to Boone," I said. "You said you had health issues."

"*Had* being the key word, kid. I'm a survivor, and Vivi and her merry little band better get used to it."

Joaquín moved to my side. "Get. Out. Vivi told you that you aren't welcome here."

The woman with Steve had out some kind of laser device and was measuring the room. Steve looked at her. "Let's go."

"I'm not quite finished," she said, pointing the laser toward the back of the bar.

"I said let's go." Steve's voice was as sharp as her nose.

She packed her things in a huffy way and hefted the satchel up on her shoulder. Steve didn't offer to carry it for her.

"I'll be back," Steve said.

He didn't sound like Arnold Schwarzenegger in the *Terminator* movies, but it still sounded like a threat. I hoped for a passing moment that someone would terminate *him*. Then I felt bad for wishing ill on him. Karma and all that.

Joaquín was muttering under his breath in Spanish, which made me know how upset he was.

"Don't worry," I said to Joaquín. "I'll deal with him one way or the other." I turned to get back to work and saw Deputy Biffle was right behind me.

CHAPTER 29

Perfect timing. By the set of his face I was certain he'd heard my comment. Joaquín turned, and his eyebrows popped up. He looked from Deputy Biffle in his mirrored aviator sunglasses to me and back again. It didn't help the situation. Maybe it was best to ignore it.

"Can I get you something, Deputy?" I asked, trying for a reasonably normal voice, but it had an edge to it that it didn't usually have. I hoped my face had lost some of the red heat I'd felt earlier. I'd seen how I looked when I was worked up and it wasn't becoming.

Deputy Biffle looked around the bar. Did I detect a hint of disappointment when he turned back to me? "I wanted to speak to you for a moment," he said. He glanced at Joaquín. "Alone."

I looked over at Joaquín. He gave a small nod.

"Why don't you use Vivi's office?"

"Thanks," I said and motioned for Deputy Biffle to follow me.

I sat in Vivi's chair and Deputy Biffle sat across from me. He took off his sunglasses, folded them, and tucked them in front of his uniform shirt. Biffle looked up at me. He had deep, brown eyes that weren't any easier to read than when he had his sunglasses on.

"This is a courtesy call, and what I'm about to say isn't public yet." He gave me an intense look.

"I won't say anything, then." I managed not to cross my heart or pretend to zip my lips and throw away the key.

Biffle continued to stare at me for a moment. "The remains found on the boat weren't Raquel Harrison's."

I sat up a little straighter. "They weren't?" That was stupid. Why would he say that if he didn't mean it? "Whose were they?" I hoped they knew.

"Susan Harrington's. She was the other woman out on the boat the night Raquel Harrison and the two men disappeared."

I didn't know how to feel. I wondered how Phillip would feel. At least he would have some closure, but that meant Ralph's family and Raquel's wouldn't. That might mean suspicion would continue to cloud Ralph and Delores. It broke my heart a little to think that.

"How did you find out so quickly? I thought these things took days."

"If we had to rely on DNA, it would have. But in this case we could use dental records. The news will be out soon enough, but keep it tucked under your hat for now. Hard to keep a secret in Emerald Cove."

He might think that, but I thought this small town had more than its share of secrets. "I will. I'm surprised you're telling me this."

"Yeah, so am I." Biffle stood, so I did too.

It made me wonder what his motive was. "Have they identified that man who rescued me?"

"Not yet."

"Doesn't that seem odd? I thought they could find almost anyone with their fingerprints."

"If they've been fingerprinted for some reason." Biffle looked at me for a long minute. "You'd best hope nothing happens to Steve Kincheloe. If it does, you'll be the first person I'll come talk to."

"I didn't mean I would physically harm him. I meant I'd do what it takes to find out the truth about the will he gave Vivi."

He gave me another hard look, put on his sunglasses, and left. While I'd have liked to hide out in here a while and absorb what I'd just found out, I had drink orders to take.

With all that was going on with Steve, I hadn't wanted to bother Vivi, about the *Fair Winds* disappearance. She knew all the players, though, so I decided I had to get her thoughts. Earlier in the day I'd asked her to stay after so we could talk.

"Why don't you pour yourself a glass of wine?" Vivi suggested as she fixed herself a glass of seltzer water. She dropped in a lemon and a lime. "Poor man's Coke."

"I'll never get used to people down here calling all pop Coke."

"And trust me, no one will understand when you call Coke pop. What's on your mind?"

We took our drinks out on the deck. It was a lovely evening. The air was still warm, and bits of laughter from the Briny Pirate drifted over to us.

"I wanted to hear what you thought about the four people who were on the *Fair Winds* the night it disappeared."

"Of course you do."

I decided not to ask her what she meant by that. "What was Cartland Barnett like? He was younger than the others on the boat."

"I know you think it's odd that our families don't get along, but Cartland is a good example of why."

"Odd" wasn't the word I'd use, but I let that pass too and just nodded my head.

"Cartland thought the world should be brought to him on a silver platter. His parents and grandparents didn't do anything to dissuade him of that notion."

"He sounds like Steve Kincheloe."

Vivi pursed her lips for a moment. "Not quite as bad. Cartland's family actually had a silver platter or two. He made it through college and was an excellent tennis player. Cartland just didn't have any ambition."

"Was he connected with anything that would have made him murder three people and disappear?"

"I can't imagine him having enough energy to plan and pull off something like that. The money streamed to him through his family. He'd be cutting off his nose to spite his face."

"What about Susan?"

"She was one of my best friends."

That was a surprise. "Did you meet her after she and

Phillip married?" Since Susan had grown up in Birmingham, it was unlikely they knew each other as children.

"No. We went to the same college and pledged the same sorority. Everyone called us 'the twins' because we were inseparable."

Vivi had suffered a lot of loss—her daughter, her dear friend, and Boone. That had to take a toll on a person.

"She met Phillip when she came home with me one weekend. He was just a bit older than us. Phillip had already graduated and was working. They fell hard and fast for each other." Vivi smiled at the memory.

"I've heard about Susan's family. Did they approve?"

"Not at first. I think they hoped she would marry one of the Long boys and solidify the relationship of the law firm partners. But Susan was headstrong, and they came around." Vivi shook her head. "It might have been better if they hadn't."

"Why?"

"I'm not sure being the wife of a defense contractor kept her in the lifestyle she was accustomed to. Her parents paid for their country club membership. There was quite a row between her and Phillip over that. But Phillip relented. He always did. However, as the years went on, they led more and more separate lives. Susan spent most of her time at the club and Phillip at work."

Wait a minute. Phillip had told me theirs was a great love story. He hadn't indicated that they had problems. Although it might explain why he followed his third wife to her tennis games.

"How did Phillip react when she didn't come home that night?" Maybe Phillip was behind the disappearance. "It couldn't be pleasant to live with someone you didn't really care about." I couldn't imagine. My parents were so in love it was almost sickening.

"He was devastated and guilty."

"Guilty because he had something to do with it?" I asked.

"Guilty because they'd grown apart. That he hadn't accepted Susan for who she was. He spent many an evening in here crying after the bar closed. I cried with him most nights."

I put my hand on her arm and she covered my hand with hers for a moment before moving away. "I've never seen him in here." Vivi's story conflicted with what Phillip had said, although maybe that was just how he wanted to remember things.

"He moved to Seaside about six months after Susan and the others disappeared. He cut himself off from everything that had to do with his old life. People deal with grief in different ways."

"Any chance he moved because he was in to something fishy? I've read lots of articles about defense contractors making deals to increase their own wealth. Maybe he was doing something illegal that ended up getting Susan and the others killed."

"I can't imagine that. He was always a straight arrow."

No one wanted to think their friends could do anything wrong. I knew that now more than ever with the whole controversy over Boone's will. "What about Blake Farwell?" He was my last hope that Vivi would say he was a drunk, drug-addicted gambler who robbed people and had a long list of charges against him. Someone I could delve into to prove Ralph wasn't involved. But inexplicably, Vivi's face softened and a smile played around the edges of her lips for a second.

I'd never seen her look like that before. Not even around Wade. I knew she loved Wade, but maybe as a friend instead of as a potential love interest. It made me think of Boone and me. I hoped Vivi wouldn't go through what I had, realizing too late I might have lost out on something special. The look also made me realize I knew nothing about Vivi's husband or what happened to him. I didn't remember seeing any photos of him at her home or in the Sea Glass. Another mystery, but one for another time.

"Were you in love with Blake?" I blurted it out. I hadn't meant to.

Vivi straightened into what I had come to call her Queen Vivi pose. No one wanted to be around Vivi when she pulled it. When she combined the pose with the drawl you knew you were in trouble. But then she relaxed. Thank heavens.

"That's none of your business," Vivi said.

CHAPTER 30

That was a yes in my book. Now I'd have to interpret everything through a lens that may be rosier than was true. "Was he in business with Jed?"

"Yes. Like so many in Emerald Cove, it was a family business."

"Did they get along?" A good family conflict would be an excellent reason for murder and mayhem. Jed certainly hadn't seemed like he was a big fan of his brother and he would know all about boats and how to sabotage one. Maybe he thought his brother would be alone on the boat that night.

"As well as anyone. They divided the business in two. Jed loved being out on the boat and Blake built the business and did the books."

"Any hint of him cooking the books, as they say?"

"Blake was kind to a fault. He helped at the animal

shelter and rescued more than one animal. If he'd been a woman, he would have been called a crazy cat lady."

Another annoying stereotype about women that didn't apply to men, but I needed to focus on the matter at hand. "So, you don't think he'd do anything illegal with their bookkeeping?"

"No." Vivi said. She stood up. "I'm tired.

Vivi rarely admitted to being anything less than 100 percent but this was the second time in a few days. It worried me. "Go home. I'll lock up."

Vivi gathered her things. "Maybe you should let this all drop."

I hated dredging up painful memories, but on the other hand I wanted to help Ralph. I didn't answer her. Vivi left and I did a bit more cleaning up, thinking about each of the people who'd disappeared on the *Fair Winds*. Delores had a reason to want Raquel gone—so she could be with Ralph. Phillip seemed to have gone through a lot of wives. Maybe he was a philanderer at heart and wanted to move on. Jed wasn't happy with his brother's work ethic. It didn't sound like Cartland was in a happy marriage, so maybe Rip's mom was looking for a way out. But all of that seemed like petty reasons for killing four people, if that was what had happened.

I locked up. Vivi may have wanted me to drop this, but I wasn't about to.

I walked out of the bar after my talk with Vivi determined to find Ann only to see her leaning against my car. That was a surprise. She wore her usual black. This time black leather leggings, biker boots, and a black, long-sleeved T-shirt.

"We need to talk," she said.

No kidding. I'd only been looking for her all over the place—well, at Two Bobs. I managed to keep that all in. "Okay. Here?"

"Let's go to your place. I don't want to risk anyone overhearing us."

That sounded serious. "Do you need a ride?"

"No. I've got my bike." She pointed to a motorcycle.

Of course she had a motorcycle—a sleek, bulletlike black one. It fit her perfectly. It was like a machine version of her. "I'll see you in a few minutes, then."

I watched as she straddled the bike, picked up her helmet, and swung her enviable, long, wavy hair over her shoulder. She snapped on the helmet, started the bike, and roared off, leaving only some dust in her wake.

Fifteen minutes later we were settled in the living room, each with a beer. Mine from a local brewery, hers from A&W. As fit as Ann was, I was surprised she drank pop. I'd offered her a glass and ice, but she'd said she preferred to drink right out of the can. Even though it was a lovely night to sit out on the porch, we were inside with the windows closed. Ann had insisted. She didn't want anyone to overhear us.

I took a long drink from my beer, bracing myself for what was to come.

"I found another red boat. It was owned by a tangle of partnerships and LLCs. But I finally found the name behind it all."

"Who?" I put down my beer, worrying it would shake right out of my hand. At last some progress.

"Rip Barnett."

CHAPTER 31

If stomachs could have pits, mine had one. Like a black hole. I stood up and grabbed my purse.

"Where are you going?" Ann asked.

"To find Rip."

"Wait. Let's talk this through before confronting him."

That made sense, but my thoughts swirled around as I pictured Rip and me out on the ocean, the red boat chasing us. Him acting like he knew nothing about it. The whole getting shot at was probably faked. I'd thought we were just lucky they didn't hit us, but instead they must have missed us deliberately. The man I thought might be my Darcy was anything but. I sat back down.

"He betrayed me," I said.

Ann stood up and started pacing around the room. She was always so still it made me nervous.

"He betrayed both of us." She shook her head, and her

hair tumbled around her. "I was feeding him information about the illegal liquor that was coming into Emerald Cove."

I'd forgotten about that. Ann had been worried a few months ago that something could happen to her. She'd confided in Rip, so if something did happen to her, someone would know what she was up to.

Part of me didn't want to believe Rip owned the red boat, but Ann had known Rip, trusted him, longer than I had. If she believed he was bad, I guessed I'd just have to accept it too. It hurt.

"What did your friend in the Secret Service say?" Last June Vivi had suspected that illegal liquor, untaxed, was being brought in and used. She'd asked Ann to look in to it. When Ann had confided in me with concerns about her safety, I'd mentioned to her that I'd read about a case in Illinois where the Secret Service had stepped in and shut down a ring similar to the one that was operating here. In the end Ann had reached out to a friend in the Secret Service.

"The trail went cold. All the sources I developed, the drop points I'd found, none of it panned out. He wasn't too happy with me and got in trouble for a wild-goose chase. It will take a while to rebuild a relationship with him."

"Is there anyone down here who isn't on the take?" If I couldn't trust Rip, who could I trust? Were Joaquín and Michael up to no good? What did I really know about any of these people? I'd only been down here for a few months. The place was up to its proverbial ears in shady pasts and shadier dealings. Maybe I shouldn't even trust Ann. Her reputation as a fixer meant she was doing things for people I probably didn't want to know about. I sagged back on the couch. Maybe this wasn't the place for me. Maybe I should go back to Chicago and live in one of my brothers' basements until I could get back on my feet. They'd both offered.

"There are good people here. But it's a hard life for most," Ann said.

"So we have to continue to look for answers," I said.

"And you have to go about like before. You have to continue your relationship with Rip so you don't let him know we suspect him."

I was shaking my head before she even said Rip. "I'm not that good an actress."

"You have to be if you want to help Ralph."

After Ann left I yanked open my closet and stared at my suitcase. It wouldn't take long to pack. The boxes of books I'd shipped down here I could ship back, or I could donate some to the library. Tears rolled down my cheeks. I wiped at them with my hand. Rip owned the red boat and must be colluding with the bad guys. Disappointment and acceptance circled like seagulls being fed on the beach.

Running was something I was good at. I reached for my suitcase. But up until now I'd always been running toward something, not away. I pulled back my hand and slammed shut the closet doors. Thankfully, I didn't see Rip that often and he didn't know me well enough to know what normal behavior was for me. I could do this. I had to. For Ralph and Vivi.

I couldn't sleep, so I took out the supposed email exchange between Steve and Boone. I got out my rarely used laptop and opened my Gmail account to find old emails from Boone. I took a couple of deep breaths before I opened the last email he'd ever sent me. I couldn't help but read the content. It wasn't about anything too significant, just how his day had gone and that he missed me. It said he'd be home in seventy-three days. We just didn't realize he'd come home in a coffin. He always signed his emails with *Love, Boone XOXOXO*. I signed mine the same way, but seeing it here, now, knowing that he was in love with me instead of just loving me as a friend made me sad all over again.

After a few more deep breaths I checked what I'd come here to verify. The address he sent his emails from. Most of them came from his own Gmail account. But some of them were from an official government account. I compared the email addresses Steve had received from Boone to the ones I had. The email addresses matched letter for letter and symbol for symbol. Darn. I'd been hoping that the address would be different. That it would be some proof that something fishy was happening. But I suppose Vivi's lawyer, Ann, or Michael would have already checked this.

It was midnight here, so it was around 9:30 a.m. in Afghanistan. I emailed one of Boone's buddies who was still stationed there. I snapped pictures of both email addresses, inserted them into the message, and asked him if anything looked off. And added a brief explanation of why I was asking.

My phone rang, and it was Boone's buddy. Before Boone was in Afghanistan I had no idea how easy it was to communicate with someone in the military if they weren't out in the field for an operation.

"Chloe. This is messed up. Boone wouldn't do that."

My heart pinged happily that he agreed with me. "Do you remember him talking about his dad?"

"Naw, but that probably doesn't mean anything. It's not like we're all out here sharing our feelings around a campfire. In our off time we're playing poker, working out, and calling home."

If only I'd kept a calendar of when I had and hadn't heard from Boone. Then maybe I would know where he was when the will was written. Even though it was never said because it couldn't be said, I knew when I didn't hear from him that he was probably off doing something dangerous.

"Did the emails look the same to you?"

"Almost anyone can copy an email and make it look legit. You need to see the account the emails were sent from. If you run the cursor over the email, you'll see the actual address."

"Of course. I should have thought of that." Getting access to Steve's email account might not be easy. I was sure he wouldn't just hand it over to me. He might if forced to by a court, but that could take months.

"Do you know the people who witnessed the will?"

"No, but there are thousands of people over here. So don't take that as a sign the will isn't legit."

"Okay. Thanks. Please call me if you remember anything else." We chatted for a few more minutes before we hung up. I was exhausted from all I'd heard today, but I needed to sleep because tomorrow might even be longer.

At nine Tuesday, after a run, shower, and getting ready for work, I called Green and Long in Birmingham. I blocked my number before I dialed. Step one in the digging I'd told Ann I'd be doing.

"Green and Long. How may I help y'all?"

The woman's voice who answered was rich, with a deep Alabama accent. "May I speak to Ted Barnett, please?"

There was a momentary pause. "I'm sorry, Ted no longer works here. Are you a current client or is this a new need?"

Now I paused while my mouth dropped open. My thoughts tumbled more than waves on the shore. If that was the case, I guess my suspicion that Steve had something on the firm was wrong. What else had I gotten wrong with all of this? "When did he leave?" My voice wobbled a little.

"I'm not at liberty to tell you that, honey."

"But I'm his girlfriend and he told me this was where he worked." I was a competent liar, which I'm not sure was something to be proud of. It started when my brothers taught me to play poker as a child. I'd lost more than my share of bubble gum and candy to them before I learned what it meant to have a poker face or, in this case, a poker voice. I made my voice wobble a little more.

"I'm sorry—"

"Please," I said, "I'm—" I paused again. "Pregnant. And I haven't seen Ted for a week." If this person had any heart at all, she'd give me some kind of information.

She lowered her voice. "Men are dogs."

I couldn't disagree with that as my thoughts flashed to Rip. "They are," I said in the wobbly voice.

"I shouldn't," she said.

"How would you feel in my place?" *Betrayed. That's how you'd feel.*

"I heard he went to Destin to practice law with his cousin."

"Thank you." This time the wobble in my voice was authentic as I thought about what a liar Rip was.

By nine thirty I'd parked by the Sea Glass and walked around to the north side of the harbor. This time I was looking for Oscar Hickle. He owned the Hickle Glass Bottom Boat company with his daughter and granddaughter. They took people on tours of the bayous and Choctawhatchee Bay, which separated us from the mainland. Oscar had been up to some mischief in June and wasn't a big fan of mine. Who knew how he'd react to seeing me?

The boat itself wasn't at the dock, so Leah or Edith must have had it out on a tour. I walked over to the small kiosk they worked out of and found Oscar reading the paper and chewing on a pipestem. He looked up with a pleasant smile until he realized it was me.

He set down the paper and pipe, got up slowly, and came over to the window. "Just read my horoscope and it said I was in for some trouble today and now here you are."

Oscar had a deep tan, like many longtime locals. It made his blue eyes even brighter. We'd seen each other a few times at the Sea Glass. He didn't come in as often as some of the other heritage business owners did. But Leah and Edith came in on a regular basis. "I've been called worse than trouble before."

"I'm right sure you have," Oscar said. He craned his head out the window, looking left and right up the harbor walkway. "Got any more fake boyfriends with you?"

"No fake or otherwise boyfriends." I had a momentary thought about Rip. "It's just me today."

"Well, get it over with. I ain't got all day and I'm guessin' you don't want to buy tickets for a tour."

"I need information."

"Call 411."

Oscar was a laugh riot this morning. I expelled a long sigh. "I know you don't have any interest in helping me out and don't exactly trust me. But Ralph Harrison is in trouble. He's been questioned by the Coast Guard. You want to help him, don't you?" I waited. "Please?"

Oscar worked his jaw around. "I guess if it will help Ralph out. He's a good man."

"Have you been out on any midnight tours?" I'd been on one with him in June. He could almost motor through the bayous with his eyes closed.

"Not since you and Ann Williams made sure that Edith took the keys away from me." He winked. "They don't know I have a spare." Oscar raised his hands. "Don't be tellin' them that."

"As long as you aren't out at midnight running illegal liquor."

"That business all dried up. Pardon the pun."

I frowned. "You haven't heard any rumors about it just shifting to somewhere else?"

"Rumors ain't facts." He leaned in. "But I did hear about a red boat been seen out late at night by a couple of the boggy boys."

CHAPTER 32

The boggy boys were people who grew up on the Boggy Bayou on the north side of Choctawhatchee Bay. They were longtime locals who hunted and fished for mullet together. There used to be a town of Boggy, Florida, but it had long since been renamed Niceville. The detail about the red boat sounded authentic. "Where?"

"Over toward Rocky Bayou."

Rocky Bayou was a section of Niceville. "Thank you."

"You aren't my favorite person." He rattled the paper at me. "You be careful trying to help Ralph. These here horoscopes say there's lots of trouble. Mercury's in retrograde."

Things were slow this morning at the Sea Glass, so at eleven I was reorganizing piles of papers, notebooks, and assorted lost-and-found items that had been shoved into the cabinet space under the cash register.

"What's this?" I held up a dusty, three-ring binder that had the word "Drinks" printed on it to show Joaquín. He sat on a barstool, drinking coffee and looking like he needed it.

"That's the drinks book."

"What's 'the drinks book?'"

"It's all our proprietary drink recipes. Haven't you been using it?"

"No. This is the first time I've seen it. No one ever mentioned it." I didn't make drinks that often, only on the rare occasion when I was here alone.

"How have you been making drinks?"

"I've been looking up recipes on my phone."

"Chloe, every bar has their own twists on drinks. That's one of the reasons the same drink tastes different wherever you go."

"Well, this is the only bar I've ever worked in." I was feeling a tad defensive, which I blamed on my restless night's sleep. "You might have mentioned it before now. I've never seen you use it."

"That's because I have all the ones in there," he pointed to the book, "memorized."

"There's more than what's in here?"

"Some that Vivi and I have developed together and haven't added the recipes to the book."

A customer walked in. The regular who always was grumpy and almost always ordered a whiskey sour. "I'll have your drink for you in a moment, sir."

"I'm sorry we never told you about the book. We've never had anyone work here who didn't have prior experience working at a bar. You wouldn't know it existed, or to look for it."

"It's okay. Things were off-kilter, first with Boone's death and then with me finding a dead body by the dumpster."

"Not to mention how crazy summers are here." Joaquín started to stand up.

"Just stay put. I'll use the book to make a whiskey sour."

"Okay."

I was surprised that Joaquín agreed. I noted some history about the drink typed above the recipe, but that would have to wait. "Egg whites?" I looked at Joaquín. That sounded disgusting.

"Don't add the egg whites. He doesn't like them, and there's always a risk of salmonella if it isn't handled properly. But they add a nice, frothy component to the drink."

"Whatever you say." I was conscious of Joaquín following my every move as I filled a shaker three quarters full of ice, added two ounces of whiskey, squeezed fresh lemon juice to equal an ounce and simple syrup. I shook it like my life depended on it, then strained the drink into a rocks glass. I scooped up one of our pink flamingo picks and threaded a cherry and lemon slice as a garnish.

I did a Vanna White flourish with my hand and Joaquín nodded his approval. I took it over to our customer.

"What's the matter with Joaquín today?"

I thought he was just tired from his two jobs, but that wasn't anyone's business. "He's training me."

The man snorted. "Just my luck."

When I first started working here this guy always made me bristle. But I was used to him now. The first drink I'd made for him in June was an old-fashioned. He didn't spit that one out, so I figured I did okay. I hovered over the man, waiting for him to try this one.

"You got nothin' better to do than watch me drink?" he asked. "I'm going to have to tell Vivi she doesn't need the extra help."

I smiled as I went back over to the bar. I'd dealt with worse at the library in Chicago. I was a bit surprised that the old man didn't know I owned part of the Sea Glass. Vivi had told the heritage owners back in June. Usually things got around faster, but I didn't fill him in.

"Joaquín, why don't you go home?" I said. "You look exhausted. It's slow, and now that I have the drinks book I'll be okay."

"I'm fine."

"At least go take a nap. Look," I pointed toward the ocean, "it's starting to sprinkle. No one will be in here."

"Or it could drive everyone in here."

"If that happens, I'll call you. You can be here in five minutes."

"You're not going to let up, are you?"

"Probably not," I admitted.

"Promise you'll call if it gets busy?"

"Yes, and Vivi should be back soon. It will be fine."

"Okay, then." He came around the bar and kissed me on the cheek. "I'll see you in a few hours."

I picked up the drinks binder and read the history of the whiskey sour. According to this, the recipe first appeared in 1862 in a book by Jerry Thomas called *The Bartender's Guide*. It also said that the recipe had been around from at least the 1700s. Drinks cycled in and out of favor. Back then, when scurvy was an issue for sailors or travelers at sea, lime and lemon juice were added to watered-down liquor, which was the origin of the whiskey sour.

A group of women came in and all wanted wine or wine spritzers. That I could easily handle. While I was preparing their order Ann Williams came in, sat at a table with her back to the wall, and pulled out a thick paperback book. I tried to read the cover from here but couldn't. It reminded me that I'd brought some books in to put on a shelf that currently held sand dollars, starfish, and a jar of sea glass.

I served the group of women their drinks, checked with the curmudgeon, who was nursing his drink, and headed over to Ann. She set her book splayed open on the table. The spine was broken. I cringed when people did that, but at least I could see the cover. *Under a Dark Sky* by Lori Rader-Day. She was a Chicago author and had spoken at our library once.

"Great book," I said.

"Has me hooked," Ann said.

"Can I get you something?"

"Just a cup of coffee. It's chilly today."

As I poured Ann's cup of coffee, I weighed what to tell her I knew. I somehow had to get my hands on Steve's email account. Even if the emails weren't essential in the legal resolution of the wills, they would prove to me that I was right about Boone. That he'd never do what Steve claimed he had.

I also had to follow up on what Oscar had told me, just in case that was tied in with what was going on now. Fortunately, I was smart enough to know I shouldn't do any of this on my own. I realized I was holding the coffeepot in my hand, so I put it back on the coffee maker and took Ann her cup.

"I need to tell you something."

Ann put down her book and picked up the coffee. "Shoot."

I flinched a bit at the word. I hoped there wouldn't be any shooting in my near future, or any future for that matter. After glancing around to make sure no one could overhear me, I explained what Oscar had told me.

"Oscar," Ann repeated. I nodded. "He told you all that?"

"Yes." I brought my brows together for a moment in a concerned look.

"I talked to that old geezer about this a few weeks ago. He swore he didn't know a thing."

"Maybe he didn't then," I said.

"I told him to let me know if he heard anything."

"You aren't always easy to find," I said.

Ann shrugged.

"I'm heading out there tonight and I wouldn't mind some company." It was my Midwestern passive-aggressive way of asking for help. I'd worked on being more direct, but when I was intimidated—and Ann definitely intimidated me—I defaulted back to my roots.

"How do you plan to get out to the bayou?" Ann asked.

"Boone's boat."

Ann almost rolled her eyes. "Boone's boat will stick out like a beacon from a lighthouse and be noisy."

"I hadn't thought of that."

"I'll pick you up at your place at ten. Dress in black."

Ann picked her book back up. I wasn't sure whether she wanted to help me or if she wanted to save me from myself.

Antsy with the anticipation of tonight's events, I decided I'd better keep busy. Since neither Vivi nor Joaquín were here I moved the sea glass, sand dollars, and starfish off the shelf and put a selection of books on it. I added a small sign that read, "Take one, return one." I put the jar of sea glass on one side to help keep the books upright. Most of the books were mysteries, thrillers, and romances. Novels that made for good beach reads. Then I added a couple of books about the history of the area that I'd bought before I headed down here.

When I finished that I made the rounds and cleaned. Ten p.m. couldn't come fast enough.

At ten sharp Ann pulled into my drive in a nondescript, slightly weather-beaten Jeep. Not what I pictured her driving, although maybe she had a warehouse full of different cars for different occasions. At least it wasn't the motorcycle. It was a new moon, I noted as I walked to the Jeep. Perfect for clandestine activity.

CHAPTER 33

"I wasn't sure you'd pick me up," I said as I climbed into the Jeep. All the windows had been removed. I was glad I'd worn black leggings with old, black running shoes and a black, long-sleeved T-shirt. It was cool enough without the car moving.

"I wasn't sure either, but I decided you provided the intel, so I might as well let you come along. Just follow my instructions."

My, aren't we bossy? Probably the only reason she'd brought me was so if I found something out in the future, I'd share the information with her again. Or she didn't want me bumbling about on my own. We took a left out of the driveway, drove over to 30A, and a short time later took a left on 98 heading toward Destin. We crossed Choctawhatchee on the Mid-Bay Bridge, paid our toll with cash, and took the first exit to the right.

"Did you tell your Secret Service contact?"

"I didn't. No point in telling him anything yet. Not until we have some facts. Plus, I'm not sure who to trust."

Boy, did I understand that feeling. Ann took a left onto a small, paved road. It became a dirt road that wound around until I wasn't sure which direction we were headed. We drove through tall pines, occasionally passing a house. But soon there weren't any more houses. Ann turned into the woods on a trail that could barely be called that. We came to a gate locked with chain link and a padlock. A sign on the gate read, "Private, No Trespassing," with a skull and bones under it. *Great.* But it was better than being out here by myself. Ann, if anything, exuded a calm confidence.

"Stay here," Ann ordered.

"Yes, ma'am," I muttered as she got out of the Jeep. I noted no lights came on when she opened the Jeep door.

She jogged to the gate and had it open in minutes. I couldn't see if she had a key or if she picked the lock. I hoped it was the former and that this land was her lair. A few night insects made their low sounds. Something small skittered in the pine straw to my right. I couldn't see it when I looked.

Ann climbed back into the Jeep and drove through the gate.

"Want me to close it?" I asked.

"We're good."

I wondered if she wanted it open in case we needed a fast escape. We drove another fifty yards or so until we came to a small, flat area on a smaller bayou or creek. Ann turned the Jeep around so it pointed toward the trail we'd just traversed. She shut off the Jeep and the lights. I couldn't see a thing. We sat for a couple of minutes and my eyes adjusted enough to see outlines of things.

"What's the plan?" I asked, my voice low. This definitely wasn't Rocky Bayou, which was wide and lined with houses.

"I figured no one would be doing anything illegal on the actual bayou. Too many people. But there's all kinds of creeks and bayous off it. I took an educated guess as to where to come. What I'd do if I was smuggling something." Ann got out of the car, so I did too. "We may be on a wild-goose chase courtesy of Oscar. He might think it was payback time for you because you got him in trouble in the first place."

Ann was the one who'd actually ratted him out, but now wasn't the time to point that out. "I hope not."

"There's a spot upstream from here with an old hunting camp. It adjoins a piece of land that has an abandoned grass airstrip. They used to use it for takeoff and landing for the planes that fly over the beach with advertising banners. Anyone could add a banner to a plane and no one would take notice about what you were really up to."

Those planes flew up and down the beach all day, advertising different restaurants, bars, and amusements.

Ann walked over to a pile of logs and brush and started tossing things aside. "Are you going to help?"

A few minutes later we unearthed a small bass boat. It was painted a dark green or black—every inch of it, inside and out. It would be hard to see this time of night. I decided not to question Ann about whose boat it was or whose land we were on. She probably wouldn't answer anyway.

We dragged the boat to the creek. I pointed at the motor. "Isn't that going to be too noisy?"

Ann pulled an oar out of the boat and tossed it at me. I managed to catch it before it thunked me between my eyes.

"We paddle. Carry your weight or I'll toss you overboard."

Shades of her pirate ancestry past. Ann would probably make me walk the plank if one was available. "No problem."

"Get in," she ordered.

I got into the front, and she shoved us off and clambered in. Well, Ann actually slid silently in. I was more the clamberer of the two of us. We paddled silently for about fifteen minutes against the slow current. The banks were lined with trees and scrub brush reaching out over the water. I hoped there weren't any snakes dangling from the branches. Occasionally, Spanish moss would brush my face making me shiver.

"Paddle to the shore," Ann said, her voice low and urgent.

I heard the whine of an engine heading toward us.

We paddled to a spot that had trees hanging over the edge of the bank. Ann tossed a rope around a stump so we wouldn't move.

"Put some mud on your face. It's too white."

I thought about arguing, but then thought about being left out here. I scooped some mud from the bank and smeared it over my face and hands. It stank of decay and rot. Maybe it was some unknown miracle wrinkle cure, not that I had many at my age. We got as low as we could in the boat and waited. Ann pulled out some kind of binoculars.

The sound of the engine got louder. My heart thrummed in time with the engine. I forced myself to slow my breathing. *Stay calm.* A slightly bigger bass boat came around the corner. Boxes were stacked in the middle. A man sat to the front and another in the back. They were only ten feet from us. If they turned, they'd see us. They pulled up even with us and I held my breath. Ann handed me the binoculars. I held them up, waiting until they adjusted to my vision. I didn't recognize the man in the front of the boat. But I choked back a gasp when I saw the man in the back.

CHAPTER 34

Jed Farwell. He was so close I could almost reach out and touch him. I wanted to drag him out of that boat and shake answers out of him. They puttered on by and disappeared around a bend. Neither Ann nor I said anything until the sound of the motor was barely louder than a cricket, and even then I spoke in a quiet voice.

"Should we go to the police?" I asked. "Or your Secret Service contact?"

Ann didn't answer right away. She was staring up the bayou in the direction the boat had just taken. "The man in the front of the boat? That is my Secret Service contact."

I let that sink in for a second. "What now?" I asked.

"We follow them. The old hunting camp is around the next bend. There's a cabin that was more lean-to than house last time I was out here. It could be where they are."

"But—"

"No buts. We don't have any evidence to take to the police. Two men in a boat with boxes don't add up to anything. I can leave you here and go on by myself. This is more than I thought it would be."

I clasped my paddle. "I'm going with you." I'd like to say it was because I was brave, but sitting out here on my own was scarier than continuing on. Alligators and snakes and bears, oh my. "Do you think the Secret Service agent is undercover?"

"I hope so," Ann said. "But I have a feeling he's not."

I nodded, even though it wasn't what I'd hoped to hear. We used our paddles to shove away from the bank and fell into a rhythmic pattern of paddling. Ten minutes later I was sweating and wondering just how far it was to the next bend. The mud on my face was drying and itched like crazy. I heard the whine of a mosquito by my ear, but none of it made me stop paddling. The sooner we found them, the sooner we could get out of here.

"When we get to the camp if no one is out, we'll paddle beyond it and find a spot near the shore to stop." Ann kept her voice low.

I didn't want to think about what would happen if someone was out and spotted us.

"I'll go up to the house," Ann said, "take a look around, and see if I can find out anything. If something goes wrong. Don't go back the way we came, keep heading up the bayou. It narrows and becomes shallower, so it will be hard for anyone to follow you. In the morning you can find a deer trail. One of them should lead you back to a road."

I was going to protest, but her plan made sense. Ann had skills that I was woefully lacking. I couldn't believe I'd thrust us into a situation that was so dangerous. That wasn't my intent. And maybe all along I'd just thought that Oscar was messing with me.

"As we go around the bend, you'll be able to see before I will. If it's safe to continue on, keep paddling. If it's not, hold up your oar."

"Then we watch?" I asked, surprised at how uncertain my voice sounded.

"No. Then we tie the boat off and I'll approach through the woods."

The next ten minutes were like a thousand hours: stroke, stroke, stroke. We turned the bend. Jed's boat was tied to a brand-new dock that looked out of place here. No one was on it and I didn't see anyone outside, although lights glowed through the windows of the cabin. It too must have been rebuilt because it wasn't at all like Ann had described.

"Pull up beside their boat," Ann said in a voice just above a whisper.

I did as I was told. Ann grabbed the other boat, so I did the same. She pulled out two oars and slid them into the water. I watched them head downstream. Ann opened the outboard motor, pulled something out, and tossed it on the floor of our boat. She motioned for me to get going.

We paddled beyond the dock and found a place where our boat wouldn't easily be seen and tied it to another stump. Ann scrambled up the bank and disappeared from sight. The quiet unnerved me along with not knowing what was happening. I climbed out of the boat and clawed my way to the top of the bank. I peeked over the top, lying on the sloped bank.

I settled in to watch through the night-vision binoculars she'd left me, making sure to keep as little of my face as possible from showing over the edge of the bank. It looked like the windows of the cabin were open. Light spilled out. Ann moved like the fog that was beginning to form. Of course that would happen.

I kept scanning the grounds as Ann peered in a window of the house. I spotted a shadowy shape slinking toward Ann. If Ann moved like fog, he moved like smoke blowing in her direction. I couldn't cry out because it would bring others. I snatched up a limb and tried to pull myself up. I lost my footing and started sliding toward the water. I pitched the limb up and over the embankment. My hands clawed out. My feet searched for something to stop the slide. Small bits of rock and dirt splashed into the water.

I latched onto a tree root just before my feet hit the water. My breath was heavy, my heart accelerated. Using the root, I pulled myself up and over the lip of the embankment. Ann still peered in the window. The man stood looking toward the creek before turning back toward Ann. I snatched up the limb and tried to move as quietly as Ann had. Every stick I stepped on sounded like dynamite exploding, but neither of them heard as I approached.

As the shadow reached for Ann, I drew back the limb like a baseball bat and hit as hard as I could. The blow cracked like someone knocked over a stack of hardback books onto a wood floor. The man crumpled to the ground with an *oof*. Ann swirled in surprise. I grasped her hand and jerked her toward the boat. We ran. As we slid down the embankment, Ann scooped up a softball-size rock. Once we were in the boat she heaved it downstream like it was a shot put. It made a huge splash. We started paddling upstream like Ann had told me to do. Shouts followed and lights flared all over the property. But we were gone. Two ghosts in the night.

CHAPTER 35

When we came to the end of the bayou we hauled the boat out of the water and hid it close to shore in some underbrush. We collected pine straw from under the trees and spread it on the ground to hide the drag marks.

"It's not perfect, but it will do for now," Ann said. "Hold on to the back of my shirt."

Ann put on the night-vision binoculars and I clung like I was a kid and her shirt was my blankie. She might think this was a deer path, but I thought a machete would have come in handy.

"What did you see in the cabin?" I asked after we'd walked for a while and I hadn't heard any sounds of us being followed.

"Tables full of guns, cash, and unmarked bottles that were probably liquor, the way one of the men was swigging from a bottle. A duffel bag was on the table."

Duffel bag? "The people on the *Fair Winds* had a duffel bag with them." Of course the world was full of duffel bags. At least Rip had said that was what it looked like. Would he tell me that if he was involved in this? Was he afraid I'd seen it too, so he had to say something? "The duffel bag could connect whatever was going on with the *Fair Winds* to this operation."

"It could," Ann agreed. "I also saw lots of turtles."

"Turtles?" That was the last thing I'd been expecting. Turtles instead of drugs. This night just kept getting stranger.

"It's illegal to sell natural-born turtles. This area is full of them."

"What kind?" I asked.

"Different breeds. Box turtles can go for three hundred a piece. Other species up to ten thousand dollars in parts of the world."

"Ten thousand? That's more than gold is an ounce." How could that be?

"Turtles represent long life and are considered lucky by some people. A box turtle can live for up to eighty years. There are people who collect turtles like other people collect books or art."

"That's awful," I said.

"They're also food for a lot of people."

I'd seen turtle soup on the menu of restaurants. "How many people were in the cabin?"

"Five. Four men and one woman. I only recognized Jed and the Secret Service agent."

"Jed will probably move his operation because he knows someone was out there."

"I agree. But I'll have someone watch the place."

I shook my head. Not that Ann could see me. I was out

in the middle of nowhere with someone who had people who could watch a place. We walked silently for about thirty minutes. Ann made a brief call. Ten minutes later we came to a blacktop road. We stopped under a pine tree and waited for another ten minutes until a battered pickup truck came down the road.

It pulled over and we climbed in. The man who'd been sitting at Ann's table at Two Bobs was driving.

"Drop Chloe off first," Ann told the driver.

She didn't give him the address, but he drove straight to my house.

Wednesday morning my arms and shoulders ached from paddling, or maybe from being tense. However, my face looked great, luminous even. Maybe I should spread bayou mud on it more often. For once I didn't bother to get up and run. Ann had instructed me not to tell anyone what we'd been up to. As if I didn't know better than that.

It didn't mean I wouldn't look into the connection between the disappearance of the *Fair Winds*, its reappearance, the red boat, and Jed Farwell. It all had to be connected somehow. Since I couldn't do anything about that right now I'd focus on what I could do. I still had to figure out a way to have a look at Steve's computer. It wasn't as if I had any hacking skills, or even knew anyone who did. So on my agenda for this morning was to find out where Steve was staying and come up with next steps.

I knew he wouldn't just hand over his computer if I asked. I couldn't decide whether to go to the coffee place on the town circle or The Diner. Both places were good for overhearing local gossip. If Steve was staying in Emerald Cove, it might be easy to pick up his trail, but if he was in Destin, it would be much harder.

I wondered if he was on social media. The old Carly Simon song "You're So Vain" popped into my head. My mom had been a big Carly Simon fan and knew the lyrics to almost every song she sang. Steve was vain enough that social media would appeal to him.

Sure enough, he was on almost every social media platform anyone his age would be. His profile picture looked like the fake ones I got requests from. The sad difference was, Steve was real, not fake. There was a picture of him on the beach in front of my house with the caption, "My new place." I closed my eyes and counted to ten so I wouldn't throw my phone across the room. Maybe I should have gone on a run this morning after all. It usually kept me calm.

Another picture showed him at the coffee shop in Emerald Cove at a corner table with his laptop in front of him. The caption read, "Temporary office. I'll soon be on to bigger and better things." Not if I could help it.

Time to get ready for the day. Small scratches laced the backs of my hands from my evening in the woods. I had no way to cover them up unless I wore gloves, which would make me look as if I'd time-traveled from some ladies' lunch in the fifties. I showered, dressed, and made a bigger effort than normal with my hair and makeup. At the last minute I remembered to stuff the copies of the Boone/Steve emails in my purse. *I'm coming for you, Steve.*

Steve sat at a table near the window when I walked into the coffee shop at nine thirty. His computer open in front of him. I wanted to go over, snatch it out of his hands, and make a run for it, but there were too many witnesses. He looked up and spotted me. Steve smiled and waved as if we were best buddies. I assumed he was putting on a show for everyone in there. I turned a haughty shoulder away from him. Yeah, I wanted to talk to him, but I couldn't be friendly all of a sudden or he'd know something was up.

I waited in line to order. While a cup of hot coffee was tempting for what I was about to do, I didn't want to injure him. I only wanted a few minutes of time on his computer. Instead, I ordered their largest iced tea and a chocolate chip scone. I went over to the coffee station, grabbed a couple of small napkins, and loosened the lid of my tea. I also took one of those cardboard sleeves you put around your cup if your drink was too hot. I stuffed the scone in my purse to eat later.

"Chloe, how's the packing going?" Steve called out to me as I walked toward the door.

Perfect. This would make talking to him so much more natural. I worked my way through the tables over to him.

As I got close, I fake-tripped. At the same time I squeezed my cup of iced tea hard. Tea arced up and splashed down all over Steve's head. Poor guy. I had to hide a smile.

"Oh, no," I exclaimed with fake concern. "I'm so sorry." I thrust a small paper napkin at him and tucked the edge of the cardboard sleeve on his keyboard so it wouldn't close all the way. I hoped that would give me a chance to open it and not have to worry about any password protection he might use if I got the chance.

Steve jumped up and slammed the lid of his computer. He took a step back so the tea dripping from him didn't get on his computer. "If you're this clumsy, there's no way I'm keeping you on at the Sea Glass."

As if it was his decision, but I kept the concerned look on my face. He lifted his hand, and for a moment I thought he would hit me. I almost wished he would so I could have him arrested for assault. Instead, he brushed some ice from his head.

"I'm usually not. I'm so embarrassed. Let me move your computer so it doesn't get dripped on." I shoved it to the other side of the table and stood in front of it so Steve wouldn't see the laptop wasn't fully closed. Everyone in the coffee shop was staring at us. This was the part that could be a problem.

Tea and ice continued to drip from his head and hair. "I'll be right back," he said. "Watch my computer."

It would be my pleasure. He was treating me as if I was his employee and not his adversary, like he thought he'd already won. As soon as he was out of sight in the rest-room, I sat in front of the computer and opened it. Whew, it was still on the page he'd been reading—a page full of fancy house designs. I couldn't let the burn of anger flashing through me distract me. I shoved the cardboard sleeve in the pocket of my dress.

My hands shook as I found his email files. I typed Boone in the search box and opened one of the emails that had the same date as the ones Steve had given Vivi. I grabbed my phone and snapped a picture of it. I hovered my cursor until the email address box popped up, show-ing the one belonging to the actual sender. I quickly took another picture. If any of the other customers thought what I was doing was strange, they didn't say anything. Most of them had returned to their own computers or phones after Steve went to the bathroom.

After I closed his emails and the computer, I ran up to the counter and borrowed two towels. When Steve returned moments later I was cleaning up the iced tea on the chair he had been sitting in. His shirt and hair were damp.

"I am so sorry," I said, managing to choke out the words with some sincerity. I hoped he thought I was groveling because I wanted to keep my job. "Good as new."

I swept my hand toward the table and pulled out the chair farther so he could sit back down. "Let me pay to have your shirt cleaned." It would be a small price if my photos showed anything suspicious. After he sat I opened my purse, took a twenty out of my billfold, and set it on the table. "That should cover the cost."

He squinted at the small scratches on my hands from my adventures last night. "What happened to you?"

"Weeding. Trying to keep things looking good at Boone's house." I started walking away.

"You'd better be packing, because your days of beach living are just about over."

As much as I wanted to turn and flip him off, I managed to walk out the door. I hurried to my car. I wanted to be as far away as possible in case someone mentioned what I'd been up to while he was in the restroom.

CHAPTER 36

I got to the Sea Glass by ten fifteen. I hurried through the opening routine so I could follow up on the emails. By the time the barstools were in place and the barback work was done Joaquín strolled in. He had on a bright orange Hawaiian shirt with green turtles on it. Turtles that reminded me of all that had happened last night.

"Everything's done?" He looked around in amazement. It was only ten thirty-five.

Considering my late night and my morning chat, even I was impressed with myself.

"What happened to your hands?" he asked.

I was uncomfortable lying to Joaquín, but for now I needed to keep some secrets. "I was weeding around the house and ran into some thorns or had an allergic reaction."

Vivi walked in as I was speaking. She came over, took my hands, and gave me a long look before dropping them. "I'll send my crew over to do some cleanup for you. Things grow so fast here, it's hard to keep up."

I'm not sure she believed me, but fortunately, no one questioned me further on that topic. "I have a quick errand I need to run. I'll be back before we open." I didn't want to tell Vivi or Joaquín what I'd been up to this morning until I knew for sure if the emails were fakes or not.

They looked at each other.

"Before you go, I have something I need to talk to you both about. It will only take a minute."

"Okay," we said in unison.

"I offered Steve a big chunk of money to go away like I did when my daughter was still alive. He didn't accept it."

That was disappointing news. "So, you think that means the will is valid?" I asked.

"It makes it seem that way, but Steve knows how to play a hand of cards. Maybe he was calling my bluff. Hoping for a bigger payout."

"He must be, Vivi," Joaquín said.

He's got to be.

"I've decided that if the will is legal, and if Steve turns out to own half this bar, I'm going to give both of you twenty-five percent ownership."

For a moment we stood in shocked silence, and then Joaquín and I began to protest.

"No way."

"You can't do that."

"This is your place."

Vivi held up her hands to the barrage of statements. "I

can't work with him. Life's too short. But you two are young and have the energy to fight him. I trust you with this place. You'll carry on its legacy."

We started to protest again.

"Go run your errand," Vivi said to me. "I've got nothing else to say."

I dashed out the door. Vivi's shocking announcement made my errand even more urgent. If Vivi decided it was time to retire, I didn't want it to be under these circumstances. As I hurried down the harbor walkway, I sent a text to Michael. **Are you home? I want you to look at something with me.**

I waited a minute.

I'm here.

Thank heavens. I was keyed up. So keyed up that I ran into someone while my head was down, texting. Rip. Ugh. That was a new reaction to seeing him. But remembering what Ann had said, I plastered on a smile. "Sorry about that."

"Hey, no texting and walking by the water."

I forced a laugh. "You're right." I darted around him. "I'm in a hurry. See you later."

"Chloe—"

I pretended not to hear him and hurried on. Michael was waiting outside on the back of the boat.

"What the heck is up with you, Chloe? You almost knocked Rip into the harbor."

It would have served him right, but I kept that to myself. I was keeping a lot of things to myself this morning. I glanced back the way I'd come. Rip was watching me, arms crossed and head tilted. I waved like an idiot. That was the opposite of acting normal. I needed to calm down. "Can we go inside?" I asked.

"Sure." Michael led me in. "Want some coffee?"

Michael's coffee was so strong it would curl my innards, but it was just what I needed this morning. "Perfect."

"Take a couple of deep breaths while I get the coffee." I leaned back against their sleek, white leather couch and actually closed my eyes and took some deep breaths. I wouldn't be of any use to anyone if I was jittery. I wasn't sure how a couch could be sleek and comfortable, but this one was.

"Here you go," Michael said a few minutes later.

He put down two mugs of coffee. I picked up mine and took a sip. It wasn't quite thick enough to hold a spoon upright, but it wasn't far off either.

"What has you all riled up?" he asked.

First I told him about what Vivi had just told Joaquín and me.

"That's terrible," Michael said. "Not that you and Joaquín wouldn't make excellent partners, but that Vivi's ready to give up."

Would we make excellent partners? I hoped it would never come to that. Then I explained to Michael what I'd done this morning at the coffee shop. His face went from shocked to almost amused to serious. He was shaking his head while I talked.

"That was risky, but well done. Let's take a look."

"I didn't want to look at this by myself. If I'm wrong, I'll be crushed. I realized, as I've thought this all over during the past few days, if the will is legitimate and Boone really did reconcile with his dad and really did this to Vivi, Boone wasn't the man I thought he was." My lower lip quivered, and I wasn't normally a quiverer.

"Let's look." Michael said it firmly yet gently.

I took the emails from my purse and spread them across their two-tiered, midcentury modern, kidney-shaped coffee table. Then I took out my phone and opened the two photos I'd taken. We looked back and forth between the picture on my phone and the paper copies.

"It looks like the same address," I said. This time not only my lip quivered, but so did my voice.

"You said you took two pictures."

I opened the other one, holding my phone between us. We stared at it and then each other. "The email address is different when the cursor is on it," I said. Hope blossomed in my chest. I threw my arms around Michael for a quick, jubilant hug.

"It is," he said.

"So this is a scam. Someone wrote emails that sounded a bit like Boone and then spoofed his email to make it look as if he was the source of the emails."

"It looks like it. Give me some time to try to track down who this email belongs to."

"You can do that?"

"I can try."

"Do you think this is enough to prove the will isn't legitimate?" I thought for a moment. "Even if it doesn't, if Steve tries to use them in court to prove the will is valid, maybe the prosecutor will be able to go after Steve for fraud." That idea perked me right up.

Michael shrugged. "I'm no lawyer, but someone might have a case for saying you obtained this illegally."

Just two days ago I would have asked Rip, but not

now. "I'll worry about that later. Please don't tell anyone else until we have a better feel for whether we're right or not."

"My lips are sealed. I'll get back to you as soon as I can. I checked on the *Fair Winds* with some of the vets over at that place I told you about in Fort Walton."

"Did you learn anything?" I asked.

"Just that it's still an active case with the Coast Guard."

"Thank you. I've got to get back to work."

"Don't knock anyone into the harbor," Michael called after me as I headed out the door.

Every minute of work felt like two hours as I waited for Michael to call me. I felt like I was in the middle of a John le Carré book or a *Mission: Impossible* movie. Only hopefully this would turn out to be *Mission: Possible*.

"Are you sure you're okay?" Joaquín asked for the twelfth time. "You keep alternating between twitching and sighing. You just walked by a tableful of people who waved and called out to get your attention."

"Sorry," I said back for what seemed like the hundredth time. I hurried over to the table Joaquín had pointed out so I wouldn't say anything else. My head felt like that children's candy Pop Rocks, and that words might burst out of me at any moment. Words I wasn't ready to say yet. The group of women, in contrast, were laughing and having a good time. I wished I could be as carefree.

"We're working our way through a *The Ultimate A-to-*

Z Bar Guide book," one of the women explained to me. "We're on the *F*s."

"That sounds like fun," I said, tempted to pull up a chair and join them.

I took their order. One Flamingo—lady with the brown bob. One Florida—big diamond earrings lady. One Flying Grasshopper—red pointy nails. And one Flying Dutchman—pink lipstick with silver sparkles.

"Have I got this?" I asked. "I've never heard of any of these drinks. You want a Flamingo, a Florida, a Flying Grasshopper, and a Flying Dutchman." *Flying Dutchman?* It made me think of the story Ralph had told me about the ship disappearing, never to be seen again. I repressed a shudder. These certainly weren't the usual beach bar drinks.

"You've got it," the woman with the big diamond earrings said. "And honey, don't you worry, because we've never heard of them either. I hope your bartender is up to the task."

"Don't you worry," I said. "He's always up for anything."

The women all laughed, and my face warmed as I realized how that might sound. "Any drink. He's a great bartender."

"Well, he looks like he'd be up for anything," the woman with the pointy nails said.

"We can only hope he is," the woman with the brown bob added, laughing.

I joined in, and it felt great.

I took the order to Joaquín. He looked it over. "Why don't you make the Flying Dutchman while I make the others?"

Of course he'd suggest I make that one, but it probably meant it was the easiest.

"You trust me after the disgustatini?" I asked.

Joaquín laughed. "Just don't let the Flying Dutchman crash."

I opened the Drinks binder and found the drink—just three ingredients: gin, triple sec, and orange bitters. Pour the ingredients into a chilled glass and stir. I finished before Joaquín did, so I read that the drink first showed up in the Netherlands during the 1950s. Once Joaquín finished, I put little paper umbrellas in each drink.

"Those kinds of drinks don't usually get umbrellas," Joaquín said.

"It makes them look happy, and we all need more happiness in the world."

Just after I placed the drinks in front of each lady, I looked up to see Deputy Biffle walk in from the beach. Thank heavens the drinks were already on the table or I might have dropped them all. He looked at me and jerked his head toward the door. At least I thought he was looking at me. I couldn't be sure with those mirrored, aviator sunglasses. So I pointed to myself and raised my eyebrows. Deputy Biffle lifted his chin in response.

"Give me a minute," I said. *What now?* I took the tray back to the bar.

"Does this have anything to do with your errand earlier or why you aren't you today?" Joaquín asked.

"I don't think so." Unless Steve was pressing charges against me for the iced tea incident. "I'll be right back."

I walked over to Deputy Biffle. He motioned for me to follow him outside. The deck was crowded, so we walked down the beach toward the water. I should have grabbed my sunglasses. The white sand was so bright I was squinting.

He stopped and turned toward me. "We have an ID on the man who rescued you."

"Oh." I wasn't sure why he was here telling me instead of making me wait to find out on the news or through local gossip. A thrum of anticipation or anxiety swept through me. I tried not to show it.

"It was Blake Farwell."

CHAPTER 37

I looked at him and blinked a couple of times. "Blake Farwell who disappeared twelve years ago with Susan Harrington, Cartland Barnett, and Raquel Harrison? That Blake Farwell?" It couldn't be. I closed my eyes for a moment and thought about the man who rescued me. I hadn't noticed a resemblance between Jed and Blake. *Jed!* Jed who was sneaking around at night, apparently involved in a smuggling ring. Was Blake too? But if he was, why did he bring me back? He could have just left me to die or taken me somewhere and killed me.

The thought that gave me pause, that sickened me, was wondering if Jed had something to do with Blake's death. His own brother. No doubt I'd been mad at my brothers often enough over the years, but I would never have killed them.

"Chloe."

I squinted up to see Deputy Biffle staring at me, a deep line between his eyes. "Yes?"

"Yes, that Blake Farwell."

I clapped a hand to my mouth like I was physically trying to stop myself from blurting out anything. I should tell him about what Ann and I had seen last night, but I'd promised I wouldn't say anything. For all I knew Deputy Biffle could be part of the smuggling ring.

"Are you sure that you don't have a connection to him? Know him from somewhere?"

"No. I'd never seen him before." If he was involved with the smuggling ring, why would he risk showing his face around here? "Have you told Jed?"

"Yes. Before I came over here."

Had Jed known all along that his brother was alive? "Why did you come tell me?"

"Because I wanted to know if you had any idea why he rescued you or why he ended up dead by your house."

"At the time I thought he was a random Good Samaritan who was out searching for me." I looked out at the placid Gulf as if it would toss an answer up on the shore. The waves were barely more than a ripple, but how deceiving that was. The Gulf could turn on you in a minute, like so many people. I thought of Rip. I wasn't ready to tell Deputy Biffle about Rip's connection to the red boat either. Ducks in a row first.

"To be honest," I said, "I thought maybe the boat ending up by my house was deliberate. Some kind of warning for me to stay out of something. But now that it was Blake Farwell in the boat, I've changed my mind. It must have been random." It wasn't.

Deputy Biffle pulled his sunglasses down his nose and studied me for a moment. "I've never trusted people who say, 'to be honest.' It makes me think everything else they've said is a lie."

Retorts circled like a school of fish in my head. "Think what you want. Do you have any other questions for me? I need to get back to work."

Deputy Biffle pushed his glasses back up his nose. "Not at this time. Do you have anything you need to tell me?"

"Not at this time." I headed back toward the bar.

"Chloe," Deputy Biffle called out.

I stopped and waited for him to walk over to me. He gave me a long, serious look, and it was tempting to melt under the pressure of that look and tell him about last night.

"Keep this under your hat for now. We've asked Jed to do the same."

"Will do." With the amount of people telling me not to say anything about something, pretty soon I would have to quit speaking altogether.

I trudged back up toward the Sea Glass.

"Chloe," a male voice called.

This time it wasn't Biffle. Even worse—it was Rip. But maybe I could dig some information out of him.

I arranged my face in what I hoped was a friendly expression. "Hi." By the surprised look on Rip's face I'm not sure I succeeded.

"Everything okay?" he asked.

"Sure. Why wouldn't it be?"

"You were just talking to Deputy Biffle, and earlier you almost knocked me into the harbor."

"It's been a busy day."

"What did Biffle want?"

"Following up on the boat that ran ashore by my

house." I paused. "Hey, I've been thinking about selling Boone's boat and getting something more oceanworthy. Something faster. Like the red boat that followed us the day we went out searching for the *Fair Winds*." *Followed us*. That was an understatement. I watched his face. He looked a little puzzled, but not guilty. Could Ann have been wrong? Or was that just wishful thinking because I wanted her to be?

"Does that mean you've heard something about Steve's will?"

"No. But if I don't keep positive, I'll go nuts." Not really a lie. I hadn't heard anything about Steve's will, but I'd seen something. I wondered if Rip was involved with that too, seeing as it was his cousin who was helping Steve. Being part of a smuggling ring and illegal wills meant he'd be in prison for a long time. I wouldn't miss him one bit. That wasn't entirely true. I'd miss the man I'd thought he was. I wondered if while he was gone all summer he'd been out smuggling.

"I'd be happy to help you look for a boat," Rip said after a couple of moments. "I'd still like to take you out to dinner—"

"Can't." I waved a hand toward the Sea Glass. "Work. I'd better get back before I get fired. Sorry."

Thursday morning I found a text from Michael that he'd sent around midnight. All it said was **Patience.**

Really? The whole time I'd run this morning my feet seemed to slap out *patience, patience, patience*. It wasn't my best quality. However, after I'd gone through my shower, breakfast, and getting ready routine, I had another text from Michael. This one said to meet him at the bar at eight, and bring Vivi.

Vivi, Michael, and I met at the Sea Glass to find out what Michael had learned. Joaquín was still out fishing.

"I traced the account. The emails were sent from an account owned by Steve."

I took Vivi's hand and gave it a triumphant squeeze. "I knew it. I knew Boone would never do that to you, Vivi."

"Or you, Chloe," Vivi said. "But don't we still have an issue, because the only reason we know this is because of Chloe's snooping? Snooping that won't hold up in court?"

Vivi didn't sound angry, which I was afraid she would be when she found out what I had done to get access to Steve's computer. She sounded matter-of-fact, with a hint of pride.

"It's a problem. But I have more information," Michael said. "I think we should call your lawyer, Vivi. We should meet with him and tell him what we know."

Vivi made the call. "I caught him on his way to his office. He has time to swing by."

I chopped fruit while we waited, too jittery to sit still and drink more of the coffee that Michael had brought along. Or maybe I was jittery from the coffee that Michael had brought. I paid close attention to what I was doing, because I didn't care to lose a finger with the very sharp channel knife I was using.

Michael strolled over to the shelf of books I'd put up. The one's Vivi and I hadn't yet talked about. Michael pulled a book from the shelf. "Oh, a Louise Penny novel I haven't read yet. I thought I was behind on her series.

And John Grisham's *A Time to Kill*." He looked over at me. "Are you the one with the excellent taste in reading?"

I glanced over at Vivi. "Yes. I loved both of them. Help yourself."

Vivi walked over and stood beside Michael. "Chloe came up with the idea. What do you think about mixing books and booze?"

"I think it's brilliant," Michael said.

Vivi smiled. "So do I, although I didn't at first. I guess we'll have to get more shelves. If you have more books you want to bring in, Chloe."

Whew. Vivi never ceased to surprise me. "I do have more books."

"I have some I can donate to the cause," Michael said. "Joaquín and I tend to overbuy. Then things get crowded, and there are only so many books you can keep on a boat."

George Colton hustled in. He wore a light-blue seersucker suit. I couldn't imagine a lawyer wearing that this time of year in Chicago. I set down the knife and washed the juice from my hands before joining the others at a table.

We laid out the case for him. I explained about the emails, my suspicion that they weren't really from Boone, and how I'd found out they weren't.

George frowned as I mentioned the way I'd gotten the emails. "What else have you found out?"

Michael told him how unlikely it was that a will would be made when a soldier was out in the field for an operation. "I've confirmed that Boone was out on an operation during the time Steve claims the will was written."

"It's the news we've been hoping for," I said. I tried to

remain calm on the outside, but inside I was jumping and yelling and shouting *Yes* and *Take that, you bucket of slime, Steve.*

"It is, but as with your email evidence, it will have to be confirmed. An anonymous source won't be enough," George said. "It's not that simple. Or quick. At the very least Steve has committed wire fraud. Perhaps impersonating a member of the Armed Forces if Steve forged the signatures." George stroked his mustache. "I think we have enough to take to a federal prosecutor."

"I can't wait to hear that Steve's been arrested and charged," I said.

"The federal prosecutor will have to agree that there's enough evidence here," George responded.

"The federal prosecutor might not take the case?" I asked.

"He might not accept any of this as evidence," George said.

"What happens if he doesn't?" Vivi asked.

"A judge would still have to look at both wills and decide which one was legal. During that process all of this would come out. Hopefully."

"What about Ted Barnett—will he be arrested too?" I asked.

"It's rare that a lawyer would be arrested or involved," George answered.

I didn't believe that Ted didn't know what was going on.

"But maybe I'll have a conversation with Ted. Lay out what we know. It might spur things on a little bit." George almost smiled at his comment.

"How so?" Vivi asked.

"I have a feeling Ted's the kind of man who'll dive off a sinking ship before the rats do. He'll point the finger at Steve. I'll call him on my way to the office," George said.

"Do I have to move out of the house like Steve told me?" I asked.

"No," George said. "You stay put until all this is resolved. And once it is I don't think you'll be moving anywhere." He stood. "I'll be in touch."

We watched him walk out.

"So Steve played his hand in hopes that we wouldn't call his bluff," Vivi said.

"But we knew Boone. Knew his heart," I said. "I think at some point Steve and Boone must have had some contact. Because the emails did sound something like Boone."

"Only instead of reconciling, Boone would have told him to take a hike," Michael said.

"That's right," Vivi said. "That was my boy."

CHAPTER 38

Around one thirty I took an order for two strawberry daiquiris up to Joaquín. He mumbled in Spanish under his breath. He often did when I brought him requests for frozen drinks. Maybe it was because of Vivi's no-premixed-drinks rules, although these didn't seem any more difficult than any other drinks he made.

"What's with the muttering every time I bring you a request for a frozen daiquiri?"

Vivi was standing at the end of the bar. "Don't get him started, Chloe."

Joaquín put his left hand on his hip and then waggled his right finger at me. "They are an abomination to the original daiquiri."

"I told you not to get him started," Vivi said.

"The original daiquiri runs the fine line between sweet

and tart. Strawberry daiquiris are just sweet. Too sweet," Joaquín said.

"Do you want me to make the strawberry daiquiris so you don't have to be offended by them?" I asked.

"Yes," Joaquín said. "Yes, I do."

Vivi's eyes were twinkling. "And when you're done and they've been served we'll have a daiquiri making contest. Me against Joaquín. Chloe, you can be the judge of who makes a better daiquiri."

"I don't want to get—"

"It's a deal," Joaquín said to Vivi. "It's been far too long since we've had a drink-off."

"I'm not sure—" I started.

Vivi held out her hand. "Shake on it, Joaquín. I wouldn't want you to chicken out, or say you're too busy like last time." She stuck her hands under her armpits and made flapping motions while she made *bwak, bwak, bwak* sounds.

My brown eyes were fairly wide normally, but now they got even bigger. I'd never seen this side of Vivi.

"I *was* too busy, and then you ran out of here like a scared little girl." Joaquín stuck out his hand and they shook.

"Once Chloe has the drinks made and served," Vivi said, "it's on."

I took out the Drinks book and found the recipe for strawberry daiquiris. I didn't want to get in the middle of Joaquín and Vivi. No good could come from picking one of their drinks over the other.

"Why are frozen daiquiris so different from the original one?" I asked Joaquín as I started adding strawberries, simple syrup, lime juice, and ice to the blender. I was still grumbling in my head about the drink-off.

"Some man in Texas saw the Slurpee machine at Seven

Eleven and thought adding alcohol would be a good idea. A whole new drink industry was born. At least ours aren't that bad," Joaquín said. "Now daiquiris are the stuff of spring-break hangovers and brain freezes. Not the elegant, simple drink they actually started out as."

"Ah," I said. I didn't think I should admit out loud that I'd enjoyed sweet, frozen drinks on a cruise I'd been on in the past. While they weren't as good as the happy drinks Joaquín made for me, they'd suited the moment. In the same situation I'd do it again. I added the triple sec, orange liqueur, and rum. I glanced over at Vivi, whose grin looked like that of the illustrations of the Cheshire Cat in *Alice in Wonderland*. *No good can come of this*, I thought again.

I hit Puree on the blender as Joaquín yelled, "No."

A column of strawberry daiquiri shot up in the air and came back down with most of it landing on my head. I stood stunned for a moment. I'd been so distracted by the upcoming contest I'd forgotten to put the lid on the blender. I glanced over at Vivi. She was laughing. Laughing! Joaquín laughed too, and held out a towel. I snatched it out of his hand.

"I'll make another batch while you clean up," Joaquín said.

Really, could his grin get any bigger? It wasn't that funny, or at least I wasn't ready to laugh about it yet. I was sure at some point I'd find this amusing. "Thank heavens I look good in red." Humor restored, I grinned back at Joaquín as I went to the bathroom.

As I looked at the sticky mess dripping down on my shoulders, I thought of Steve and the icy tea I'd poured on him. That was karma for you. I cleaned up my shirt the best I could. As I was about to leave the bathroom, some-one knocked on the door.

"Chloe, I brought you a clean T-shirt."

I opened the door to find Michael holding a gray T-shirt.

He handed it to me. "Joaquín called and said you might need a fresh shirt."

"Thank you. I'd give you a hug, but—" I gestured to my sticky shirt.

"I'm fine," he said, backing away, hands out. "Happy to help out."

I quickly changed into the T-shirt that was just shy of dress length on me. *Go Navy* blazed across my chest. I stepped back out into the bar.

Vivi whistled sharply, to my surprise. "Listen up, peo-ple. We are having a drink-off."

The crowd started to whoop. Even the old curmud-geon banged on his table and yelled. This must be some tradition I'd missed out on.

"Joaquín and I are both going to make a daiquiri and Chloe, here, will blind taste test them and decide who the winner is," Vivi announced.

I did a small curtsy. Thank heavens it would be a blind taste test. That way I couldn't be accused of having a fa-vorite—which I did, but no one needed to know that.

"In case you don't know the origins of the classic daiquiri," Vivi said, "it was created by Jennings Cox at a party when they ran out of gin. It was named for the nearby town of Daiquirí, Cuba." Vivi turned to Michael. "Please escort Chloe out back. The rest of you will be getting a master class in daiquiri making."

*   *   *

Michael and I stood by the harbor, looking out over the water.

"I've never seen this side of Vivi before," I said.

"Until Boone died, this was the Vivi we usually saw."

I pondered that as we waited to be called back in.

"Are you doing okay, Chloe?" Michael asked.

"I'd be doing better if they found out what happened to Raquel, Susan, and the others, so Ralph and Delores would be off the hook."

"They will," Michael reassured me.

"I hope you're right. A lot of people had reasons for those four to disappear." But who other than Jed had a reason to kill Blake?

Joaquín stuck his head out the door. "We're ready."

"I feel like I can't make a right decision here," I said to Michael.

Michael patted my shoulder. "They've been doing this for years. They don't hold a grudge. At least not for long."

So comforting.

Two beautiful daiquiris sat on the bar in coupe glasses—the flat, wide glasses often used for champagne. Each had a lime twist in the drink. Joaquín and Vivi stood at the far end of the room with their backs to the Gulf. Michael went and stood between them. They all stared intently at me, along with the rest of the people in the bar. *No pressure.*

I picked up the first glass and sipped. The balance of sweet and tart was almost perfect. It didn't scream that sugar or lime was the main ingredient. I always felt elegant drinking out of a coupe glass, even in an oversize T-shirt with sticky hair. I set down the first glass, took a drink of water, and picked up the second. It too had a delicate balance of flavors, although this one was slightly sweeter. However, I enjoyed the sweetness.

I took a drink of water and tried both again, this time in reverse order. The crowd in the bar was quiet. I mulled the tastes over in my mind.

"Both are delicious," I said. The crowd cheered. "But this one," I pointed at the first one I'd tried, "wins by a hair."

Michael held up Vivi's hand as if she'd just won a boxing match. When he dropped her hand Vivi strutted around the bar with her hands clasped above her head. She looked at Joaquín, made an "L" for loser with her fingers, and held it to her forehead. He tapped a fist to his chest as if he was wounded. Then he bowed to her several times.

"I told you turbinado sugar in the simple syrup was the key ingredient," Vivi said to Joaquín.

I was laughing so hard I had tears in my eyes. Steve walked in from the deck. That sobered me up fast. Vivi, Joaquín, and Michael all turned around and spotted him.

"Well, well," Vivi said. "If it isn't my brand-new partner."

Steve stopped, and for a moment the arrogant look on his face flashed to surprise. It didn't last.

"Sounds like you're coming around," Steve said.

He sounded disappointed.

Vivi gave a snort of laughter. "You wish. We know that you faked the will and the emails." Vivi looked at the silver watch on her wrist. "I'm guessing your lawyer is with the federal prosecutor right now turning state's evidence."

"You're being ridiculous," Steve said, but his usual bluster had an edge of uncertainty to it.

"Am I, Chloe?" Vivi asked.

"Nope. Was it wire fraud, mail fraud, and impersonating a military officer? I can't quite remember the exact charges," I said. "Oh, look, there's the deputy now."

Steve paled and whipped around. Of course no deputy was there. That was wishful thinking on my part.

Steve turned back to us. "We'll just see about that." Then he hightailed it out of the Sea Glass.

"George said it would take a while for the case to go to court, Vivi," I said.

"Steve isn't the only one who can bluff," Vivi said.

I guessed he wasn't.

"Daiquiris on the house," Vivi called out. "Let's get this party started."

"Classic daiquiris," Joaquín added.

After work I walked down to Two Bobs to look for Ann, still smiling from the drink-off and the satisfaction of seeing Steve run out of the bar. This time Ann was at her regular table and alone. I sat down across from her.

"We need to talk," I said. It sounded like a bad line from a D-list movie.

"Agreed. But not here."

"I thought you always conducted business here."

"There's business and there's this." She gestured between us. "I don't want anyone to overhear us."

CHAPTER 39

"Your place or mine?" I asked. That sounded like a bad line too. Maybe I should take up writing terrible screenplays. I had no idea where Ann lived, but it would be interesting to find out. I pictured her living on a three-masted ship tucked in a quiet cove somewhere. One that could glide out quietly in the night to do whatever Ann needed to do.

"Your place. I'll meet you in thirty minutes."

Before Ann showed up I scrubbed off my makeup and showered off the remnants of my day—strawberry daiquiris were surprisingly sticky, or at least the one I made was. Rookie mistake, not putting the lid of the blender on and having the drink spray all over me.

I changed into old leggings and a Chicago Bears

sweatshirt that I'd stolen from a long-ago boyfriend. It was soft and comfy. When I heard a car pull up I peeked out the drapes to confirm it was Ann. I was still worried that Jed and his gang had somehow figured out that it was Ann and me in the woods.

Ann climbed out of the passenger side of her Jeep. Why did she have a driver again? It made me wonder what she had planned after she left here. Or maybe she was worried about Jed too. Whatever she was doing after our conversation at Two Bobs I hoped it hadn't involved me. I opened the door and let her in. We sat in the living room, on opposite ends of the couch.

"Do you want anything to drink?" I asked. Ever the hostess. My mom would be so proud.

"No. Have you been okay?" Ann asked. "No one's following you?"

"If they are, I haven't noticed." I paused. "We have to tell someone what happened. What we saw at the camp."

Ann nodded. I was surprised.

"I agree," she said. "I've been trying to figure out who."

I could understand her reluctance after what had happened with the Secret Service agent. "You're sure your friend isn't running an undercover op?"

"He's been around too much. They would have brought someone else in to infiltrate Jed's organization."

That made sense. "What about reaching out to Deputy Biffle? He seems like a straight arrow, but you've lived here longer than I have." I didn't really know much about Ann, or how long she'd lived here, or where she'd lived before.

Ann did a slow nod. "Let's call him."

"Right now?"

"Yes. I think they're moving camps tonight. It would be best to catch them in the act."

That explained the driver and the Jeep. I took out the card Deputy Biffle had given me with his cell phone number on it. I hoped I wasn't waking him up. I didn't want to reach him through the sheriff's office.

"Biffle."

He sounded alert. "This is Chloe Jackson. I have some information that I think has something to do with Blake Farwell's death. Can you come over?"

There was a pause. I assumed he was thinking it over.

"I'll be over in ten."

I ended the call and turned to Ann. "He's on his way."

Ann got out her phone and sent a text. Seconds later I heard the Jeep start up and leave. Ann Williams, international woman of mystery. Whatever. I didn't really care what she did or didn't want Biffle to see.

We waited in silence until he knocked on the door. Ann seemed a little tense, but I was too. I got up and let him in. Biffle's eyes swept the room and settled on Ann. His facial expression didn't change, but I thought I noticed a slight tensing of his shoulders. Hmmm, did they have a past? Deputy Biffle didn't wear a wedding ring. Straight-and-narrow Biffle and bend-the-rules Ann would be an interesting combination for a couple.

I went through my hostess routine, which he rejected. We sat at my kitchen table and filled him in on what had happened the other night. Well, "we" was a stretch. I did most of the talking, starting with my conversation with Oscar Hickle, telling him about seeing Jed Farwell and the Secret Service agent, and ending with us getting away. I left out the part about getting picked up and driven home.

Deputy Biffle deserved an Oscar nomination for playing a wooden board. His facial expression was set to neutral, and he barely moved. If it wasn't for the occasional blink or breath, I'd have thought he was in a trance. Oh, or maybe spellbound by Ann. I shoved that thought aside to focus on next steps.

"This is all conjecture, but what if the smuggling ring has been around for years?" I asked. "The *Fair Winds* somehow came upon something that night that they shouldn't have. Maybe the smuggling operation. Blake threw in with his brother to survive."

"He was probably supposed to kill Chloe," Ann said. "But for some reason didn't."

It was strange to hear the thing I'd been worrying about voiced out loud. I wondered if I'd ever have an answer to that question.

"We didn't know who to trust." That's what I finished with. Neither Ann nor I mentioned Rip and the red boat. Maybe some small part of both of us hoped he wasn't involved.

Deputy Biffle studied Ann for a moment. From anyone else the look would be nothing. But because it was Deputy Biffle I assumed that this was an expression of great surprise. He was surprised Ann trusted him. This was getting better and better.

Ann finally spoke. "We think they're moving tonight."

"We need to go in quiet, but we'll need a few more people," Deputy Biffle said.

"People you trust, Dan."

That was the first time I'd ever heard Deputy Biffle's first name. I looked back and forth between them. Caught a momentary softening of both their features. Or maybe I was just tired and imagining things.

"I'll call a couple of people," Deputy Biffle said.

"I'll meet you in forty-five minutes. I'll be your guide. Observation only," Ann said.

That confirmed they had some kind of history. "Do you want me to come along?" I asked.

"No." They said it in unison, and then they left.

A knock on my door at six thirty Friday morning surprised me as I was getting ready to head out on my run. I opened the door and found Ann standing there, with two cups of coffee no less. She held one out to me. That was when I noticed a bruise on her cheekbone.

"Thanks," I said. "Living room or porch?"

"Let's sit on the porch."

Once we'd settled on the porch Ann seemed content to take in the view. The sun was rising with some showy pinks and oranges. Gulls were swooping and calling, a line of pelicans flew by skimming the water. It felt like heaven must as a gentle breeze blew the salty Gulf scent to us.

"What happened?" I asked. While Ann might be content to take in the scene, I was antsy as a kid waiting for the next page of a beloved book to be read. "I thought you were there to observe only." I tapped my cheekbone in the place she had her bruise.

Ann did a minisnort, which seemed so un-Ann like. "That's what I told Biffle so I could go with him."

Hmmm, she was back to Biffle instead of Dan. Maybe he wasn't too happy with her. I got that, because Ann was driving me crazy. "How did you get the bruise?"

"I tackled the man who snuck up on me the other night. No one gets the jump on me." She took a drink of her coffee. "If you hadn't been watching the cabin, it would have been bad. So he had some payback coming. When I saw him make a run for it I stopped him."

"Let me guess, you have a small bruise and he has a large one."

"Several. I also heard his shoulder might be dislocated. He must have stumbled on something in the dark."

Humph. I was guessing the only dark thing he stumbled on was Ann in her black outfit. "Who else was out there?"

"They've got Jed and the Secret Service agent in custody. Plus the others I saw out there that night. The Secret Service agent was already pleading that he was undercover, but I don't still buy it."

"How many of you were out there to round up everyone?"

"Biffle obviously, me, two other Walton County deputies, and the police chief from Fort Walton Beach, Chuck Hooker."

"Why the police chief?"

Ann raised and dropped her shoulder. "He and Biffle go way back, I guess. Because of you lots of guns are off the street, turtles have been saved, and a long-running liquor-smuggling operation has been broken up. Hopefully, Biffle will get confessions out of some of the men and the tangled mystery of the *Fair Winds* will finally be resolved." Ann downed the last of her coffee. "Have a good run. You don't need to see me out."

That was about as near as Ann got to thanking someone. It felt pretty darn good to be me right now. I finished my coffee watching the sun rise. After some stretches I set out on my run wondering when I'd hear anything about arrests.

CHAPTER 40

Deputy Biffle had a smug smile on his face as he sipped a beer at the Sea Glass. He'd stopped in just before we closed—out of uniform for once, although his jeans and short-sleeved shirt had crisp ironing marks. Ann, Joaquín, Michael, Vivi, and I sat with him at a high-top table. Deputy Biffle's back was to the wall. Before the bar opened I'd filled Joaquín, Michael, and Vivi in on what had happened the other night on the bayou and what Ann had told me this morning.

Vivi had been shocked and disappointed that Jed Farwell had been involved. The heritage business owners were so close.

For once Deputy Biffle didn't have his aviator sunglasses on. As I put a beer in front of him, I noticed that his gaze lingered briefly on the bruise on Ann's cheek. She'd lifted her chin a bit as he did it.

"Jed Farwell sang like he was Renée Fleming singing Bellini's 'Casta Diva.'"

My eyebrows wanted to pop up in surprise, but I managed to keep my facial expression set to neutral. I never would have guessed Deputy Biffle was an opera fan. People down here in the Panhandle continued to surprise me, making me realize my Yankee self had biases I wasn't aware of.

"I can't believe he talked," I said. Everyone else nodded. I also couldn't believe Deputy Biffle was in here filling us in.

"A lighter sentence for giving up a bigger fish," he said.

"The Secret Service agent?" I asked. I glanced at Ann. She wasn't fooled easily, so I knew that having the Secret Service agent double-cross her stung.

"Yes." He took a drink of his beer as if it was the best thing he'd ever tasted. "Although Jed doesn't realize some of the other people we picked up are talking too."

"What happened on the *Fair Winds* the night it disappeared?" Vivi asked. Deep lines cut across her forehead.

She'd lost friends that night, and maybe more when Blake Farwell disappeared. I thought again of the wistful look on her face when I'd first mentioned him to her.

"According to one of the men we brought in, the *Fair Winds* inadvertently came upon Jed and the smugglers transferring liquor from one boat to another. It was a common practice, so if law enforcement was on to one boat, they'd switch things up. When the suspected boat showed up at port it was free of anything illegal."

"So they've been at this a long time, and up until Vivi started asking questions about possible liquor smuggling in June, no one knew," Ann added.

"How could no one know for so long?" I asked.

"Because they kept moving their operation around," Biffle said. "They stayed out of Emerald Cove because it was too close to home, but their greed got in their way."

"But why did they kill Cartland, Susan, and Raquel?" Joaquín asked.

"Witnesses. Cartland was shot and killed right away when he tried to get one of the smugglers' guns. They dumped him overboard," Biffle said. "Then they tried to stage some debris and a scarf to look like the boat had blown up."

So, Rip's dad was a hero and his son a smuggler. How ironic was that?

"Blake didn't know what his brother was up to until that night. After Cartland was killed Blake got the women to agree that they wouldn't tell anyone. But Jed didn't trust them, so he took them to a remote island in South Florida where he had an encampment. Raquel tried to swim away and perished not long after they were taken to the island. Susan pretended to fall in love with Jed. They had an affair for years sailing the *Fair Winds* together, until she was caught trying to radio for help."

"But why were her remains on the boat? It couldn't have been floating alone for years," I said.

"It's disgusting. She was a warning to those who interacted with Jed and Blake of what would happen to them if they were crossed. They've been using the boat for years in southern Florida. Painting it and repainting it with different names."

"Who shot at me when Rip and I went out looking for the *Fair Winds*?" I asked. I knew it wasn't Jed because he'd been out on a charter.

"Some of Jed's men. They swear they were just trying

to scare you off so they could retrieve a duffel full of money that was left behind when Blake abandoned the *Fair Winds* during a storm."

We were all pale and quiet when Deputy Biffle finished.

"What about the *Fair Winds* ending up on the beach here?" Vivi asked.

"I did some digging and found out that last summer there was a Mayday call from the *Fair Winds* during a hurricane down in southern Florida. The Coast Guard rescued a man—I'm convinced it was Blake Farwell, but he was using a false name."

"So the *Fair Winds* has just been drifting around since then?" Joaquín asked.

"It was. It might have gotten caught in the Loop Current, and then the storm blew it this way. It's not the first time an abandoned boat has ended up in this area," Biffle said.

"Why did Blake stay in town after he saved Chloe?" Vivi asked.

"We brought Jed's son in for an interview. He turned on his father pretty quick when we explained how things were shaking out."

Jeez, there were more people turning on one another than in *And Then There Were None* by Agatha Christie.

"According to Jed's son, Jed was tired of Blake's screwups, like leaving the cash behind when Blake was rescued from the *Fair Winds*. Also, Blake was tired of being on the run and wanted to get out of the business. So he could return, Blake came up with a story that he'd been kidnapped by smugglers and hit over the head and had been wandering around with amnesia all this time. Jed didn't react well to that."

"Maybe that's why Blake didn't kill me," I said.

"I'm not sure," Deputy Biffle said. "Maybe he wanted to redeem some of his wrongs. We'll never know for sure."

Or maybe Blake wanted to win Vivi back.

Biffle finished his beer. "Most of this will be coming out in the next few days. Until then you don't know a thing. We're working with the Coast Guard special agents to build the cases. They're still looking into the stain you spotted on the floor, Chloe, and why Raquel's ring was there. We might not ever have an answer to that."

We all nodded. Deputy Biffle strode out of the Sea Glass looking like a happy man. He'd closed a few cases. The aftermath would linger for a long time. Ann stood up. She looked at me and gave me a quick flick of her head.

"I need to get going," she said. "Vivi, if you need anything get hold of me. I can't imagine what you must be feeling."

I stood up. "I'll walk you to your car." Or motorcycle, or whatever mode of transportation Ann was using today. At this point it wouldn't surprise me if a helicopter swooped in to pick her up. Everyone gave me a look, because if anyone needed walking to their car, Ann would be the last on the list. She managed to project a don't-mess-with-me attitude. Her comment to Vivi was the most vulnerable I'd ever seen her. It made me wonder how she became a fixer in the first place. It wasn't as if you applied for a position like that, or advertised what you did.

Instead of heading to the parking lot we walked down to the edge of the Gulf. We both looked out at it.

"The Gulf looks so mild and yet hides so many secrets," I said. "It makes me wonder what else is happening out there."

"You probably don't want to know," Ann said. "And you haven't seen it during a hurricane. I hope you never do."

I'd seen some violent thunderstorms and the waves they produced. I'd read about the category five storm that had hit fifty miles east of here in Panama City and Mexico Beach. They were still recovering three years later. A hurricane in Emerald Cove would be unimaginable. "I hope I never do either."

"Rip didn't know about the red boat being in his name," Ann said.

My eyes widened. "How did you find that out?" It was amazing the way she rooted out information.

"I asked him."

Well, that was one way to find out. "You went from not trusting him to trusting him? Why?"

"Things weren't adding up. No one from last night mentioned Rip to Deputy Biffle or he would have been brought in too."

"Did I just get run over by a truck? Because I sure feel like I have whiplash." I rubbed the back of my neck.

"I get it," Ann said. "I was wrong."

"What did he have to say that made you change your mind?"

"His family has layers of different corporations and LLCs. That the boat was in his name was news to him. It was one Cartland owned a long time ago and was stolen at some point. Even though red boats are unusual here, they aren't so unusual that Rip would assume the one you saw was his dad's stolen one."

"What did he say when you asked him about it?"

"First he was mad that I'd even considered him to be involved in anything that might hurt you."

"And then?" I had a sinking feeling in my stomach.

"Then he asked if you knew."

"Oh."

"I told him you did. He said that explained why you'd acted so funny around him lately."

Ann didn't bother to add that she'd asked me to behave as usual around him. No acting awards were in my future.

"He's leaving tonight," Ann said.

"For where?" I asked.

"I don't know. We hurt him by not trusting him. By not asking him immediately."

My shoulders sagged. "I didn't know him well enough to trust him." That might sound as if I thought Ann should have. "And I don't mean to imply you should have. The evidence was damning."

"It was. If you want to see him, he might not have taken off yet."

I kicked off my shoes, picked them up, and took off running. Did I mention I hate running in soft sand? I cut up the beach. I turned back to shout a thank-you and saw that Deputy Biffle had joined Ann at the water's edge. They were standing so close to each other that you wouldn't be able to slip a picture book between them. Interesting. "Thank you," I said, but not loud enough to interrupt them.

I set off again, and popped out onto the harbor walk between the Briny Pirate and the condominium building. I took a left and ran down to the arm of the dock where Rip kept his boat.

Rip looked up from untying his boat when he heard

me pounding toward him. The vapor light lit his face. I slowed at the look of disappointment when he saw me. I stopped at the edge of the dock and looked down at him.

"Ann told me you're leaving. I'm sorry."

"Me too."

He wasn't apologizing to me. He was disappointed in me. "I don't know you that well. What did you expect me to think when I found out you owned the red boat? It made me view everything that had happened through a different lens." I wouldn't point out that Ann had known him longer and had doubts too.

"Why would I have collaborators who went out of their way to shoot at me? And you? In my own boat."

"I thought it was to throw me off. To make me believe you were a good guy."

"I am a good guy." Rip paused. "People have to trust one another."

"Trust has to be built and earned. It doesn't just happen. It's not like being innocent until proven guilty." I'd heard my dad say that many times. I gestured toward the boat. "We won't ever be able to learn to trust each other if you leave."

"What are you saying, Chloe?"

I hated having to spell it out. It made me mushy inside, and scared. I'd been rejected by my share of handsome men. It probably contributed to my suspicions of Rip. "Don't go. There's something between us. I'd like to find out what it is."

Rip bent back over the rope. Disappointment cascaded through me. I should have kept my big mouth shut. My face heated up. He'd probably be telling everyone the story of the loser girl who liked him. I had my answer and turned to go.

"Chloe."

I paused at the warmth in Rip's voice.

"I'm tying her back up. I was planning to go away for the weekend. Ann knew that."

Ann! She'd tricked me into believing he was leaving for a long time. I turned back around. Rip reached his hand up to me. I put my cold one in his warm one and stepped down onto his boat.

ACKNOWLEDGMENTS

Thanks to everyone who takes the time to read my books. This is book number eleven for me, and I always have to pinch myself to believe the dream of being published really did come true. I'm so blessed to have Gary Goldstein as my editor at Kensington and John Talbot as my agent. The team at Kensington is amazing and I have to give a special shout-out to Larissa Ackerman. I'm so lucky to work with her.

Thanks so much to The Wickeds—Jessie Crockett, Julie Hennrikus, Edith Maxwell, Liz Mugavero, and Barbara Ross. We've all grown so much since our early days together and I can't imagine better blog mates and friends than all of them.

Barb Goffman, independent editor, always reads an early draft of my books. And by early I mean a bunch of scenes strung together that she somehow manages to make sense of. If there are mistakes, it's on me, not her.

Shari Randall is my go-to children's librarian. I send her questions asking, "What would Shari do?" She always has an answer for me. Shari also writes amazing novels, so check them out.

Another thank you to Shari's husband, Bill Randall, Coast Guard Commander (Ret.), for sharing his expertise with boats and the Coast Guard. All mistakes are mine!

Thanks, Vida Antolin-Jenkins, Captain (Ret.) JAG Corp, for your advice on military wills and what could go wrong with one. It was brilliant! And again, if there are mistakes, it's my fault.

To all the Coast Guard spouses that reached out when I asked a question on Facebook—thank you! And a huge thanks to the spouse and her active-duty Coast Guard husband who helped so much but wish to remain anonymous!

To my three beta readers extraordinaire, Jason Allen-Forrest, Christy Nichols, and Mary Titone, thank you for always dropping everything and reading for me. An extra thanks to Mary for a second last minute read through. This book is so much better because of your contributions. I'm a lucky woman to have all of you supporting my stories.

Also, thanks to Jen; you are so much more than a virtual assistant.

To Clare—now my angel. A couple of years ago she handed me a newspaper clipping about a ghost ship washing up on the beach of Destin, Florida. It's what set this story off. I miss you, but know you are still here helping me with my books.

And as always to my fabulous, funny family—you make life an adventure. I wouldn't want it any other way!

Don't miss the first book in the *Chloe Jackson
Sea Glass Saloon Mysteries*!

FROM BEER TO ETERNITY
by Sherry Harris

With Chicago winters in the rearview mirror, Chloe
Jackson is making good on a promise: help her late
friend's grandmother run the Sea Glass Saloon in the
Florida Panhandle. To Chloe's surprise, feisty Vivi Slidell
isn't the frail retiree Chloe expects. Nor is Emerald Cove.
It's less a sleepy fishing village than a Panhandle hotspot
overrun with land developers and tourists. But it's a Sea
Glass regular who's mysteriously crossed the cranky
Vivi. When their bitter argument comes to a head and
he's found dead behind the bar, guess who's the number
one suspect?

In trying to clear Vivi's name, Chloe discovers the old
woman isn't the only one in Emerald Cove with secrets.
Under the laid-back attitude, sparkling white beaches,
and small-town ways something terrible is brewing. And
the sure way a killer can keep those secrets bottled up is
to finish off one murder with a double shot: aimed at
Chloe and Vivi.

Look for FROM BEER TO ETERNITY on sale now!

CHAPTER 1

Remember the big moment in *The Wizard of Oz* movie when Dorothy says, "Toto, I've a feeling we're not in Kansas anymore?" Boy, could I relate. Only a twister hadn't brought me here; a promise had. This wasn't the Emerald City, but the Emerald Coast of Florida. Ruby slippers wouldn't get me home to Chicago. And neither would my red, vintage Volkswagen Beetle, if anyone believed the story I'd spread around. Nothing like lying to people you'd just met. But it couldn't be helped. Really, it couldn't.

The truth was, as a twenty-eight-year-old children's librarian, I never imagined I'd end up working in a beach bar in Emerald Cove, Florida. In the week I'd been here I'd already learned toddlers and drunk people weren't that different. Both were unsteady on their feet, prone to temper tantrums one minute and sloppy hugs the next, and they liked to take naps wherever they happened to be.

Go figure. But knowing that wasn't helping me right now. I was currently giving the side-eye to one of the regulars.

"Joaquín, why the heck is Elwell wearing that armadillo on his head?" I asked in a low voice. Elwell Pugh sat at the end of the bar, his back to the beach, nursing a beer in his wrinkled hands. I had known life would be different in the Panhandle of Florida, but armadillo shells on people's heads?—that was a real conversation starter.

"It's not like it's alive, Chloe," Joaquín Diaz answered, as if that made sense of a man wearing a hollowed-out armadillo shell as a hat. Joaquín raised two perfectly manicured eyebrows at me.

What? Maybe it was some kind of lodge thing down here. My uncle had been a member of a lodge in Chicago complete with funny fez hats, parades, and clowns riding miniature motorcycles. But he usually didn't sit in bars in his hat—at least not alone.

Elwell sported the deep tan of a Florida native. A few faded tattoos sprinkled his arms. His gray hair, cropped short, and grizzled face made him look unhappy—maybe he was. I'd met Elwell when I started working at the Sea Glass. I already knew that Elwell was a great tipper, didn't make off-color comments, and kept his hands to himself. That alone made him a saint among men to me, because all three were rare when waitressing in a bar. At least in this one, the only bar I'd ever worked in.

It hadn't taken me long to figure out Elwell's good points. But I'd seen more than one tourist start to walk in off the beach, spot him, and leave. There were other bars farther down the beach, plenty of places to drink. So, Elwell and his armadillo hat seemed like a problem to me.

"Elwell started wearing it a few weeks back," Joaquín

said with a shrug that indicated *what are you going to do about it*. Joaquín's eyes were almost the same color as the aquamarine waters of the Gulf of Mexico, which sparkled across the wide expanse of beach in front of the Sea Glass. With his tousled dark hair, Joaquín looked way more like a Hollywood heartthrob than a fisherman by morning, bartender by afternoon. That combination had the women who stopped in here swooning. He looked like he was a few years older than me.

"It keeps the gub'ment from tracking me," Elwell said in a drawl that dragged "guh-buh-men-t" into four syllables.

Apparently, Elwell had exceptional hearing, or the armadillo shell was some kind of echo chamber.

"Some fools," Elwell continued, "believe tinfoil will stop the gub'ment, but they don't understand radio waves."

Great, a science lesson from a man with an armadillo on his head. I nodded, keeping a straight face because I didn't want to anger a man who seemed a tad crazy. He watched me for a moment and went back to staring at his beer. I grinned at Joaquín and he smiled at me. Joaquín didn't seem concerned, so maybe I shouldn't be either. I glanced at Elwell again. His eyes always had a calculating look that made me think there was a purpose for the armadillo shell that had nothing to do with the "gub'ment," but what did I know?

CHAPTER 2

"Whatta ya gotta do to get a drink round here?" a man yelled from the front of the bar. He was one of two men playing a game of rummy at a high top. They were in here almost every day.

"Not shout for a drink, Buford," Joaquín yelled back. "Or get your lazy as—" he caught himself as he glanced at Vivi, the owner and our boss, who frowned at him from across the room, "asteroid up here."

Vivi's face relaxed into a smile. She would have made a good children's librarian considering how she tried to keep things PG around here. Joaquín tilted his head toward me. I took a pad out of the little black apron wrapped around my waist and trotted over to Buford.

"Would you like another Bud?" I asked Buford. "Or something else?"

"Sure would," Buford said. There was a "duh" note in

his voice suggesting why else would he be yelling to Joaquín.

"Another Maker's Mark whiskey?" I looked at Buford's card playing partner as I wrote his beer order on my pad.

"You have a good memory," he said looking at his half empty glass. "But I'm good."

Good grief, I'd been serving him the same drink all week, I'd hoped I could remember his order. I made the rounds of the other tables. By each drink I wrote a brief description of who ordered it: beer, black hair rummy player; martini, dirty, yellow Hawaiian shirt; gin and tonic, needs a bigger bikini. I'd seen way more oiled-up, sweaty, sandy body parts than I cared to in the week I'd been here. Not even my dad, a retired plumber, had seen this many cracks at a meeting of the Chicago plumbers union.

Those images kept haunting my dreams, along with giant beach balls knocking me down, talking dolphins, and tidal waves. I'd yet to figure out what any of them meant—well, maybe I'd figured out one of them. But I wasn't going to think about that now.

Nope, I preferred to focus on the scenery, because, boy, this place had atmosphere—and that didn't even include Elwell and his armadillo shell hat. The Sea Glass Saloon I'd pictured before I'd arrived had swinging, saloon-style doors, bawdy dancing girls, and wagon-wheel chandeliers. This was more like a tiki hut than an old western saloon, though thankfully I didn't have to wear a sarong and coconut bra top. I could fill one out, but I preferred comfortable tank tops. Besides, the Gulf of Mexico was the real star of the show. The whole front of the bar was open to it, with retractable glass doors leading to a covered deck.

The Sea Glass catered to locals who needed a break from the masses of tourists who descended on Emerald Cove and Destin, the bigger town next door, every summer. Not that Vivi would turn down tourists' money. She needed their money to stay open, as far as I could tell.

Like Dorothy, I was up for a new adventure and finding my way in a place that was so totally different from my life in Chicago. I only hoped that I'd find my own versions of Dorothy's Scarecrow, Tin Man, and Cowardly Lion to help me on the way. So far, the only friend I'd made—and I wasn't too sure about that—was Joaquín. He, and everybody, seemed nice enough, but I was still trying to adjust to the relaxed Southern attitude that prevailed among the locals in the Panhandle of Florida. It was also called the Emerald Coast, LA—lower Alabama, and get this—the Redneck Riviera.

You could have knocked me over with a palm frond when I heard that nickname. The chamber of commerce never used it, nor would you see the name in a TV ad. But the locals used it with a mixture of pride and disdain. Some wanted to brush it under the proverbial rug, while others embraced it in its modern-day form—people who were proud of their local roots.

The Emerald Coast stretched from Panama City, Florida, fifty miles east of here, to Pensacola, Florida, fifty miles to the west. The rhythm and flow was such a contrast from the go, go, go lifestyle in Chicago, where I'd lived my entire life. The local attitude matched the blue-green waves of the Gulf of Mexico, which lapped gently on sand so white you'd think Mr. Clean came by every night to tidy up.

As I walked back to the bar Joaquín's hips swayed to the island music playing over an old speaker system. He was in perpetual motion, with his hips moving like some suave combination of Elvis and Ricky Martin. My hips didn't move like that even on my best day—even if I'd had a couple of drinks. Joaquín glanced at me as he added gin, tonic, and lime to a rocks glass. I'd learned that term a couple of days ago. Bars had names for everything, and "the short glasses" didn't cut it in the eyes of my boss, Vivi Jo Slidell. And yeah, she was as Southern as her name sounded. I watched with interest as Joaquín grabbed a cocktail shaker, adding gin, dry vermouth, and olive brine.

"Want to do the honors?" Joaquín asked, holding up the cocktail shaker.

I glanced at the row of women sitting at the bar, one almost drooling over Joaquín. One had winked at him so much it looked like she had an eye twitch, and one was now looking at me with an openly hostile expression. Far be it from me to deprive anyone from watching Joaquín's hips while he shook the cocktail.

"You go ahead," I said with a grin and a small tilt of my head toward his audience. The hostile woman started smiling again. "Have you ever thought about dancing professionally?"

"Been there, danced that," Joaquín answered.

"Really?" the winker asked.

"Oh, honey, I shook my bootie with Beyoncé, Ricky Martin, and Justin Timberlake among others when I was a backup dancer."

"What are you doing here, then?" I was astonished.

"My husband and I didn't like being apart." Joaquín started shaking the cocktail, but threw in some extra moves, finishing with a twirl. "Besides, I get to be outside way more than I did when I was living out in LA. There, I was always stuck under hot lights on a soundstage. Here, it's a hot sun out on the ocean. Much better." He winked at the winker, and she blushed.

The women had looked disappointed when he mentioned his husband, but that explained Joaquín's immunity to the women who threw themselves at him. He didn't wear a ring, but maybe as a fisherman it was a danger. My father didn't wear one because of his plumbing, but he couldn't be more devoted to my mom.

"Put three olives on a pick, please," Joaquín asked. While he finished his thing with the shaker, I grabbed one of the picks—not the kind for guitars; these were little sticks with sharp points on one end—fancy plastic toothpicks really. Ours were pink, topped with a little flamingo, and I strung the olives on as Joaquín strained the drink into a martini glass.

"One dirty martini," Joaquín said with a hand flourish.

I popped open a beer and poured it into a glass, holding the glass at an angle so the beer had only a skiff of foam on the top. It was a skill I was proud of because my father had taught me when I was fourteen. Other fathers taught their daughters how to play chess. My friends knew the difference between a king and a rook. Mine made sure I knew the importance of low foam. You can guess which skill was more popular at frat parties in college.

As I distributed the drinks, I thought about Boone Slidell, my best friend since my first day of college. The promise that brought me here? I'd made it to him one night at the Italian Village's bar in downtown Chicago. We'd had so much fun that night, acting silly before his deployment to Afghanistan with the National Guard. But later that night he'd asked me, should anything happen to him on his deployment, would I come help his grandmother, Vivi. He had a caveat. I couldn't tell her he'd asked me to.

"Yes," I'd said. "Of course." We'd toasted with shots of tequila and laughter, never dreaming nine months later that my best friend in the world would be gone. Twenty-eight years old and gone. I'd gotten a leave of absence from my job as a children's librarian and had come for the memorial service, planning to stay for as long as Boone's grandmother needed me. But Vivi wasn't the bent-over, pathetic figure I'd been expecting to save. In fact, she was glaring at me now from across the room, making it perfectly clear that she neither needed nor wanted my help. I smiled at her as I went back behind the bar.

Vivi was a beautiful woman with thick silver hair and a gym-perfect body. Seventy had never looked so good. She wore gold, strappy wedge sandals that made my feet ache just looking at them, cropped white skinny jeans, and an off-the-shoulder, gauzy aqua top. I always felt a little messy when I was with her.

"A promise made is a promise kept." I could hear my dad's voice in my head as clear as if he were standing next to me. It was what kept me rooted here, even with Vivi's dismissive attitude. I'd win her over sooner or later. Few hadn't eventually succumbed to my winning personality or my big brown eyes. Eyes that various men had described as liquid chocolate, doelike, and one jerk who said they looked like mud pies after I turned him down for a date.

In my dreams, everyone succumbed to my personality. Reality was such a different story. Some people apparently thought I was an acquired taste. Kind of like ouzo, an anise-flavored aperitif from Greece, that Boone used to drink sometimes. I smiled at the memory.

"What are you grinning about?" Joaquín asked. Today he wore a neon-green Hawaiian shirt with a hot-pink hibiscus print.

"Nothing." I couldn't admit it was the thought of people succumbing to me. "Am I supposed to be wearing Hawaiian shirts to work?" I asked. He wore one every day. I'd been wearing T-shirts and shorts. No one had mentioned a dress code.

"You can wear whatever your little heart desires, as long as you don't flash too much skin. Vivi wouldn't like that." He glanced over my blue tank top and shorts.

"But you wear Hawaiian shirts every day," I said.

"Honey, you can't put a peacock in beige."

I laughed and started cutting the lemons and limes we used as garnishes. The juice from both managed to find the tiniest cut and burn in my fingers. But Vivi—don't dare put a "Miss" in front of "Vivi," despite the tradition here in the South—wasn't going to chase me away by assigning me all the menial tasks, including cleaning the toilets, mopping the floors, and cutting the fruit. I was made of tougher stuff than that and had been since I was ten. To paraphrase the Blues Brothers movie, I was "on a mission from" Boone.

"What'd those poor little limes ever do to you?"

I looked up. Joaquín stood next to me with a garbage bag in his hand and a devilish grin on his face. He'd been a bright spot in a somber time. He smiled at me and headed out the back door of the bar.

"You're cheating," Buford yelled from his table near the retractable doors. He leaped up, knocking over his chair just as Vivi passed behind him. The chair bounced into Vivi, she teetered on her heels and then slammed to the ground, her head barely missing the concrete floor. The Sea Glass wasn't exactly fancy.

Oh, no. Maybe incidents like this were why Boone thought I needed to be here. Why Vivi needed help. The man didn't notice Vivi, still on the floor. Probably didn't even realize he'd done it. Everyone else froze, while Buford grabbed the man across from him by the collar and dragged him out of his chair knocking cards off the table as he did.

I put down the knife and hustled around the bar. "Buford. You stop that right now." I used the firm voice I occasionally had to use at the library. Vivi wouldn't allow any gambling in here. Up to this point there hadn't been any trouble.

Buford let go of his friend. I kept steaming toward him. "You knocked over Vivi." I lowered my voice, a technique I'd learned as a librarian to defuse situations. "Now, help her up and apologize."

He looked down at me, his face red. I jammed my hands on my hips and lifted my chin. He was a good foot taller than me and outweighed me by at least one hundred pounds. I stood my ground. That would teach him to mess with a children's librarian, even one on a leave of absence. I'd dealt with tougher guys than him. Okay, they had been five years old, but it still counted.

He turned to Vivi and helped her up. "I'm sorry, Vivi. How about I buy a round for the house?"

Oh, thank heavens. For a minute there, I thought he was going to punch me. Vivi looked down at her palms, red from where they'd broken her fall. "Okay. But you pull something like that again and you're banned for life."

Connect with

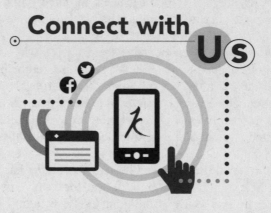

Us

Visit us online at
KensingtonBooks.com
to read more from your favorite authors, see books
by series, view reading group guides, and more.

Join us on social media

for sneak peeks, chances to win books and prize packs,
and to share your thoughts with other readers.

facebook.com/kensingtonpublishing
twitter.com/kensingtonbooks

Tell us what you think!

To share your thoughts, submit a review,
or sign up for our eNewsletters, please visit:
KensingtonBooks.com/TellUs.

Grab These Cozy Mysteries
from
Kensington Books